THE MISSING TAYLOR

BY
RC Cameron

Printed in the United States of America

First Printing, 2019
ISBN 978-1-9995071-0-7

RC Cameron Books
Pompano Beach, FL 33062

www.rccameron.com

To my fantastic wife and dear children who encouraged me on this great adventure. And to Jérôme, Lola, Charlie, Louis, and Rafael, when you set your mind to it, anything is possible.

Table of Content

PROLOGUE

A dozen officers were consumed by absolute silence as they took their positions alongside a vintage garage in an industrial zone of Chicago while the sun peeked just over the horizon. We were expecting an empty garage. So, the plan was to break the door, seize the material, and return to the office - a run-of-the-mill FBI raid.

However, our group leader suddenly raised his arm, causing everyone behind him to stop as they awaited his instructions. When another hand created a telling sign, a colossal man with a battering ram broke rank and ran ahead to reach the entry point. A third sign started the action. The door resisted the ram initially but gave way and flew wide open on the second try.

A terrifying explosion practically flung the bulky man like a piece of paper and sent him crashing back against a fence. Black smoke erupted where a door once stood as debris flew everywhere, accompanied by a sound that I had never heard up-close. We would later discover that the booby trap would kill anyone who entered the garage, unaware of the bypass method. Shrapnel flew in all directions. Several agents fell and were engulfed by the black cloud that resulted from the explosion.

Upon regaining consciousness, the first thing that I noticed was the smell. The smoke lifted, and the horrific scene appeared. An acrid smell replaced the fresh morning air. Lying on my back, I tried to get up, but to no avail; I couldn't move my legs. I could move my head toward the right and left, but my lower body seemed to ignore my brain's orders. The first word that my recuperating mind formed was "paralysis." Suddenly, I became nervous.

A half-dozen officers lay on the ground, groaning, while some remained motionless. That's when I saw our leader—he was beside me, lying on his stomach. His head was turned in my direction, and his eyes were wide open. Blood oozed out of a wound in his neck. I attempted to reach out and apply pressure. However, my arms wouldn't budge, and the look on his face told me that it was too late. His heart was just pumping out all the blood in his body. His carotid artery was severed, I would be informed later. He died almost instantly as I was left to deal with the loss of a close friend for the first time.

A week ago, the planners in the FBI situation room chose four locations, which were linked to a gang of criminals who were manufacturing and distributing controlled substances in our district. In the ghettos, these addictive drugs would often prove to be fatal for young users. We teamed up with the Chicago police—my former employer. The plan was to arrest the people responsible for this nuisance and destroy the production site. It was a major undertaking. Expectations and stakes were high.

Our primary targets were half-a-dozen individuals, including the mastermind—Bruce Steiner. The fifty-four-year-old Caucasian had a long history in the drugs business. However, he had always avoided getting captured miraculously. After sightings in Los Angeles, Denver and New Jersey, he shifted the operations of his illegal activities to Chicago, my hometown. We had adequate data to identify him easily. He wore a tattoo on his face—a tiny cat surrounded by nine small dots on his right temple, echoing the nine lives he claims to enjoy. The other characters we hoped to capture included two couples and a few young men who were involved in distribution around the city. They primarily worked in the downtown area and the North side of Chicago. Each of these individuals had long rap sheets of drug-related offenses. But Steiner, the kingpin, was the prime target. The plan was to raid his residence and a garage shop, which concealed his true activities. It looked like a regular garage but had a sizable backroom, where the manufacturing operations supposedly occurred.

As part of our preparation, we had surveillance on each target location. Our goal was to identify the residents of those houses and associated individuals such as wives, girlfriends, or children. We expected individuals to be at home, naked in bed, with no intention of resisting arrest. The garage itself was supposed to be empty at the time of our arrival. A judge signed the warrants a day in advance, a textbook operation.

The crucial day began at 4:00 am for our attack team, which included ATF, FBI, and Chicago PD officers. The team met early for one last update and review. By 4:30, the vehicles took off toward the targeted sites while it was still dark outside. An ambulance followed my convoy as a precautionary measure. We aimed to execute the final assault at 5:30 am.

Once the air cleared up after the explosion, officers secured the scene, and medics rushed in to treat the wounded ones. To honor those who died during this operation, they slipped a cover over their body. Amid the debris, the odors, and the shouts, the sun still rose over the horizon. Life would continue its everyday shenanigans.

Face guards and body armors had absorbed large chunks of the blast. Arms and legs, which enjoyed limited protection, received the rest of the brunt. Our group leader and two FBI agents died on-site, including the ram operator. Other ambulances arrived within minutes to carry away the wounded.

When I informed the medics that my legs seemed immovable, they put a neck brace on and carefully placed me on a stretcher. Lights and sirens led us to the University of Chicago's trauma center.

Although the other raid locations resulted in five arrests, our main target, Steiner, fled before our team had arrived. The cat had lived through another episode, as he was secretly informed about the operation before the raid. Never would the FBI discover the source of the leak. But one thing was certain: I would never forget that man.

"You lost a lot of blood, Sir," a man dressed in blue and sporting a stethoscope around his neck informed me at the hospital. "We'll get some new blood into you. Then it's off to the X-ray machine to look at the spinal cord for your back injury. We'll do something for the pain also," the doctor added.

When the staff rolled me back into the emergency room, the doctor and a colleague were examining the X-rays on their machine. I tried to clear my mind of negative thoughts as I waited. A few minutes later, both the doctors approached me.

"This is Doctor Ferguson. He's a spinal cord specialist; I'm Doctor Carter. You can't move your legs yet."

"Impossible."

"Don't worry. We think you suffered a mild compression of the lumbar spine when the bomb blast projected you backward. We

4

believe that the inflammation prevents the signals from reaching your legs. By treating this condition, we believe everything will return to normal," Doctor Carter said.

"What's the treatment then?" I asked, still worried about anything related to my spinal cord.

"It's like treating any inflammation, cold at first, heat later, steroids can help as well," continued Dr. Ferguson.

"Any permanent damage?" I asked.

"Don't get ahead of yourself. Let's work on the inflammation, and we'll see after. Right now, you need some rest."

Nurses transported my injured body to a private room. My wife Laura was awaiting my return in the wing, walking back and forth and looking down at something invisible. She ran in my direction upon spotting the stretcher rolling down the corridor.

"Jason Tanner, don't you dare do this again, you understand me?" she said, her voice trembling. The love of my life, right from my high school days, was now by my side.

The fifth morning after the incident, I woke up to realize that I could move my toes, my feet, and even my legs. I called Laura at home all excited to tell her the good news. She cried over the phone. Mid-morning, Dr. Ferguson was at my bedside testing the nerves in my lower body. He asked me to walk, which I did with some difficulty. Pleased with the results, I complained about increasing back pain. He prescribed some medication and signed my release papers. I could go home the following day and start my rehabilitation.

I spent hours at the rehab clinic five days a week for the next six months. While the results took long to materialize, I could almost walk like a normal person except with some persistent back pain, which the OxyContin helped ease.

One afternoon, when I returned home, potentially bad news awaited. Laura's doctor wanted to see us both after her "routine" examination.

Chapter 1

Seven years later, a lot had happened, not all for the best. Since my wife Laura's death, I moved to South Florida and became a private investigator, living aboard a small but comfortable yacht.

I was enjoying a late midweek afternoon at the Marina with the sun slipping over the horizon and the heat now becoming bearable. My five o'clock cocktail hour was in full force. Amid the area buzz, I heard footsteps on the wooden planks leading to my floating home. These ambient sounds would not distract me in normal times, but these seemed like high heels, rare for the Marina crowd. On the aft deck of my yacht, in my most comfortable chair, a martini in hand, I listened to approaching steps.

"Excuse me... Mister Tanner?" said a low voice.

Dressed in my most basic clothing accessories, T-shirt, shorts, and topsiders, I was not expecting anyone this afternoon, and indeed not a fine-looking lady. She had black hair pulled back in a ponytail, glasses that made her look smart and attractive, and a red suit over a white top. Classic, but stylish.

"Yes?"

I did not wear my best attire, but still, a mere 52 years old, trim because of my marines, police, and FBI background. Short black hair, for the same reasons. My complexion changed from fair to tan because of my presence in the sunshine state.

"Excuse me, Mister Tanner, I'm Nadine Taylor, and I would like to hire you."

"Is that so?" I replied, using my most pleasant voice.

Dressed in a professional suit, I examined my visitor, uncertain of what to expect.

"Won't you come aboard?" I said as I got up and opened the transom door to avoid my guest the uncomfortable move over it, in heels and short skirts. She seemed to appreciate the consideration and smiled at me. She wore a subtle perfume that brought back memories of Laura; nothing intense, just a delicate smell.

I asked her to wait a minute while I stepped inside. As the lone resident living aboard, table or seating arrangements are not group-friendly. I got her a chair which I placed in front of mine, asked her to sit, and reached down for my glass.

"Can I offer you anything to drink, Miss Taylor?"

"Mrs. Taylor, but call me Nadine. I'll have a glass of water if you don't mind."

When I returned with a small bottle of water, she said, "That's fine. Thank you."

She swallowed a small amount of water, put the bottle down, looked up, and after some hesitation, said, "I need your help."

I heard this opening line so many times.

Many private investigator cases involve following a cheating husband or wife to gather proof for an upcoming divorce. But

8

somewhat, my instincts told me she's not looking for this kind of service.

"How did you get my name, Mrs. Taylor?"

I must admit to a problem using first names when meeting new people.

"A Miami Police captain I know recommended you."

"And this captain is?"

"Russell, John Russell. He sends his best."

"In my profession, I run across many policemen, but John is special. He's a fine man, and if he sent you here, it's because he believes I can help. What can I do?"

"Mark, my brother, disappeared six months ago, and nobody has seen him since. Captain Russell says you have a gift to discover missing people. The police investigation has stalled, and they're only waiting for new leads, which are not coming. I need a full-time investigator to find my brother, dead or alive."

"Well, I have a certain ability to find lost souls; it's a fact."

I devoted a lot of time to investigative work with the Marines first, the Chicago Police Department, then the FBI, and now as a private detective. Missing person cases are common, and all kinds of information, public or not, are available to locate a person.

"It will be my pleasure to help, Mrs. Taylor. I charge a daily fee plus expenses. I give no absolute assurances I can find Mark. The police have more resources, Mrs. Taylor. But it's your call. You understand?"

"Yes. We can pay your fees, do not worry."

"We?"

"My father is an interested party. Let me provide you with background information if you don't mind."

"Please do," as I sipped my drink and looked into her eyes.

"Wayne Taylor, my father, built a chain of retail stores in the 1990s with the principle that women could buy brand name clothing for a reasonable price. At first, with a single store, he soon expanded to five, fifty, a hundred, and more. In 2005, my father received an offer from JTX stores to participate in their growing empire and decided it was time to let go of his dream. He'd spent enough resources building the Taylor brand. He was approaching his retirement and believed he should concentrate on other matters. With his financial security established, he now wished to teach younger entrepreneurs how to succeed."

"And he is not with you today?"

"He lives in Chicago, but you can contact him by phone if you wish."

Chicago, a place I knew well.

# # #

Nadine's soft voice reminded me of my mother's and the sensation of slow passing time during my childhood. From my early days in Illinois, playing cops and robbers with my brothers, I always chose the policeman role, on the side of justice, that was me. Not surprisingly, law and order positions attracted me later in life.

When I played with Carl and Freddy, they were bad guys, and I was a cop sent to find and arrest them. Both of my brothers now live in South Carolina. Once or twice a year, we talk but are not close. If I get a call from one, something is wrong. I have nothing against them; I am just different.

The Missing Taylor

Born in Springfield, Illinois, before Carl and Freddy, I wound up my high school and expected to join the local police force and the academy. Complications appeared as I lacked a college education. In its absence, combat experience would compensate. With the Vietnam war over, training by the Armed Forces while drawing a paycheck was an attractive plan. Not waiting, I joined the Marines and drove to San Diego for my boot camp basics of thirteen weeks. These were the hardest three months of my life, but I graduated on Family Day when my whole family, brothers included, flew west for the ceremony. It was my proudest moment.

Back home for ten days of leave, I continued to Camp Pendleton for Marine combat training. After another four weeks of hard work, I needed to make choices. Marines have hundreds of jobs for enlisted men or officers, from logistics to running ships to flying airplanes and many more. Where would I fit best?

When told the Military Police (MP) was not only a bunch of guys wearing MP on their sleeves and picking up drunk sailors from Saigon bars, it got me all excited. These officers performed real investigative work, which I wanted to do. As a result, I requested to become an investigator, and for three years, I served on various Marine bases.

After returning to Springfield and my family, I gained an excellent education, proper training, and now had good investigating skills. I looked forward to the next chapter of my life, the Chicago Police Department (CPD).

One may think it is challenging to become a member of the CPD; it is not. But it requires motivation to stay there, at least for me. I wanted to become a full-fledged detective, but management had a different view of my career. They preferred I spend months and years as a regular patrolman. In due time, whenever that was, I could consider taking a detective exam. Too slow for me, I needed a more expedited way of reaching my goal. After a few years of walking the beat, with no sign of becoming a detective, I made an important decision: I forwarded an application to the Federal Bureau of Investigation.

But a problem remained; the FBI also requires a college education. I had skipped college to train in the Armed Forces to become a policeman. Now, I had a significant obstacle, and the rejection letter was disappointing. Therefore, my options were few: I could get a degree after investing four years but was unsure how to manage the financials. Savings would not carry me to the end. The additional education costs were not bearable by my parents either.

After getting reference letters from my high school, the Marines, and the Chicago PD, I asked to meet my local senator. I had nothing to lose. Experience has shown that it's a great habit to get local representation involved in your case when dealing with the government. To see a Senator in person is a rare incident. Political aides, clerks, chief of staff, or other people are running interference for their leader.

One of his aides received me, and I presented my case like a pro. In preparation for that day, I practiced in front of a mirror to achieve a certain skill level. I left the aide a brochure explaining what I was looking for, including all my accumulated reference material.

Unsure if the difference was the vocal delivery or the brochure, but three weeks later, an invitation arrived from the FBI local office to visit the recruitment center in Chicago. Next, on my slate, sign up to become an FBI Special Agent in Charge (SAIC). I was on my way.

Many months later, after classes and specialized training, I moved into my dream position, Special Agent—Criminal Investigations Division, where I worked in Chicago, close to my hometown.

The Missing Taylor

With my career settled for a while, I envied my colleagues when they returned from their weekend and described their activities with families and children. It was time I looked into building a family, someone told me. One day, my friend John, another special agent, introduced me to Laura through a blind date. We connected, and four months later, we celebrated our marriage in Springfield with all my family attending along with several FBI agents from the Chicago office. A secure marriage, you could say.

After our first year together, Laura gave us a lovely daughter, Cynthia. Not long after her birth, the FBI moved me to different offices in the country. It was a pleasant experience but also challenging to displace a wife and child every time. The second kid never arrived as we were often on the move.

Back in Chicago, Laura, now forty-five, passed a routine exam. They discovered lumps in her breast. Even after the multiple treatments available, she passed away two years later. The house was now empty. Back in Denver, Cynthia had moved in with two friends where she worked as a registered nurse.

When my father also died not long after Laura, I now had no family, or they lived far away. I had friends in the Bureau but scattered around the country. My two brothers, who left the cold temperature of the North for the most pleasant climate of South Carolina, were also far away.

Two years after Laura's unexpected passing, I was eligible to collect my pension from the FBI, and I retired after over twenty-five years of service. Nothing much held me back in Illinois. My father, my last living parent, had left my brothers and me a sizable legacy of almost two million dollars amassed in his later years. With my FBI pension, my financial future was pretty much guaranteed.

After my retirement, I decided to put the house up for sale. It was already too big for a single person, it also reminded me so much of Laura. On the second day, I tackled the disposal of furniture, clothing, books, and other knickknacks, keeping enough items to leave the house presentable. I sold the property in less than a full week. With the sale document signed, I used extra days to get rid of the remaining furniture and handed the keys to the new owner.

Dr. Ferguson, who treated me during my stay at the hospital after the bombing incident, remained my doctor and I reached out to inform him of my move to South Florida. Concerned about the pain medication I was taking, he told me he was also retiring and could not write me a new prescription. He strongly recommended I connect with a pain clinic in my future neighborhood to search for alternative solutions for my back problem. My new doctor would prescribe painkillers if no alternative treatment remedied the situation. I thanked him for his support and decided to follow his advice over the years. Little did I know my good intentions would take me somewhere totally different.

Alone, I packed my life belongings, except for winter clothing, in my Ford Escape and headed south. Stopping in South Carolina to see Carl and Freddy, we reminisced and enjoyed a good time together for a few days. Because our mutual lives were far apart, we often did not see each other. The traveling inhibited a better relationship. We still had a pleasant time sitting around the dinner table. When I left my brothers, I promised I would be in touch more than I had in the past. I also gave them an invitation to visit once settled.

My next stop was Florida. That was my end game. I have stayed and visited many of our 50 states, and Florida was at the top of my list. It had a warm climate, the sea, the fishing, and I hoped I could find something to keep me busy.

The Missing Taylor

"Hold on a minute, Mrs. Taylor." I apologized and entered the yacht's main salon to retrieve a small notepad. I returned to my seat and scribbled a few words while trying to smile and look sad at the same time.

"So tell me, in what circumstances did your brother disappear?" I asked.

"It happened back in September, Mister Tanner. From what I understand and what the police have put together, my brother Mark showed up for work at the Black Cat Bar in South Beach on a Friday night, a popular site. At closing time, he left the bar, as usual, never seen again."

"And that was his regular job at this bar?" I asked.

"He worked as a barman, just one of many livelihoods he experimented. After college, he worked a few jobs, never for a long time. He also performed contractual work, just a few months at a time. I think he accumulated a few dollars and then stopped working for a while. On occasions, he would tend bars, one of his talents. Even as a bartender, it was never permanent. He replaced regular staff during their absence. Often at the last minute, he got called at 7 pm to show up at 8 pm, you see."

"Yes, I understand. Not a line of work to plan a budget, a family, a livelihood," I concluded. "Mrs. Taylor, do you know who was the last person to see your brother before he left for his job that day?"

"No, I don't. My brother lived in a small apartment, alone, as far as I know. I am not aware if anyone was with him when he left that day. Is this important?"

"Well, it could be. Should Mark be down or depressed, that could influence what he did that night."

15

I looked at Nadine and wondered why she waited six months before restarting the investigation. I assumed she harassed the Miami Police during all that time and gotten nowhere. The Miami Police detective unit runs dozens of inquiries at the same time. When a new case appears on his radar, a typical detective will concentrate on it for the next 48 or 72 hours. After that period, the case will see less and less interest. After a few months, the file sits on the desk and sees no action.

"Does Mark have a regular girlfriend?"

After taking a few seconds to answer, she admitted, "Not that I know. I have seen Mark with a few girls, but never the same."

"If ever you can dig up any name for me, that would help us, anyway. Is bartending his only occupation?"

"He told me he contracted work for some IT firms. I don't know which one."

"Are you aware of his responsibilities in these positions?"

"No, I know it was contractual work and not full-time."

"Did your brother own a car? Did he drive it to work on that last Friday?"

"He owns an old Toyota. My husband and I found the car parked close to his apartment. Did he use it that night and come back? Nobody can confirm."

"How long has he lived in Florida?"

# # #

Was I a long-time resident myself? Far from it. After visiting my brothers in South Carolina, I headed to South Florida over interstate 95, Fort Lauderdale, my ultimate destination. I preferred the East Coast with its real ocean waves compared to the West Coast and its anemic water movements. Miami is too busy, West Palm Beach too quiet, Fort Lauderdale seemed like a good fit.

With a sufficient supply of capital to get started in Florida, I now required a place to camp and located a small but decent motel in Lauderdale-by-the-sea and paid for the first month. I then shopped for homes close and far from the beach. A million dollars or a hundred thousand, these were my options. My budget allowed either one. But I rejected both; another idea was shaping up in my mind.

Back in Chicago, I owned a modest fishing boat used on occasions. With Laura and Cynthia, we would cruise along Lake Michigan on Sunday mornings, enjoying the fresh air and the sightseeing. Other times, alone or with some friends, I went out to fish for bass.

A yacht I could live aboard tempted me. As a result, I could fish or coast around South Florida with my "house." That became my new game plan. I opened my laptop and shopped for a residence. I scrutinized many YouTube videos testing various yacht types, called around, visited dealers, and consulted experts. As a result, I decided and ordered a 35-foot trawler big enough to live aboard but still a size that a single person can handle. While waiting for my new toy delivery, I looked for a berth. After visiting the immense Fort Lauderdale Marina, I chose a smaller, friendlier location in Pompano Beach called the Sands Harbor Marina on the Intercostal Waterway.

When the dealer turned over the yacht, I hired a local captain for a few days. He taught me new skills around the area and perfected my talent to maneuver in windy situations and varying currents. I then docked the yacht at my new Marina and moved my few belongings aboard, leaving my temporary housing.

Although the trawler is not enormous, equipment is plentiful, and it's roomy enough for one or two people aboard. The main salon holds a large sofa, a dining table, and a storage space with a pop-up

TV screen. Amidships, a well-equipped galley on the port side, and a pilot's cockpit on starboard. Upfront, a guest room appears on the port side. On starboard, we found a micro bathroom and shower, an owner's suite in the bow.

On top, the flybridge is another location to control the ship. It possesses a lovely seating arrangement with a work table. I store a tender on the aft portion. It's a small boat I can lower to the sea when necessary.

My setup was complete now, and I could proceed with my next big project.

# # #

"How long did Mark live in Florida, you ask? Let me see. It must be almost three years now. I came here in 2011 when my husband transferred to Miami. Mark arrived three or four years later."

So I picture our missing person, in Florida for three years, still drives an old Toyota, has no steady girlfriend or a permanent job, and is not attending classes. I wonder what he does with all his time.

"Would you have a recent picture of him?"

"Yes," as she reached for her bag beside her chair. She extracted a 4X6 picture of two couples, a young blond male with Nadine and a man; I assume he is her husband. I don't know the fourth person.

"Is this your husband?" I asked, but I knew the answer already.

"Yes, Joe Patry. I kept the name Taylor. Besides me, Mark and the girl, Diane. She was with him that day at the beach. The picture dates back to last summer in Miami Beach."

I kept adding these tiny pieces of information in my notebook while flipping back and forth between pages. We both were silent for a moment. A bell sounded close by, and I noticed Nadine looked around for the source.

"Raising the bridge," I said. She nodded, having crossed that bridge on her way over.

A few hundred feet away, where Atlantic Boulevard crosses the Intercoastal Waterway, a bridge opens on the hour and the half-hour to let taller boats go by, mine included.

"Mrs. Taylor, what did your brother do with his time? He has a part-time job, part-time girlfriends, and is not in school. What am I missing here?"

"An excellent question Mr. Tanner. Whenever we chatted, and that was rare, he was always elusive. He surfs a lot, he tells me; it occupies most of his mornings. He spends time with his buddies at South Beach, I imagine. And he has a computer contract here and there and works behind the bar but part-time only."

"Does he travel?"

"He went to South America a few years ago, but I am not aware of any past or future travel plans."

"Do you believe he was into drugs?"

"I don't think so," she said with her eyes flicking to a small boat passing by and then back at me.

Did she tell a lie?

I decided not to pursue this line of questioning today. Opportunities would come up later. In my capacity as a PI, I would have other occasions to revisit the subject.

# # #

A private investigator was how I intended to keep myself busy in sunny South Florida. Once I got settled in my new toy at the Marina, I needed a part-time occupation to live: something to keep my gray cells working and to have activities other than fishing or sunbathing.

One evening, after cleaning the galley, I opened my laptop on the salon table. I typed: becoming a private investigator in Florida. The search engine located over 4 million results. I concentrated on the first page and found a website that showed the requirements to become a PI in the sunshine state. Eighteen years old, a legal resident, and with no criminal record, I met the criteria. A good moral character I also had. No history of mental illness, I didn't think so. Free of illegal drugs and alcoholism, all I took was above board. Finally, I needed at least two years of equivalent experience. So far, I have met all the requirements.

The next step was to complete the specialty training for the job. I possessed all the mandatory training with my 25 years of FBI experience. I only had to read class material addressing specific Florida requirements. A week of study would be sufficient in my estimate.

The next problem to solve was carrying a concealed firearm. I needed 28 hours of training, according to the website. I received plenty of FBI tutoring in firearm safety and usage during my career. Maybe I could skip right to the exam because of my existing skills.

So I jumped into my studies, devoting close to ten hours a day. I needed to be ready for the written test in West Palm Beach, the nearest examination facility. As a side benefit, it would allow me to take my first cruise and experience the world of planning and executing a boat trip. I was looking forward to this occasion.

The Missing Taylor

I took the exam, received my grades, and applied for my class C private investigator license in Florida. Once I received it, I could now work cases.

On the personal side, my back problems persisted, and I eventually got in touch with a pain clinic, as Dr. Ferguson suggested. A search of these institutions near me proposed more than a dozen. I selected one close by and scheduled the first evaluation.

After filling out a lengthy questionnaire, I met a specialist who reviewed my answers. It did not take him long to conclude I was running full steam ahead toward addiction. I may even have arrived. Symptoms were numerous: I appreciated the quiet euphoria it provided. I displayed several unpleasant physical symptoms, such as abdominal pain, sweating, and dizziness. My preoccupations for getting OxyContin were important, another telling sign. I had to come to grips with my situation and accept to enter a pain-management program. They scheduled my first meeting in three weeks, about the time my prescription ran out. I hoped everything would work out.

Now, on the business aspect of investigations, I needed to inform my potential customers I was now open for business. Publicity today involved running a website and advertising on Google or Facebook. It was not my intention. I wanted a low-keyed operation, few cases, enough to keep me occupied part-time. I needed to inform my contacts in Florida about my new status. I knew several police detectives in Jacksonville, Miami, Naples, and other places. One by one, I would contact them.

The next day, I put the plan in motion by purchasing the documentation and started my studying period. I resolved the firearm training issue to my satisfaction. After a few weeks, I registered for the PI licensing examination to occur in the next ten days. Because of this schedule, it would leave me time to review the material and get to West Palm Beach, a three-hour ride by boat.

Two weeks after my exam, I received my private investigator's license at the post office. I called a local lettering company to come to paint the name of my boat: "PRIVATE EYE."

Chapter 2

"Ms. Taylor, how did the police get involved with the investigation?" I asked after a long silence.

"I contacted them after I could not reach Mark. At the beginning of the week, I called to invite him for brunch on the following Sunday; I had not seen him in ages."

"What date was it?" I asked.

"It was on September 13. He did not answer his phone, but I left a message on his mobile. A few days later, I called again, the same result. Saturday afternoon, I drove by his apartment and knocked on the door; no one was present. I asked his closest neighbor, who said he had not seen Mark all week."

"What happened next?"

"I called the police reporting a missing person, my brother," she said and lowered her head at the same time. I let her have a moment. It was painful, I could see. After a few seconds, she lifted her head. She looked stronger now, a more determined expression on her face. "The police arrived at the apartment and got a key from the building manager. The two police officers entered and came out a minute later:

nobody was home. At least they had not discovered a dead body. I was relieved."

Nadine continued her story. "The officer asked me some questions, and when I returned home that afternoon, two detectives showed up."

"I'll need their names," I said.

"Someone called Freeman, Wayne Freeman. I don't remember the other, but Captain Russell would provide the information, I believe."

"And the police never found him," I said, stating the obvious to get her talking again.

"They tried without success. I had several calls from Freeman, daily at first, every few weeks after that, to tell me the same thing. No sign of my brother, like he disappeared from the face of the earth. One day, I asked to speak to Freeman's boss, and that's when I reached Captain Russell."

"And..."

"He had the same message as Freeman. They investigated, questioned neighbors, people at the bar, they found nothing. A picture of my brother appeared on the Miami-Dade website for missing people, but that has generated no leads so far."

I noted this while thinking with all the local police resources assisted by federal agencies. It astonishes me a person vanishes.

"Do you know if the police pulled your brother's phone records?"

"Yes, they did; Freeman told me so. They have looked at his incoming and outgoing calls from the phone company's records and found nothing of interest other than the last call was on September 10. After that date, nothing. I also know they asked the communication provider to locate his phone, to no avail. No more signal, they told me."

"How about his personal affairs?" I asked.

"After a few months of looking for Mark, my husband and I arranged his affairs. We settled with the owner of the apartment he was living in, we picked up his mail and rerouted it to my home, we also settled some outstanding bills. His old car is on our property; whatever he had in the apartment, we boxed and put in storage."

"Excellent, if you don't mind, I will need access to the storage locker and whatever documents you have in your possession, such as mail which you can send here, to my attention."

"Not a problem, Mister Tanner. I will have the documents delivered to you tomorrow."

# # #

The sun was disappearing from the horizon, and I stepped inside a minute to turn on some lights. I also picked up a standard retainer document to present to my new customer. I laid it on the table and invited her to come in and discuss it.

"Have a seat, Mrs. Taylor," as I showed her the sofa. I sat next to her, and I placed the retainer in front.

"I require some administrative work to launch the investigation. This document is a standard retainer for a Private Investigator in the state of Florida. Please review it. My fees are $500 per day plus expenses, and I will ask for a $2,500 retainer in advance. I will send an invoice biweekly if I can. Don't worry if I don't; it could be because I'm too busy. If you could write your name and address, this is where I will send my bill. I can also work with an email address."

She read the document, filled in the blanks, signed it, and handed it back. She pulled her checkbook from her purse and wrote one, leaving it on the table.

"I will need more information which you can fax to this number," as I handed her my business card. "You can also secure a file by email by using the password PRIVATE EYE, that's the name of my boat. I will need Mark's home address, social security number, any credit or debit card he may possess. I will also need names and phone numbers of girlfriends, surfing buddies, and places you know he worked at, both bars and technology firms. If you don't find all the phone numbers, don't worry, I can manage."

"Fine."

I asked for her father's phone number, which I jotted in my notebook.

Nadine got up and looked me in the eyes, "I hope you find my brother, Mr. Tanner; I wish you luck. I will make certain the storage space is accessible tomorrow. Wait for my email to confirm."

She turned around and exited the yacht with caution, uncertain of her footing on a moving platform. When she reached the shore, she opened the passenger door of a white SUV as the engine roared into life. Strange, I thought, her husband was present, but he did not come aboard with her. I closed the transom doors and went inside to plan my newest case.

# # #

It was too late to call Captain Russell now and thank him for the referral. It would have to wait until tomorrow. I closed the lights, locked the doors, and headed to my stateroom. It's an impressive name for a bedroom with a single bed taking much of the space in the ship's bow.

The Missing Taylor

The following morning, I awoke around 6 am, the sun still coming up at this time of the season. I prepared a coffee and headed to my all-in-one lunch, dinner, office, and work table, the main attraction in the salon. I turned the TV on and listened to the local news with one ear as I read the rest of the information on my tablet. An hour later, after a quick breakfast, I was out the door for my morning march around the neighborhood. After a good hour's walk, I sat at Starbucks on Federal Highway for my second coffee. I got my phone out and noticed Nadine had already forwarded the information we discussed the night before.

Back on PRIVATE EYE, I showered in my mini-stall, dressed, and opened my MacBook to review Nadine's communication. She had compressed several documents into a single file protected by a password, smart woman, I thought.

In law enforcement, I learned from experience you needed several tools to combat organized crime or even regular criminals. You required information. I had developed, over the years, a unique tie with an individual able to provide data on just about anybody. How he did this, I was clueless but impressed. I paid him his due whenever he sent me the info I requested. Hank Hackman, no kidding, from New Jersey, was efficient and expeditious. I grabbed the phone.

"Yes."

"Hank, it's Jason. How are you?"

"I'm fine, Mister Tanner. I heard you now enjoy living in Florida?"

"Correct. I purchased a yacht, and I live aboard now. I passed my PI license a few months ago, and I work on the sporadic case. I want to keep my brain functioning instead of frying, if you know what I mean."

"Mister Tanner, I understand. What can I do for you?"

I explained the case and told him I was looking for information on a male subject, Mark Taylor. I would transfer Nadine's file after the call. He should examine telephone records going back a year if he could. I was also seeking financial information from his bank and transactions from his credit and debit cards for the last six months. He should also search for any arrests in the subject's history, court filings, the works. I confirmed the standard pricing for this request and ended the call.

I then buzzed John Russell. Not wanting to discuss the case over the phone, but I was planning to sail to Miami tomorrow; it would be nice to see John and chat. He suggested we meet for lunch near his office. Given that I needed a few hours on the water and additional time to visit the storage locker, I asked him to set up a 5 pm meeting, my treat. Perfect, he said. So I filled PRIVATE EYE's diesel and water tanks, ready for an early departure.

Examining Nadine's file on her brother, I noticed the names of what looked like companies, not bars. I called the first one and asked for the personnel office. Directed to a young voice, I used my private investigator persona to ask questions about Mark Taylor's activities at their firm. They told me he worked part-time over six months for a customer revamping their website to add online transaction processing, whatever that was. I asked which company, they could not provide that information; it was confidential. They also mentioned it was the only contract with Mark they executed. Other opportunities came along, but Mark refused to join the newest projects.

The second business also provided related info; a fix-term contract for a third party looking to revamp a website. It seemed like Mark specialized in this area. Again, other occasions appeared, but Mark turned them down. Although both employers recommended his work, he seemed to lack interest in these projects. I put that data aside for now.

The Missing Taylor

#

I turned on the single diesel engine ten minutes to 7 am to benefit from the rise of the Atlantic Bridge on the hour. It was already 80 degrees on the intercostal. Being one foot too tall for this bridge, I had to wait. When I use the northern Lighthouse Point exit, with its 21-foot clearance, I need not wait. But traveling southbound, I do. My favorite route is the Intracoastal Waterway up to the 17th Street Bridge and then out to sea, due south toward Miami. I could use the Waterway to Miami if I wanted to, but it's slower with added traffic.

Once I hit the ocean, I relaxed and used the automatic pilot to get me to my destination. But because of the heavy traffic in the area, I stayed at the helm. When it got warmer, I moved onto the flybridge upstairs to run the yacht and enjoy the view as I brought up a fresh cup of coffee. If my new career included these kinds of moments, I masterminded a great move. I put my feet up, tuned in some Neil Young music, happy to sail with a purpose.

I missed my daughter so far from me. She loves her new environment, but I would prefer she lived closer. She said she would come and see me soon. I was looking forward to her visit.

I had called the night before, but now I confirmed my arrival at the Miami Beach Marina using my VHF radio. They require reservations even for a short stay. Winter is a busy time for the marine industry. On my way over to Miami, I received an email from Nadine informing me the storage facility had approved my access to the unit. Once moored, I walked to the Marina office and concluded the registration. I then headed for the closest main street to grab a cab. I did not wear my sidearm, as I saw no use for it at this point.

At the storage facility, I trotted to the main office and presented my new Florida Private Investigator ID credentials with pride. Without the key to access the locker, the young service desk clerk called an

29

employee to accompany me. A key opened the front access, which rose just like a garage door. It was a typical locker, about 10 feet by 15 feet. Inside, an odor of mildew. From the size of the space, I figured dear Mark got an unfurnished apartment, and he bought furniture at Rooms-to-go upon his arrival. A mattress and box spring rested on the wall. A nightstand, a dresser, a kitchen table with chairs, a sofa with a recliner, and half a dozen cardboard boxes filled the space.

The boxes interested me the most. I pulled the dining room table, picked the first box I saw and opened it: mainly clothes. I used my magic marker to initial the box, showing I had examined it. Old habits from the FBI never die. The second box was identical; another set of initials went on.

The third one must have been the dresser's top drawer, smaller belongings; a few rings, a nail clipper, old and expired credit cards, a set of keys opening God knows what. One of them got my immediate attention. It looked like a safe deposit box, so I pocketed the set of keys.

A pile of pay stubs clipped together. I photographed them to get an idea of where Mark worked in the past few years. I noticed a small life insurance policy where Nadine was the beneficiary, uncertain she was aware of this. Maybe it was for his funeral service, who knows.

The rest of the cardboard boxes yielded no treasure. I was wondering where the passport was, unseen yet. With no more cardboard boxes, I examined the furniture: tables, chairs, dressers, not much there. I looked front and back, underneath, nothing.

A large sofa topped by cushions, hidden in the back, got my attention. I had to displace several boxes and other items to get at it. Since it was the most significant piece of furniture, it was the first one to enter the space; that's why I found it at the back of the storage unit. I looked at the sofa, front and rear, nothing extraordinary. When I lifted the two cushions, dirt and chips and other sofa excrement appeared. I noticed a small plastic bag, about one inch by two inches. It looked empty. A closer examination showed small white grains. I put the bag in a ziplock container I had brought. Before, I used to call this an evidence bag. I replaced everything and closed the front door of the storage unit. I informed the manager, and I left the premises.

Back on the yacht, I called Nadine on her mobile phone, hoping I could catch her during her dinner break; it was a little past noon already.

"Hello."

"Nadine, good day, it's Jason; how are you?"

"Fine, you?"

"Thank you for the information. I received it this morning. It's what I wanted. But I have another question for you if you don't mind. Did your brother have a safe deposit box by any chance?"

Seconds later, she said, "Yes, he did. He told me a few years ago that he had named me a joint renter. If anything happened to him, I would find his important papers there. I never thought of that. But I don't have a key."

"I believe I do, Nadine."

# # #

At 4:30, seated at The Melting Pot, a favorite sports bar and grill near the Miami-Dade police headquarters, I waited for John or JR, as folks called him. Not expecting him before 5 pm, I ordered a beer and got news updates from my cell phone. Dozens of TV screens encircled the bar, showing basketball or pre-season baseball games.

I worked with John several years ago and always kept in touch. As an FBI Special Agent, the first case I consulted on was the disappearance of a Cuban family, mother, father, and two kids living in Miami's Little Havana District. Neighbors placed the first call when strangely, the family missed a get-together on a Sunday. When someone approached the family's house, no one answered the door, even when their car sat right out front. We discovered that a Cuban gang kidnapped the family because the father owed money. They murdered the entire group, including two innocent children. They found their bodies in a gravesite close to the Everglades, all shot in the head.

Other opportunities to work with John appeared later on the radar. I was reminiscing these other cases when I heard, "Hey buddy!" John was extending his arm from his over six feet frame. Standing up, I looked at his smiling face.

"I am doing well, oh, tall one."

"And your daughter?" he asked.

"Cynthia is well, still living in Denver. I hope she'll be able to visit soon. She has not seen my new living arrangements."

"And how do you like it on the water?" he continued.

"So far, so good. It's small but comfortable. I had to come to Miami today, so I moved the entire house. The best thing is the lack of traffic compared to I-95."

"For sure my friend. I live in Miami Lakes, so I don't use the interstate, but still, there's a tremendous amount of traffic in the area. The city of Miami may hold only 460,000 residents, but when you add in the metro area, we are close to 5.6 million people. It's not small by any means."

"I saw that on my way over this afternoon," I added.

"And how is the new business going?" John asked.

"Well, since I got my license, I had three or four cases already. I am working on a few, including the Taylor investigation which you referred; I thank you for that."

"The case is not cold yet, my detectives are still working on it, but no investigative leads arrived recently. New inspectors should examine the case, but I have no one available. We manage a limited staff, as you know."

I informed him of my search this morning at the storage facility and the discovery of a key to a safe deposit box. I planned to access it Monday. Could I reach out to the detectives and get a copy of the case documentation? I asked John.

"I'll have someone at the office copy the case file, and the detectives can bring it to you when you meet."

"That would be perfect. Thank you." I reached inside my pocket and retrieved a ziplock containing another plastic bag. "I also found this. There's a white powder inside. Do you think you can get it analyzed? I don't have access to the FBI labs anymore."

"Sure, buddy."

"One thing is puzzling me, John, from my search this morning. It's something I did not find."

"And what's that?" he asked.

"Mark Taylor's passport."

"Does he have one?"

"He should; his sister told me he flew to South America a few years back. He may have it with him; that's also a possibility. Do you think you can ask the Homeland Security boys to see if Mark had a passport issued and whether he used it recently?"

John would ask Freeman to request the information from Homeland Security, and we continued talking for another hour of people we knew in common and cases we worked together. We concluded with my invitation to go fishing once things were quiet. He happily accepted, and we both left the bar early, knowing John had to rejoin his family in Miami Lakes.

I returned to the Miami Beach Marina, had dinner, and opened my notebook to update my investigation. At the FBI, we had all kinds of applications to document our progress. As a PI, I limited myself to a notebook. I opened the laptop and accessed my small business accounting program to record my time and expenses of the day. If I didn't do it every night, I would forget it.

I went to the flybridge with a cup of tea to enjoy the setting sun. I had a particular thought about Laura. I wonder if she would have treasured life on the water as I did. She liked the sea and the beach but trying to get her aboard a ship for a small excursion was impossible. If she were alive, we would be close to the sea, but not right on it.

Chapter 3

The next morning, I got up at my usual time and took in the early day activities around the Marina. Saturday is a period when most owners have time on their hands to take their boat to sea, work on it, or stay aboard for a while.

I walk the docks trying to find someone who would at least look like a fisherman. It was difficult; people mostly arrived in bathing suits.

I found a senior man, bringing out fishing rods and setting them in holders on the aft deck, so I approached him. "Pardon me, sir, with all the rods I see aboard, are you familiar with the good fishing spots in the area?"

He looked at me. "Are you a new resident of the Marina?" he asked. "Temporary," I replied. He shook his head. His gray hair showed even if he wore a baseball cap, the oldest hat I ever saw. His hair matched the white beard surrounding a mouth with a few holes and yellow teeth.

"What kind of fish do you want to catch?"

"I like to eat pompano, grouper, and yellowtail tuna. Any of those around here?"

"Pompano, you can catch at the fishing pier just like any tourist in the area. Grouper and tuna, you need to outsmart them, as I do. Why don't you come with me? I'll show you a few spots."

"You are serious? I was planning on taking my boat, but your invitation sounds better; I'll share in the expenses."

"Fine. Get your gear. Meet me here in 30 minutes or less if you can."

"Count on me," as I rushed to PRIVATE EYE to gather a few essential elements like food, water, sun protection, rods, reels, a hat, and a few cold beers. I was back on his boat within 15 minutes and realized I had ignored his name.

William Tudor, he told me after I introduced myself. The diesel engine was already humming. I handled the mooring lines as per his instructions directed from the flybridge up above. He had an old 1980 Tiara 33-foot boat with a light-green hull, while the rest was a perfect white. He seemed to maintain his ship well.

I joined him on the upper deck, and after an hour, I knew a lot about the man.

William is a 73-year-old history teacher who enjoys tree-shaping, gardening, and relaxing. He's British and defines himself as a calm person. My newly found friend got a postgraduate degree in European history and sails because of a severe phobia of flying. After the Second World War, he reached the United States on a cruise ship at a young age.

He grew up in an upper-class neighborhood in Columbus, Ohio. Raised by his mother, his father died when he was young. He is single. William's best friend is a personal trainer called Neal Walsh.

The Missing Taylor

They have a fiery friendship. They enjoy working in the garden together. When he wants to relax, he comes aboard his ship named Rock Steady. Neal hates the waves and gets seasick, so he rarely shows up aboard unless the boat stays tied to the dock.

William is still in good shape. He is of average height with bronze skin, white hair, green eyes, and stuck-out-ears.

I enjoyed a great time aboard, and he shared his knowledge of fishing the sea around Miami. He showed me where to drop my line, how to bait, and the ideal depth to fish. We caught a dozen species but returned most to the sea except those we could eat in the days ahead.

We came back to port late afternoon. I helped William tidy his ship and wash it clean from saltwater. I invited him to come aboard the PRIVATE EYE and have dinner with me. We both would appreciate our freshly baked grouper, and he accepted.

My yacht fascinated him, even though it's about the same dimensions as his. The contrast is age; his ship is over 30 years old, mine onto its first year. Technology allows small refrigerators, grill oven, showers, large windows, and much more. It makes a big difference.

As the grouper cooked in the oven, I prepared a martini which he accepted graciously. He asked questions about my years in the FBI, my family, and my current occupation. He still showed curiosity, given his age.

It was a great day, and I enjoyed every minute. When William left around 9 pm, he shook my hand, wishing we could meet again. Possible, I told him, South Florida was now my permanent home. On Sunday, I took a tour of the city of Miami with free time on my hands. I visited the Seaquarium and took in the feeling of South Beach.

# # #

At 10 am sharp on Monday morning, at the corner of South West 72nd Street and South Dixie Highway in Miami, Nadine was walking down the street in my direction. She had discarded the business suit she wore during our initial meeting for more relaxed jeans with tank tops and flip-flops. She walked rapidly, with her purse on her shoulder. I had arrived somewhat earlier, not knowing the Miami traffic. I grabbed a Starbuck coffee on my way and sat on nearby stairs while waiting close to the First National Bank of Miami.

"Good morning," she said with a broad smile extending her arm. She looked in a better mood than during our initial encounter.

"Good morning Nadine. You look fine on this beautiful South Florida day."

She smiled again.

"I love this area, Mister Tanner. Knowing you're a latecomer to the region, I trust you will love it too."

I reviewed the reason for being here and explained how our visit would proceed to the best of my knowledge. As a co-renter of the safety box, she has access to its content. She needed to sign the registry, and they would grant her access. I would act as a simple observer. I handed her the key recuperated from Mark's storage locker.

We entered the bank and proceeded to the service counter, where Nadine asked to access a safe box. She did not know the number, but she was listed as a co-renter and had possession of the key. We waited while the personnel performed the necessary verification.

After checking her credentials, we passed behind the service counter and descended to the basement. The vault was directly ahead of the stairs. Following our guide, we entered and moved to a wall full of safety boxes of varying sizes. Our guide inserted the bank's key into the one numbered 256, and Nadine did the same. The door opened, revealing a metallic box which our guide pulled out. He asked that we follow him into another room where they provided private areas for owners to manipulate their box's content. The guide exited the room and waited just outside, giving us some privacy.

I lifted the metal cover and saw a brown envelope on top, with other papers in the bottom. I grabbed the unglued envelope. Inside, a stack of money materialized. I extracted it and aligned the bills on the table. A quick count gave me close to sixty thousand dollars. I examined the rest of the papers in the box, and they appeared to be life insurance documents naming Nadine as the beneficiary. I wondered who keeps that amount of money in their safety box. A few rich people maybe, but Mark wasn't wealthy as far as I knew. Something wasn't adding up.

I turned to Nadine, and her eyes told me she was expecting a question.

"How did Mark get his hands on close to sixty thousand dollars as a replacement bartender? That's a lot of tips."

# # #

I contacted Wayne Freeman, the lead detective on the Taylor investigation from the Miami-Date police before leaving for the bank this morning. We agreed to meet at the Melting Pot again, around 4:00 pm, hoping to beat the traffic when returning to the Marina and to enjoy the rest of the day. I told Wayne I would sit at the bar, ask the barman to point me.

He was right on time, and I appreciated this virtue, too often neglected. We moved to a booth when he arrived to get some privacy. He had a blue suit with the ugliest yellow tie. He would be easy to pick out in a lineup. Freeman set a brown envelope that appeared full on the table between the two of us as if delivering a package. I thought, for a moment, he would ask for a signature like FedEx. His lips pressed together; he looked furtively at me. I understood the message: he was irritated because his superiors passed the baton to an outsider.

I needed his support, his cooperation, not his bad mood. Smiling, I rehearsed my speech in my mind, and when I was ready, I looked into his eyes.

"Sit down, Wayne. Thank you so much for making time to see me. It's nice to meet you in person."

He sat down and crossed his arms. Not one word yet, his features remained tight. I intercepted our server to get Freeman a beer. Maybe that would lose him up.

"I understand you guys did a top-notch investigation in the Mark Taylor file. His family has only good words for the police department and the work you did. John Russell also appreciated your efforts, and he mentioned it a few times when I met him. You have been unlucky so far; that's something that can happen in the best-run investigations."

I stopped, waiting for a reply. Silence greeted my introduction, so I continued.

"The family asked I look into Mark's whereabouts. I'm not here to replace you but add to your team. You guys are busy surely, I enjoy some available time, and I intend to continue the investigation with your help if you don't mind."

He shook his head in approbation, the first positive sign so far. JR must have prepared him before.

"Your buddy could not come?" I asked.

He replied, "No, his kid had a soccer match tonight."

At that moment, Freeman's beer arrived, which seemed to please him.

"OK, let me share new information with you then. Today, I visited the First National Bank of Miami branch on Federal where Mark owns a safe deposit box."

He moved forward, curious to hear the rest. He may not have known this information yet. It wasn't surprising. By a fluke, I discovered a set of keys and noticed the particular form of the safety deposit key.

"We found around sixty thousand dollars in cold hard cash in there. Not a bartender's earnings."

"No kidding, that's a surprise," he added.

"He hid the key in his personal effects, almost impossible to find. That discovery may throw new light on his disappearance. Any idea of how he would have gotten his hands on such a stack of cash?"

"No, we know he worked professional contracts in the technology sector in the past, but they wouldn't pay him cash," he suggested.

"Drug dealing, maybe?" I offered.

"It's possible at this stage, but my partner and I verified with the narcotics division. He's not on their radar, never has been."

If Mark wanted to disappear, no doubt he would have brought money with him and unusually cold hard currency. If it was still in the bank, it's because he didn't have access to it. Why? That I didn't know yet.

"We didn't find a passport either, so I asked Russell to look into it. Where are we with our request to Homeland Security?" I asked.

"Sent yesterday; we're awaiting a response, Jason."

Jason? He was now on a first-name basis.

"OK, case information?"

"You have the full documentation in the envelope right in front of you."

"The plastic bag analysis?"

"In the works, I expect the lab to send us results in a few days."

"Excellent, Wayne, we'll be a great team."

We continued our discussion for another fifteen minutes before I apologized; I had to return. We exchanged business cards for future contacts, and I left the bar, a package under my arm.

I got back to my yacht and advised the local harbormaster I would stay an extra day because of the thickness of the file handed me tonight. After dinner, I brought my cup of tea to the aft deck and examined the case data.

A lot of paperwork resulted from police activities. If you sneezed, a form existed for that. I read through a good part of the paperwork that evening. Police reports contain the detective's notes after meeting a witness during the case. Occasionally, the police will ask for a formal statement. Nadine, the neighbor, and the Black Cat manager all provided statements, the strict minimum I reflected. I read them carefully, but nothing special stood out. I went to sleep with doubts about the police investigation's intensity. The file was thick, but the results were pretty thin.

# # #

The Missing Taylor

The next morning, I untangled the trawler and headed to my home Marina, adopting the Intercostal Waterway back. The route is slower because of "no wake" zones here and there, but it's a fun ride.

I cruised up to Pompano at around 10 knots when the procedures allowed it. On a sweltering day, the breeze generated by my forward progression was more than welcome. Once I secured the boat and attached the power cord, I turned the air conditioning which was an excellent option on the trawler as the absence of wind heated the interior today.

I installed my laptop on the salon table along with the sizable police file when my phone buzzed. Hank Hackman's face showed up on my display.

"Hank, I expect you to have great news for me."

"I did find some information. Let me go down the list. First, Mark Taylor has no arrest or criminal history on the judicial front, at least at the federal level and in Florida. I did not examine all the states."

"He comes from Illinois; look over there if you can."

"OK, regarding his finances, I found transactions at the First National Bank of Miami where Taylor kept a simple checking account. It shows just a few operations used to manage his living expenses, such as phone bills, rent, and other small stuff. Payroll deposits appear inconsistent; some months there is none. I will forward you the documents by email, Mister Tanner."

"Great, anything else?"

"Yes, your guy has two credit cards, according to his Equifax profile. I peeked at 12 months as you asked and looked at his transactions. The last ones originated from Marathon, in the Florida Keys."

"Fascinating, on what dates?"

"September 11 and 12."

"Just around the period he disappeared, excellent Hank, send me the data as promptly as you can."

"It's on its way, thanks."

I hung up the phone and got my investigative logic going. Mark made transactions on the 11th and 12th of September. His sister tried to reach him on the 13th, to no avail. And he did not answer a few days later. Maybe something happened to him after September 12 if he's the one using the credit cards. It is common to see a victim's credentials used, often by the murderer himself.

My laptop sounded the new email melody shortly after. Hank was on time again.

I examined the transactions with interest. A charge of $12 appeared on September 11 at Barnacle Barney's Tiki bar and grill, the day after, $52, same place.

I grabbed my phone and called Nadine. I had a few concerns.

"Nadine, sorry to bother you, but I have a quick question. Did your brother have friends in Marathon, or did he go there occasionally?"

A slight hesitation, then, "I don't think so, why?"

"I received information Mark used his credit card two days in September, just before his disappearance. I want to understand why he traveled to Marathon; any girlfriends in the area?"

"I don't know, sorry."

"Another puzzle to resolve is why he left his car at the apartment."

"A surfing expedition maybe, a bunch of friends get together, pack a minivan with their boards and head to the beaches?"

"Possible, thanks, Nadine." And I hung up.

Could surfing the seas around the Keys be a possibility? And then an accident? Which nobody noticed? Unlikely.

I made more calls to surf shops to discover that Marathon was not Mecca for surfers. The Keys configuration did not produce the large wave surfers crave. All the folks I talked to offer better alternatives. A few searches on the Internet allowed me to conclude Marathon was a fishing capital, not a unique surfing opportunity. I doubted Nadine's hunch would materialize.

I pulled the police file out of the large envelope and dug in for a report in particular. The detectives had questioned someone at the Black Cat bar. There, I found it. Freeman interviewed the manager, Jorge Garcia, on September 20, some 48 hours after Nadine first reported her brother missing, not quite an example of immediacy.

I read the file. It said the bar manager called Mark late afternoon when the regular barman complained of having laryngitis. It was not the only time Mark had replaced someone last minute. The manager trusted him, so he called him first. He was available and arrived at the bar around 7 pm. The manager didn't notice anything strange, and it was a typically busy night at the Black Cat.

Jackson, Freeman's partner, found a few regulars at the bar who were present the previous week. On Friday night, one of them did notice two individuals seated at the bar. Mark talked to them occasionally, a standard duty of a bartender. The unusual thing is when Mark ended his shift around midnight, he then left with the same two guys, Asians he specified. The bar manager could not confirm this statement when questioned again.

Old friends, new ones, acquaintances, partners, what were these two Asian guys to Mark Taylor?

I got up and pulled an opened bottle of white wine from the ship's refrigerator, which I brought to the table. My back was hurting again, and I reached for my pain medication. With only a few tablets left, I needed to refill soon, but examining the label, I noticed that I required a brand new prescription. With Dr. Ferguson retired and three postponements of my pain management meetings already, I was running out of options.

Would I rely on the street to get my drugs after all these years in law enforcement?

I parked my thought temporarily and picked up my phone and searched for Detective Freeman's number from his business card.

"Wayne? Jason Tanner. How are you?"

"Fine. Are you still in Miami?"

"No, back in Pompano, it's as warm as Miami."

"Not a surprise. What can I do for you?"

"I read in your report the interview with the Black Cat manager and other bar regulars. Someone stated that Mark left with two gentlemen of Asian descent. Were you able to trace these guys?"

"No, we did not. We examined the night's billing report. They paid cash. The manager didn't know them, only that one witness who saw them leave; we had no other leads."

"I see, and it's understandable. But I believe Mark may have spent a few days in Marathon after his shift at the Black Cat."

"And how do you know?"

"Don't ask. But it's reliable."

"OK, I won't."

He would have found out the same information if he had dug a bit more.

"Mark spent time at Barnacle Barney, a bar in Marathon, on both Saturday and Sunday evening. I suspect he must have slept in a motel, not on a park bench. Now you guys have more leverage than I have. Could you call around Marathon and look for a motel or hotel near Barnacle Barney? See if you can find Mark on the 10th, 11th, or 12th day of September. Begin with the cheapest places. He would not splurge three hundred dollars a night."

"I'll get my partner on this and get back to you."

"Thank you for the continuing effort, Wayne. Did you receive any news from the Homeland Security people?"

"No, and nothing from the lab either. As soon as I know, I'll call you."

"OK, thanks, Wayne."

I moved outside to my favorite chair with my glass of wine, trying to arrange my thoughts and speculate on what could have happened to Mark Taylor.

Mark, a solitary man, not married, has no steady girlfriend with a temporary replacement job as a bartender, meets two individuals while working and leaves with them. He drives his car back to his apartment and hops with the two guys, direction Marathon, I speculate. For what reason? Not to surf, he left his board in Miami. A temporary bartending gig? Maybe. More likely, it's to meet someone down there. Otherwise, they could have talked right here in Miami and saved a three-hour drive. But who would they be seeing?

And if he attended a mysterious meeting, what went wrong for Mark to disappear from the face of the earth?

Another thought crossed my mind. Why didn't the detectives issue an ordinary subpoena to access Taylor's credit card transactions? I received the information using my source, but the police had a simple process to get at it legitimately. Why would they not examine this avenue? Were they just lazy, or did they not want to shake the branches too much and risk something to fall?

I moved back inside to see about getting dinner ready. In the afternoon, I had walked to my Publix market and purchased a whole red snapper. I prepared it and brought it to the Rusty Hook Tavern cuisine, where my new buddy Jeff was operating the stoves. The restaurant is just off the Marina.

"Jeff, can I deposit my red snapper filet on your fire?"

"Be my guest Jason, use space over here," as he pointed to a free area on his dual grill. Being a friend of the chef was nice. "But have dinner inside once in a while," he added with a smirk.

After an excellent meal while I watched the news, I started up my web browser to explore Marathon and its hotels, restaurants, bars, Marina, and the information I needed should I sail over there.

The phone rang. I looked at the caller ID and smiled.

"Hey young girl, how are you?"

"I'm fine, dad. Can't be better."

"That's nice, still saving lives in Denver, gorgeous?"

"I will not be for the next few days, Dad. The hospital owes me vacations, and if I don't take them before the end of March, I will lose them."

"And what were you planning to do?"

"I was thinking of coming down to Florida and staying with you for five or six days. Do you think it's possible?"

"Of course. I am preparing to sail to Miami and Marathon in the Florida Keys. I am working on a case but not full-time. You can help me solve it. Father and daughter detective team that would be nice. Veronica Mars and her father, in Neptune. What do you think?"

"You know your TV series. It sounds great, Dad, where shall we meet? Fort Lauderdale?"

"Hum. I am planning to travel to Miami in the morning. When would you arrive?"

"I would leave the day after tomorrow."

"Then that would be perfect. Go to Miami International Airport, more choices are available, and it will be easier. From there, grab a cab. The Miami Beach Marina is thirty minutes away. I will be there waiting for you. Just ring me when you land."

"Great. I miss you, Dad."

"Me too, darling; we'll have a great time, I'm sure."

After ending the call, I was elated. I had not seen Cynthia for quite a while. With my move to Florida, the boat, the PI license, I had been too busy to visit her in Denver.

I returned to my computer. In my search, I found a Facebook page for missing people in South Florida used to communicate unresolved disappearance or the discovery of unidentified bodies. I could post information here to advance my case.

I first got the picture Nadine had provided. I used my phone to make an image and transferred it to my Photoshop application. I then isolated Mark from the rest of the group and added a neutral background. The result provided me with a solo picture of Mark. I would post it on the Facebook page with a short story on his disappearance from Marathon in September last year. Any person with information could get in contact with me through Messenger.

I returned my attention to the police reports to see who the detectives questioned during their probe, other than the Black Cat manager. They talked to employees, but few knew of Mark; he replaced only occasionally at the bar. They questioned Nadine and Mark's neighbors without ever discovering any real information. Nadine told me her brother surfed the beaches of Miami. The police should have questioned people practicing the sport in the area, but no witness fits that description in the investigative report. Nadine didn't mention any surfers in her notes to me; I needed to check out this avenue. I had my work cut out for tomorrow.

# # #

Up early the next morning, I began searching for Mark's surfing companions. I had hoped the police would have located and interviewed some of them, but as captain Russell said, a limited staff has limited capabilities. Unless a celebrity or a young child disappears, the public shows little concern. Without the media pressure, the authorities dragged their feet on occasions.

While traveling to California once, I observed a group of surfers, all gathered together. The waves were large where they assembled. It was not a surfer every 500 feet spread out, more like every 10 feet, often less. So I needed to discover similar sites where they gathered on the beaches of Miami.

First, I looked into Miami Beach surf shops. I called a sizable group, each time asking where to find the most exceptional surfing locations. I cross-referenced the data with a Google search of Miami's best beaches for surfing. Several options appeared, and my map grew with possible candidates. I figured Mark would frequent a site close to his apartment. A list of nine such locations now emerged from the lot, all recorded on my portable GPS. I planned to arrive from the sea on my tender; it's easier to park than by car.

Checking my email, I only had a short message from Hank: "No activity in Illinois," a dead end.

I published the Facebook page asking my friends to share it to increase the number of people able to offer information on Mark Taylor's disappearance. You never know. I prepared for a new journey to Miami by resupplying PRIVATE EYE.

Chapter 4

Again, I got an early start, heading north toward Hillsboro Inlet. The tide was coming into the Intracoastal. I didn't have to wait for the draw bridge; the clearance is 21 feet here, and I can easily pass under. I navigated at low speed while studying a half-dozen fishermen trying to catch tonight's dinner. From the absence of movement onshore, I gathered the fish was not collaborating and pizza night was the alternative.

Once I was out by at least one mile, I set the automatic pilot for Miami Beach then made myself a fresh cup of coffee. After two hours of smooth sailing, my phone rang, Detective Freeman was on the line.

"Good morning Jason, I hope I am not disturbing you?"

"No, I am enjoying a nice cruise down the coast of Florida, headed to your city. As long as I have you, if you are available, why don't you join me for dinner aboard tonight? Nothing complicated."

"Maybe. I'll call you back around five o'clock to let you know. Will that work?"

"Sure."

"Russell asked me to call you. We received the lab reports for the plastic bag you brought in. They conclude it's fentanyl."

"No shit."

Fentanyl and the opioid crisis were all over the national news, not just in South Florida. Fentanyl, an opioid used to relieve pain, is at least 50 times more potent than morphine. While it's available in a medical setting, its bad reputation comes from illegal usage. Mixed with other drugs, it becomes OxyContin or Xanax sold on the street and consumed as a potent analgesic for chronic pain.

When no time or money is available to fix a medical problem, sometimes it's easier to take a cheap fake opioid and get a 12-hour relief. Artists like Prince died from an opioid-induced overdose, as have other major names in entertainment. Who would have thought?

"Wayne, I hope you find a few moments to come tonight. It is a serious business."

"I'll call you later," and he hung up.

Strange, Russell asked Freeman to reach out to me. Was a little push necessary to get the detective's cooperation with my investigation?

Good thing JR is on my side.

With an eye out for traffic out at sea, I powered my laptop while the Internet signal was strong enough. I needed to get up on fentanyl. This twist would complicate my investigation. Cash and drugs together spell bad news. If you translate the situation to a Family Feud trivia question, you will get something like, "Name things you find in a drug dealer's house." The top two answers would be drugs and cash; guns would not be bad either. We found most of these items in Taylor's belongings. Was he a dealer himself?

The research I consulted showed an increase in death rates by overdose because of mixing fentanyl with cocaine. Why would you add a deadly drug into an existing one? It seems the combination makes for a more potent mix, more addictive, and so brings more money into dealer pockets. I also read most of the fentanyl comes directly from China. Was there a link with the Asians in my investigation?

Scanning the news, a story caught my attention. Fentanyl was imported as a finished product from China and through Mexico. The cartels were quick on finding new revenue streams. But although the drug was banned, its primary ingredients were not, or very little. Was I the only one who found this situation a bit ridiculous?

Around eleven o'clock, Miami Beach was getting closer, so I turned the automatic pilot off and slowly maneuvered my yacht to the Miami Beach Marina. With my reservations in order, I slipped into berth H9, bow first needing to unload my dinghy over the stern. My next activity consisted of reaching my first high-priority surfer site: South Point Park. Located just off the Marina where I stayed a few days ago, this area is an urban park and quite popular with tourists and residents alike. As the name clearly says, it is the southern point of the Miami Beach area.

After I lowered the tender and tied it to the transom, I grabbed a small backpack and filled it with my long-range binoculars, portable GPS, and Glock 17 sidearm. If I left in an hour, it would put me on the site around 4 pm, an excellent surfing period. Hoping that Freeman would join me later, I expedited the dinner preparation. Should he make it, I would return aboard. Otherwise, I would continue my search for Mark Taylor's friends into the evening finishing with a late lunch if needed. Both possibilities worked for me. Still early, I walked to a Total Wine store nearby to replenish my inventory, ensuring I had an excellent Bordeaux for tonight.

The Missing Taylor

I prepared to leave at around four o'clock, dressed in shorts and a tee-shirt with rubber flip-flops. With my phone in my back pocket, business cards in the front, and my notebook bearing Mark Taylor's picture in my tee-shirt pocket, I was ready. I put on my backpack and got into my tender. Inflated, this tiny boat is V-shaped upfront with a driving station in the middle and an outboard motor in the back. The little boat can carry one person comfortably with a small load, or it can transport a second party without pleasure.

I pumped gas into the engine, pulled once, twice, and that was enough to create the gentle sound of my Honda engine. Fumes told neighbors that a motor was active. I untied the tender, pushed the gear forward, and slipped out of the Marina toward Government Cut, which provided access to the Atlantic Ocean. I went around South Point Park Pier and the breakers. The surf beach was on the other side of the rock formation used to secure Biscayne Bay's entrance.

As I rounded the breakers and performed a one-hundred-and-eighty degrees turn, I saw people in the water, sitting on their boards, dressed in black one-piece swimsuits. A few brave, or unfortunate, surfers only wore regular trunks. In March, the water temperature was not collaborating.

I looked for a place to beach my craft and found an isolated area where I saw no one close. I sped up, and at a safe distance from the beach, I shut it off, turned around, and lifted the outboard motor's foot out of the water. I got out and hauled my small boat onto the sand. I removed the key, not wanting anyone to grab it and disappear for a fun ride.

I meandered down the beach, always looking for surfers doing their things. It took tremendous abilities to maneuver a surfboard as they had. When a surfer got out, joined a companion, or just took a break on his towel, that was my trigger. I would approach them, comment on their physical abilities, and ask them if they knew the man in the picture in my notebook. When someone asked why I wanted this information, I told them the truth. His sister hired me to look for him. I handed them a business card in case they remembered something later.

Nobody recalls seeing Mark at South Point Park, so I moved to my next site, the beach at 3rd Street, just a little way from my initial landing. Heading up north, I used my GPS to give me an idea of the exact location. When you drive around the city, it's easy to locate 3rd Street. Signs are posted on street corners. From the sea, it's more complicated, and my GPS was useful. I found a parking space for my dinghy and questioned the crowd in that area as well. No success there either. Nobody knew Mark Taylor, the surfer.

My phone rang as I was about to leave and investigate the beach at 12th Street. Freeman was available tonight and would show up for dinner. I gave him directions to my yacht and headed back to meet him. When I got to my watercraft, I noticed one side of the dinghy had collapsed. As I approached closer, I saw a one-inch tear. A knife had perforated one side, it looked like. Someone did not welcome my being here. I had only talked to a dozen people and already got someone mad at me, so much for making a good first impression.

A small compartment inside my tender held patches and a portable pump. In about 10 minutes, the problem was solved, and I was on my way back.

When Freeman arrived, dinner was almost ready; only the steaks waited for their hot spot on the ship's grill. Freeman stepped aboard, and I offered him other footwear to save my teak floors. I had set up two chairs on the aft deck, and he sat in one, at least not my favorite one, so I offered him a drink. He liked beer, and I had Blue Moon aboard, so that's what I brought him while I fixed myself a dry martini.

The Missing Taylor

In the spirit of exchanging information, I told him I was back in Miami to look for Mark's surfing buddies. He admitted his squad lacked enough time to research these connexions. I informed him of the attack on my tender, and that prompted a long silence. After a few seconds, he suggested, "Accidental?" I didn't think so.

It was such a beautiful and warm evening. I moved the dining table outside where we could eat under the stars. I gave Freeman plates to set while I handled the grill. A few minutes later, we were enjoying our red meat.

"Wayne, with today's lab reports, it opens a whole new line of thinking about this case. Maybe Mark was buying or selling drugs or even fentanyl."

"We have no solid evidence yet. Someone else could have left the bag, and we have no prints on it. As a curiosity, do you know what we call cocaine or crack pushers in American punk slang?"

"No."

"A bartender."

"Well, well," I said. "Isn't that a strange coincidence?"

"So, what is your plan for the next few days?" Freeman asked.

"I will continue to chase surfers on the beaches from right here."

"Check the Northside. A lot of surfing happens over there too. I will follow up with Homeland Security on the passport question."

Freeman may not be my favorite person yet, but I found him more enjoyable today.

"Sounds like a plan. I'll drink to that," as we raised our wine glasses and watched the sun slowly disappear from the sky.

# # #

The next day, I got up early to catch the surfers in their morning session. I would try to visit as many of the previously identified sites. Cynthia was arriving today, so when she called, I would return home and act as the perfect host. My first stop of the day was the beach at 12th Street. I used the same approach as yesterday with one exception: I kept a closer watch on my tender.

During my morning expedition, I questioned at least thirty surfers and was running out of business cards. My watch showed almost noon, and I was hungry, so I returned to the Marina. As I approached my berth, I noticed two pairs of eyes on a bench near the docks and looking my way. Probably two friends enjoying the Marina views.

As I unlocked the main cabin door and set foot in the salon, my phone rang. I examined the number on the screen, unknown, but the 305 area code told me it was a call from this neck of the woods.

"Hello."

"Mr. Tanner?"

"Yes, this is he. Who is this?"

"I'm Jeff Mason, sir. I understand you were at South Point Park yesterday, looking for people with information about Mark Taylor."

"Yes, I was." Thanks for calling me.

"A buddy yesterday was talking about you, but I was in the water the whole time; the surf was superb then. When I got out, you had left, but my friend gave me your card, and here I am."

Finally, I was getting a break, maybe.

"Possible we meet today, Jeff? Are you surfing tonight?"

"Yes, I am."

"I suggest we meet at the South Point Park Pier. I am close by. Will that work for you?"

"Fine, around 6:30 maybe; it will give me time for a few runs."

"Fantastic, I will wear a Chicago Black Hawk hat."

"Fine, I'll be in my black wetsuit, as usual."

"Perfect, see you later." I created a phone contact using the last number on my screen, and I added Jeff's name.

I picked the pier location for its closeness. It would be a short walk for Jeff, hardly five minutes, fifteen for me, a public park, safe and quiet, nothing would happen there.

After lunch, Cynthia checked in just as her plane landed. I expected she would arrive in less than an hour, so I used the time to clean the guest room where some stuff had accumulated behind the closed door. This room serves as a storage area when I'm alone, now it would have a real guest. I made it pleasant by removing and storing the ship's equipment in their rightful lockers. I cleaned the floors; it now had a pleasant aroma and was ready for occupation. Her private bathroom checked out as well; everything was in order.

I went upstairs to the flybridge to await Cynthia's arrival.

The phone rang again, another unknown number from the 305 area code.

"Hello."

"Mr. Tanner, this is LeBron Jackson from the Miami-Date Police department, I'm Wayne's partner, and I have information for you."

"Hi, LeBron. Nice to talk to you."

"Same here. I located the place Taylor stayed for those two nights back in September."

I got my notebook out, "Yes?"

"It's called Captain Pip's Marina and Hideaway, and the address is 1610 Overseas Highway, the phone number 305-743-3044. It is one of the cheapest motels in the area, as you had assumed. He stayed there on September 11 and 12."

"Excellent, LeBron, great job, that will serve us well."

"Happy to contribute. Captain Russell would like to talk to you when you have a minute."

"I will call him this afternoon, promised. Thank you again, LeBron."

I moved to the main salon and got my computer powered up. I searched for Captain Pip's Hideaway and looked at pictures of the main building, the accommodations, and the Marina. It was all third-rate except for the $165 daily fee for a single room. I could not imagine what the berthing rates would be for my yacht. Other Marinas in the area were available, but I preferred staying where Mark had spent a few days.

As I was looking at other images of the region, I heard a car door close, and as I looked up, Cynthia was getting out of a white Tesla. I rushed outside and down the docks to greet her and grab her luggage. I walked to the point of almost running, so happy to see her.

"Hey, Dad!"

"Nice to see you, Cynthia. How have you been?"

"Fantastic, look at you now, all trimmed, fit, and bronzed. You impress me."

"The tan is not mine; a greater authority controls it. I should put more protection. But I have no one on my case now."

"I'll try to give you better life manners while I'm here."

I grabbed her backpack and walked toward the dock and her new residence for the next few days. "You sure travel lite," I said.

"Shorts, T-shirt, swimsuits, how heavy can that be?"

"You have a point there, young lady," as we neared our floating home.

"So this is your new toy. It looks wonderful, wow. Give me the official visit, will you?"

We spent the next twenty minutes touring the yacht. Cynthia had pertinent questions such as why a trawler; for fuel economy, a single-engine, easy maintenance. She appreciated the reasonable size but still large enough for a comfortable living. Small for a two-person setup, but just for me, it was perfect. I could control and man the ship solo.

We proceeded to the flybridge and talked for over an hour under the roof, protecting us from the setting sun but still savoring the warm climate.

My 6:30 meeting was coming up, and I told Cynthia. She should look around the galley for the pasta dish I had prepared for tonight. I stepped into my cabin, got the Chicago Black Hawk hat, told Cynthia that I would be back around 7:00, and strolled toward my rendezvous. I gazed at my watch, 6:15; I should be there just in time. The maritime traffic around Biscayne Bay is dense, with both small and large vessels coming and going. As I approached the meeting place, I looked for a man wearing a black wetsuit. I saw only one standing around, and I marched right toward him.

"Jeff?"

"Yes, Mr. Tanner?"

"Glad to meet you, let's sit here," as I showed a bench close by.

"Jeff, thanks for contacting me; I appreciate it. The Taylor family hired me to locate Mark. I understand he loved surfing, and I hoped some of his comrades might know his whereabouts. You knew Mark, I assume."

"Yes, I did. I met Mark when he first joined our little brotherhood of surfers two years ago. He would come around in the morning and late afternoon."

"He had plenty of time thus."

"Yes, he worked nights mostly. On occasions, Mark worked a full-time job lasting a month or two barely."

"And you got to befriend Mark?"

"I did. I work in a large engineering firm, and I struggle to find time to surf. But not Mark. He never had this problem as he only worked part-time. It always amazed me how he could manage, but he did. Money was not a problem; he earned just enough, I guess."

"Are you aware of what he did for a living?"

"He told me he worked in nightclubs as a replacement bartender. He also said he did contractual work on occasions. And I understand his dad has plenty of money."

"Did you guys meet at other places than the beach?"

"Sometimes we had a drink in a small bar close to the beach after surfing."

"Are you aware of any girlfriend?" I asked.

"No, he was a solitary guy. He met women at bars sometimes, but they were for one night only, never longer."

"What were his favorite subjects? Do you remember?"

"We talked a lot about sports, that's for sure. His other interest was surfing. He also enjoyed reading about federal politics, especially our strange president."

"Interesting, do you know if he was into drugs? Did he talk about that?"

"I have no reason to believe he was into drugs, Mister Tanner. I never observed him use. But something is strange. He talked about some places he worked where drugs were being distributed almost freely. He saw people with no education make thousands of dollars by delivering a bag of pills. He worked hours before making that kind of money."

"Do you know what places he was referring to?"

"No, I think he talked about bars in general, at least those he worked at."

"Hum, I need to ask, do you know anyone who would want to see him dead?" I had to ask.

Jeff looked at me and said, "Dead? Do you think it's possible?"

"It is Jeff. He vanished over six months already."

After a brief pause, he said he did not know of anybody that hated Mark and thus could see no reason to harm him. I inquired if Mark had other friends, and he had a few people to suggest, so I noted their names and phone numbers. I thanked him, and he left toward the beach area while I wrote some notes on the bench.

# # #

I got up and walked toward my boat, where Cynthia waited aboard for our first dinner in ages. The pier sector is quite lovely, surrounded by trees and bushes planted by the city, making it a pleasant, peaceful zone. I noticed a few people walking around the area, and I wondered why; it was so beautiful here.

Lost in my thoughts, someone hit me behind the head by what I figured must have been the most massive baseball bat in the world. I closed my eyes in pain, fell to my knees, and lost consciousness.

When I woke up, Cynthia was next to me, and I heard sirens in the backdrop.

"Don't move, you may have a concussion," as an experienced registered nurse would suspect.

I moved onto my backside, knowing right away that was an ill idea. As soon as I rested my head on the ground, my once terrible headache pulsed again. Because of the grimace I made, Cynthia put a sweater underneath my neck, so my head rested on something other than the hard cement pathway, a welcome idea.

"What happened?" I asked.

"I don't know, Dad," she answered. "You were late, and I was getting anxious, so I walked toward the point, following your steps. In the distance, I could see a group of people gathered around. When I arrived, I found you here, unconscious. Someone had already called 911. The ambulance arrived shortly after. Stay calm."

Easy for you to say kiddo, I thought. I touched the back of my head. It was wet with a large lump already pulsing. When I brought my hand back, I could see plenty of blood on it. The paramedics arrived and moved me onto a stretcher and into the nearest hospital while Cynthia held my hand.

A dozen sutures and a few painkillers later, I was better while still hearing a buzz between my ears. Without surprise, the doctor told me I should stay overnight. I answered I had a personal nurse handling my case. He looked at Cynthia, smiled, and signed my release papers while she was arguing, "I am a nurse."

We arrived on PRIVATE EYE around 10 pm with our stomachs crying for food. Cynthia moved to the galley to get the pasta going to relieve our appetite.

"You must have a theory of what happened, don't you?" she said.

"Not sure. Well, let me rephrase that. I have been asking around about Mark Taylor all over the beaches of Miami. Someone I questioned did not revel in my inquiries."

"You suppose, Dad?"

"Not too many options, dear. Someone mugged me, and my wallet is still in my back pocket. My Timex is on my wrist. What else could it be?"

"A message, but which one?"

"It's clear. Return to where you came from, stay away from this Mark Taylor investigation. We don't need you snooping around here."

Bad guys react when you are getting closer to them and the truth. But in my case, I was getting closer to what? I was clueless so far.

Chapter 5

I enjoyed a good night in my boat's comfortable bed with a few painkillers. Cynthia endured the guest room's small bunk. All the windows were open, and a cool breeze with rolling waves transported us both in a deep sleep.

Up before sunrise, I started the coffeemaker. I reviewed my notes again at the central table while planning my day's activities. First, I needed to talk to JR; I forgot about calling him yesterday. Next, I would reach out to Mark's friends as Jeff Mason had suggested. We also had to prepare for our excursion to Marathon. When Cynthia got up, she reached for the coffee machine, ate a few fruits, and went outside for her morning run, saying she would return in an hour. I told her to beware of South Point Park pier. She smiled, marched onto the dock, stretched, and jogged as soon as she reached the shore.

I cleaned the galley from yesterday and prepared for a more hardy breakfast upon her return. When I opened the guest room's door to tidy up, I faced pieces of clothing everywhere; so I closed it. I kept looking at my watch to call John early once he made it in the office. Marathon was a six-hour journey at my standard cruising speed. If I wanted to get there before dark, I needed to start no later than one o'clock, giving me the morning hours to handle a few loose ends.

At 8:01, I placed a call to John Russell, who answered at once.

"JR, sorry I didn't call you yesterday. I was busy, and around dinner time, when I could have spoken with you, I was unconscious."

"What happened?"

I informed him of my recent search since my arrival in Miami and how someone attacked me from behind while I returned to the Marina. It surprised him I didn't report the incident, but I said it was a waste of time. I saw nobody, and no witnesses came forward when Cynthia asked the group gathered around me that evening. I saved Miami-Dade's police a few hours of unnecessary work.

"You wanted me to call you, Detective Jackson informed me."

"Yes, I did. I have strange news to report. Homeland Security replied to the query we launched about Taylor's passport."

"Yes, you have the information I gather."

"Yes, we got an answer back, NSF."

"NSF. What is this?"

"No Such File. It means no data is available on this passport. We provided a name, date of birth, and Social Security Number. They must trace this person with this data; unless.... Unless they don't want to offer the information."

"It's impossible they don't have a file on this person," I objected.

"With politicians, stars, or any 'special' people, they hide information from us. It started when a Senator got a call from a constituent policeman to complain in person. Now, the government looks after the elite's privacy."

"Hum, so Mark Taylor, a common American working bars, is elite? He's not a politician, not a celebrity, and we have no indication he's a terrorist, at least, so far. What sort of 'special' person could he be?" I asked.

"CIA, NSA, FBI, or others," answered John, trying to find a legitimate response.

"I guess it's possible, but it would surprise me in this case. From Mark's background information provided by his sister, I see no period when Mark could have trained for one of these agencies. It is not in the cards." After a few seconds, I added, "Anything else, John?"

"Yes, someone told us to stop collaborating with you at once, or I should say yesterday."

"Oh yeah? Did they give any reasons?"

"None. Between you and me, Jason, call me on the number you see on your phone, it's my private line, to discuss any issues. I'll be available."

"Interesting. I may call upon you, John. Thanks."

"Thanks, Jason. You be careful now."

While waiting for Cynthia's return, I reserved a berth at the Marathon Marina for tonight, plus a few extra days in case. I called Nadine, but she must have been at work. So I left a message telling her I was heading down to Marathon, having received new information showing Mark spent a few days in the vicinity before he disappeared. I abstained from telling her about my encounter with a baseball bat. She did not need to know.

When Cynthia returned, she got into the shower while I completed breakfast which we enjoyed outdoor.

"So, what is the plan for today?" she asked.

"You and I will watch surfers this morning, and then, we hit the road, or I should say hit the sea, and sail to Marathon."

"When do we start our stakeout?"

"Right now," I said. We cleaned the table. I grabbed my backpack, locked the doors, and headed out.

"Where to, Dick Tracy?" she asked.

"We are going to South Point Park, but this time, incognito."

After a 15-minute walk, we stepped onto the warm sand. We observed several surfers honing their skills on the fiberglass boards this Saturday morning. We stayed far away from the group and rented a cabana beach setup which included two chairs and a half-moon top to protect us from the sun.

I pulled out my ship binoculars from my backpack and brought them to eye level. I examined the group of surfers while being a quarter-mile away, they couldn't see me, but I did. I looked for Jeff Mason to no avail.

A movement attracted my attention. Two men were walking along from the nearby pier in the surfer's direction. While most people on the beach wore swimsuits or shorts, these two guys donned pants and Polo shirts, shoes in hands. I trained my binoculars on the curious couple. I adjusted the focus and discovered two Asian males in my sight. One was tall and bulky while his companion was a few inches smaller and skinny. The image of Laurel and Hardy popped up. Laurel, the tall one, had an oval face, tiny lips, and his eyes were behind a pair of large round sunglasses. His hair was short and black. He resembled Psy, the Korean singer in Gangnam style. Hardy, his smaller buddy, also wore glasses, rectangular but clear. His distinguishing features were a set of long blond hair on top of a black base, colored for sure.

I watched them approach the surfers and stop in front of the group. One figure emerged from the sea with a board under his arm, walked toward the two men, and then, all three gathered around a backpack. The surfer reached in, extracted a towel, and dried off. Boy, I would love to hear this conversation. I pulled my notebook out and handed it over to my assistant.

"Get your cell phone and dial this number, and then this other one? If anybody answers, hang up."

"Why?" she asked.

"A hunch."

I extracted my Nikon camera from my bag. Equipped with a decent size zoom, it recorded the three men together. I kept watching the trio, snapping pictures, while listening to Cynthia key in the numbers on her phone. When she got to the second call, the surfer bent down toward his backpack, extracted a phone, and put it to his ear. I heard my assistant investigator say, "Sorry, wrong number."

She had reached Yang Nelson, one of the two individuals Mason said was friendly with Mark Taylor. How interesting was this? The beach discussion continued for a few more minutes, and the trio then separated. Laurel and Hardy turned toward the pier where they came from while Nelson picked up his surfboard and walked toward the nearby parking lot.

"Cynthia, can you follow those two guys but be careful? Stay far away. See where they go if you can. Get a license number if they drive off. We'll meet up aboard the yacht afterward."

Cynthia knew who I was referring to. She got up and walked toward the pier, like a professional tourist, keeping the couple in her sight. When Nelson left the beach through an access corridor, I picked up my bag and walked to the next passageway, a few hundred feet away. He hoisted the long surfboard on top of his jeep and extracted himself from his wetsuit using a towel wrapped around him. With this technique, Nelson emerged in pink shorts with a white polo shirt, his thick black hair combed backward. He hopped in the open-air all-wheel-drive vehicle and accelerated away from me. I raised my binoculars once more and got the license plate number, which I noted.

While I walked back to the yacht, I called Hank Hackman and asked for a full rundown of Yang Nelson. I provided his license plate number, figuring this should be enough to identify him.

Back aboard, I called Cynthia's name, to no avail. I raced up to the flybridge, no sign of her either, I worried. I hoped no one would spot her trailing the Asians, most importantly, not the ones she was following. All kinds of terrible scenarios erupted in my head, and my skin prickled. I rushed down the ladder, all sorts of evil thoughts in my head, and came face-to-face with William Tudor, his yellowing teeth smiling at me.

"William!" He hated to be called Bill. "What's up?" I said.

"I thought you had gone for good, but you're back. You must like Miami Beach."

"I do. But right now, I have a big problem. Can I ask you a favor, William? My daughter has gone out, and I need to find her right away. But if I leave and she comes back, she'll just try to track me down again. Could you stay here and tell her, when she returns, to just wait for me."

"I can manage, brother."

"Go inside, grab a drink in the fridge; it is past noon here and 5 pm somewhere in the world. I will join you when I come back. It shouldn't be too long."

"Got it, Jason."

I hurried over the back rail and ran down the docks in search of Cynthia. From the Marina, Alton Road runs only in one direction, northbound. I figured people coming to the area parked near the A1A Bridge and walked south toward the Marina or the South Point Park Pier. Closer to the bridge, I looked for either Cynthia or any of the two guys I asked her to follow without too much reflection. I could see no one. I looked everywhere but could not find her. I kept walking, sometimes running forward until a wider street appeared just ahead, 5th Avenue. I headed in that direction, still looking for any sign of my daughter. Then I recognized her coming out of a Burger King, of all places. She saw me and stopped in mid-stride. I ran to her. "Where have you been?"

"Well, I followed them as instructed, Dad, and as I arrived on Alton Road, gone, they vanished. I looked around to no avail. I walked to the bridge, and still, no trace of them."

"And then?"

"Well, Burger King got my attention. I don't go there often, but I was hungry and away from my buddies in Denver, impossible to resist."

"Well, you scared me. But it's fine now. Let's go back."

We trudged back. I had my arm around my daughter's shoulder. When we reached the ship, we discovered William crouched over the table, in the salon, inanimate. I rushed to his side, put my fingers on his neck, right beside the back of his jaw, nothing. Cynthia got close to William and tested another pulse point on his wrist, nothing either. William was dead. I examined the surroundings; other than the body, everything looked normal to me. The back door was still open. I pulled out my phone and dialed 9-1-1, reporting a dead body on my boat.

No visible sign of violence. It could be a basic heart attack, I told myself. The autopsy would confirm. Overwhelmed. I asked Cynthia to step off the boat, and I followed her to protect the crime scene, just in case the death was not natural. My FBI instincts at work. Minutes later, sirens erupted around the Marina, and uniformed officers rushed in to investigate the reported call.

A few minutes later, an unmarked car with a red beacon flashing on the roof arrived with screeching tires. Two guys in suits came out and walked toward my yacht; I recognized one. I walked in his direction. When he saw me, he paused for a second. Detective Freeman seemed surprised to see me.

# # #

Later that night, after our terrible day, Cynthia and I got our living space back after the judicial system brought in their crime scene units to the Marina. After my call, the ordinarily quiet area saw its fair share of ambulances, police cars, coroner, and forensic experts on site. Plenty of lookers just sat around waiting for God knows what.

They dispatched Wayne Freeman and his sidekick LeBron Jackson to the incident's location to lead the initial investigation. They did not call it a crime scene at first. They found the victim sitting on the main salon couch, his head lying on the table, a drink spilled on the floor. Will his death be classified as natural or violent? Hard to say. An autopsy will be performed to determine the official cause of death.

Freeman asked me a few questions while Jackson spoke to my daughter. After the interview, they compared notes; it was standard protocol. We received instructions to come to the station and fill out a statement. We complied. While we were away, other officers questioned folks at the Marina, both owners and guests. The detectives solicited harbor management to give whatever video surveillance footage they possessed. The Marina has about 12 parallel docks with boats moored on either side. A camera sat on top of a post at each door leading to the dock and recorded arrivals and departures. The camera looks at the door, not the boats. The harbormaster assistant, a young lady behind a large desk at the central harbor station, prepared a DVD and handed it over to one of the detectives after proper identification.

I had known William for less than a week but grown to like the man. He would have made a fantastic fishing companion with the knowledge of history he possessed. I will miss him. At 73, heart failure can show its ugly head, I told myself.

Cynthia and I were brought to a location where they collected our fingerprints. The request surprised Cynthia, but I explained that the technicians needed to identify the inhabitants and figure out what prints were supposed to be there. Before leaving, Freeman asked me if I wanted to review the camera footage before I returned. My daughter and I had not eaten yet, and I was getting tired. If he could give me a copy, I had time on my hands to review it tomorrow while on our way to Marathon. We waited ten minutes, and then he brought us a small plastic container with a disk which I put in my backpack. He mentioned that the video showed people moving around the Marina but nothing criminal at first glance. A cruiser drove us back, and we were both hungry, I could sense it.

"Hungry? I have chicken breasts in the cooler. I can grill while you make a healthy salad?" I said.

"What if we go out? I located a Brazilian steakhouse on my last run, just a five-minute walk. Want to try it out?"

"Sure, honey, let's go."

Once seated with a glass of white wine for her and a martini for me, Cynthia told me how the unusual situation affected her.

The Missing Taylor

"It's quite a story so far, Dad, but I feel bad about a tragedy in your living room. I'm not sure the yacht will be a happy place anymore."

"I understand, Cynthia. William was a true gentleman, and, unfortunately, he died. But remember, he loved boats, fishing, and Marinas, so he died in a place he cherished, rather than in his small apartment downtown."

"And you only met him once?"

"Is this amazing or what? We clicked right away. Already, we had agreed on repeating the fishing expedition soon. We were planning to use my boat next time."

"I see your point. It may take a while to get used to it, but I'll manage, I guess. I'm hungry."

As she was expressing her feelings, our plates arrived, and we ate in silence, both of us lost in our thoughts. We returned to the boat around 9 pm, just as the last police officer guarding the scene told us we could go in now. He departed and removed all the remaining yellow tape.

Our initial reaction as we entered the salon was to look at where William's life ended. We both passed the table, walking toward the galley and our sleeping quarters. I made a small pot of tea as Cynthia showered and prepared for the night.

At around 10 pm, I made a final check, all the lights extinguished, doors secured, with my gun close on my side table.

#

We both overslept till eight o'clock the next morning, so tired after a horrific day. I got the coffee going before preparing the boat for a southbound six-hour run, direction Marathon. I opened the engine room access door while Cynthia called friends in Denver. The gas reservoir was full, bilge pumps and water-level alarms functioning,

VHF radio operating, AIS systems online. The fridge held food and ample drinking water.

I moved the table to the aft deck. Cynthia loved to eat breakfast outside with the rising sun. The night was restful as we talked over eggs, toast, and fruits, happy she felt better to continue.

Mid-morning, with the preparations completed and Cynthia away for a run, I reviewed my case notes. I had not called Mr. Taylor yet; an excellent opportunity presented itself now. Nadine had provided her father's number. The conversation was friendly, and he supported his daughter's quest to locate Mark. He was far from Florida; that's why he preferred Nadine handling the case. I asked him a tough question.

"Mister Taylor, did you provide financial support to your son?"

"No."

I had not expected this answer. If Mark didn't receive financial support from his family, where else? His part-time bartender job limited ownership of an apartment, even a car. He needed another source, legitimate or not. Which one was it?

Because of the earlier answer, I risked another. "Was Mark slated to inherit part of your estate after you're gone?"

"Absolutely not. I advised both Nadine and Mark long ago of my wish to leave my fortune to a charity upon my death. Their financial success would come from their efforts."

"I understand, sir. I needed this information. Thanks."

His response was clear. I could ignore the idea Mark was treading water until the inheritance arrived. I learned no fortune was coming. For Mark's future to materialize, he would have needed a steady job, the opposite of his recent actions.

The Missing Taylor

When Cynthia returned, she showered while I plotted our course to Marathon. She joined me on the flybridge where I summarized my call with Mr. Taylor.

"You are a lucky person," I told her. "Upon my death, you will inherit whatever I failed to spend. The Taylor offspring will receive nothing. The patriarch, worth more than a hundred million dollars, will donate everything to charity. Don't you feel blessed?"

"I do, dad. Bless his heart for caring about the needy. But a few million would have helped his children, and the charities wouldn't mind, I'm certain."

I could not disagree with her opinion.

With Cynthia's help, I let PRIVATE EYE go off the mooring lines as I piloted the boat toward the inlet then the Atlantic Ocean. Cynthia stayed by my side to absorb as much information as possible on maneuvering the yacht. After all, she just learned she would inherit my home. I described all the maneuvers in simple terms. Once in the open, I asked Cynthia to skipper. I showed her to hold a course. While she was taking us to our destination, I wanted to perform a few computer searches while the signal was still active.

I got my laptop set up on the work table on the flybridge, just behind the new female captain. She looked to enjoy running the yacht, and I kept an eye on her. I first viewed the Florida Keys missing person page on Facebook, nothing exciting. I had received no private messages from my post. I didn't hold too much faith in social media to help me with this case. I pulled my phone out to access my photo gallery. I had taken shots of Mark's pay stubs during the storage unit visit. A half-dozen from four different organizations, bars I presumed. Curious, I mapped the locations of these four places to discover they're in the same area, within a half-mile radius. A coincidence? Was this a hotspot for spare barkeepers or a territory?

Was he assigned this area to sell dope? The punk slang called a cocaine pusher a "bartender."

I remembered what John Russell told me during our last phone call: they are not to offer collaboration. What was that about? The local police contacted Homeland Security, and a message came back: do not help the investigation. Did I step on someone's toes? Homeland Security collaborates with law enforcement, both local and national. The federal level agencies, such as the CIA, NSA, FBI, DEA, and others, could interfere with local authorities. As a result, I needed to reach my friends at the FBI and see if they could help me.

Barry Gilmore, a native of California, has been an IT specialist working at the FBI for the last 20 years. He got his bachelor's degree from UCLA because he came from a middle-class family. He could not afford the non-resident fees applicable to other, well-known, out-of-state universities. With UCLA still classified as one of the best Information Technology campuses in the country, he put all his efforts into his studies and passed with "A" grades.

After a few jobs in the commercial world, including IBM, he joined the FBI and moved to Washington, where I enjoyed the opportunity to work with him multiple times. He provided the technology side of the equation, and I brought the investigative thinking, a fantastic team.

Barry can be a strange persona. He likes listening to music, swimming, and adores video games. Usually calm, he becomes agitated only in front of the gaming addiction he carries, even on his cell phone. Single, he's been living for years with a girl he met in school.

I collaborated with Barry on a famous case in Clark, New Jersey, in 1998. As her mother reported, Timothy Poupart, a ten-year-old boy, did not return home after a visit to a state fair. Local law enforcement searched the house, the fair, and the routes leading to it to no avail. Barry investigated his mom's lifestyle both before and after Timothy disappeared and discovered a terrible contrast. From a life of poverty, Marguerite Poupart, calling herself Sandy Heaven now, was living it big as a prostitute in New York City. She became our number one suspect then.

A year after her son's disappearance, a passerby discovered the body of a young boy in a Maryland field. The crime lab identified the body as the missing boy in the Poupart investigation. The mother confessed a few weeks later after I conducted a lengthy interrogation. She is serving life in prison today.

The bars on my phone still displayed an acceptable level. I located Barry's mobile number, and he answered after the first ring.

"The real Mister Tanner on the phone, or is this a pocket call?"

"It is a live person Barry. How have you been?"

"I'm great, and I must apologize for not going to your retirement party. I wish I could have been there."

"Not a problem, my friend. I know you're busy and indispensable to the FBI. They would have you work even during a government shutdown."

"Won't happen, Jason. It's impossible," he replied.

We addressed the story of our last FBI director fired by the new president and how the morale of the entire group suffered. Knowing how dedicated the people working for the Bureau were, he and I believed the agency would survive this setback.

After summarizing my activities since retirement and my new pass time, I got to the object of my call.

"I am investigating a six-month-old disappearance. Miami-Dade police have contacted Homeland Security to get some history on the movement of my missing person. It came back NSF, plus: don't bother us anymore."

"Hum. I can't check Homeland's files, but I can verify ours and see where that leads us. How can I reach you, Jason?"

I provided the information as he promised to get back either today or tomorrow and ended the call.

Chapter 6

As we approached Marathon, I took the helm; it was a little past 4:30. The map on my multi-function screen showed Captain Pip's Marina. Electronics sure make it easy to navigate today. A call on the VHF radio informed the Marina operator we were closing in. When we approached, an employee directed us to an available berth. The Marina could hold maybe 30 boats, and it was half-full.

The initial impression of the Marina was quite a contrast from the one I just came from. If Miami displayed a 21st-century design, this look was more like the 19th century. Docks and ramps were surely painted over a dozen times, the old colors showing at multiple places. My yacht looked spiffy around here because all the other boats were much older. No fancy electronics existed either, no free Wi-Fi.

During my preparation to come down here, I discovered a website that promoted the Marina. Pictures on the web showed room decors to date from my parent's youth. Some TVs were more massive than the neighboring stove. The only reason I could fathom Mark would come to this hideaway, as it was called, was low prices. But still, $165 a night was pressing the lemon to the max.

Once moored, I walked to the Marina office to complete the paperwork. An old sailor with a worn pipe operated the counter. His cap displayed Captain James in yellow letters. Uncertain this was his real name, I hesitated to use it.

"Captain, what is your recommendation on a decent watering hole in the area?"

"Hum, there's Porky's back there," as he pointed toward the front of the docks. "Otherwise, Barnacle Barney is around the corner. There's also the lighthouse grill a few streets down. And the young ones hang out at TJ's Tiki Bar."

I looked at Porky's, built to complement the ugly Marina. "Barnacle Barney, is it far from here?" I inquired.

"Close. Walk down Route 1 on this side of the road and turn left after the Mexican restaurant. It's behind the motel, near the water."

I thanked him and pulled out my notebook with Mark Taylor's picture, which I showed him.

"Have you seen this man around here?"

He stared at the picture before announcing: "No, can't say I did."

I wished him a good evening, and I returned to the yacht to get Cynthia and walk to Barnacle. The exercise would be beneficial. As soon as I exited the Marina office, Captain James was on the phone telling the party he had reached, "I need to talk to him as soon as he can."

# # #

Walking on the firm ground toward a restaurant provided a pleasant relief from the waves endured most of the day on our way to the Keys. It brought us back to earth. "Tonight, we explore the environment," I explained to Cynthia. We're not making any particular inquiry. We were just having a father-daughter dinner.

Barnacle Barney's bar sits right on the beach, next to a pool, not even a ten-minute walk. The inside harbors a large u-shaped bar capable of seating at least 20 people. Another dozen tables inside and just as many outside completed the decor. The place looks old but still clean. Fishing and sports artifacts appeared on the walls in a display of primitive imagination.

I did not see a hostess, so I assumed free seating was the norm. We picked a table inside but with a view of the pool and the patrons outdoor. A minute later, a middle-aged woman with a blue apron brought two menus to our table and took our drink order. When in a bar, I guess they expect you to have a pint of something? A sign on the wall read, "You can't drink all day if you don't start in the morning." We each ordered a Sandbar Sunday, a beer brewed in Islamorada, a small city nearby.

"How is Denver treating you?" I asked.

"In the wintertime, the temperature is bearable; in the summer, though, it gets hot. The city is clean, promotes good public transport, and has plenty of entertainment."

"And the hospital where you work?"

"Love it, except for the night shifts. Otherwise, it would be perfect."

A few minutes later, our waitress was back to take our order. Cynthia let me speak first while still deciding on what to eat. I handed the menu back and looked around, examining the attendance. I noticed the tall barman staring at us once again. An old guy like me with a young lady raised eyebrows. Was this his interest in us? Or my daughter? Difficult to say. I noticed he wore a tattoo on his neck, typical of people who spent time inside. Not what Cynthia would like. His chances of dating my daughter just got worse.

Someone at the bar shouted, "Tony, let's have a couple more over here." The barman turned around and grabbed some beer for his thirsty customers.

Our plates arrived in the middle of profound talks about a new friend back in Denver, not her boyfriend yet, but from her tone, I expected an announcement soon. She continued chatting about him, without me having to ask questions, a sure tell of a closer relationship around the corner.

We got up to leave. As I turned toward the barman, he was still checking us out. This time I looked at him and held his stare. He pivoted and got busy with something. I've never seen him, but I will remember him.

# # #

The next morning, Cynthia jogged in the streets around the Marina while I kept busy with a little housekeeping on the yacht and washed part of my dwindling collection of T-shirts at a nearby laundry. Close to lunchtime, my phone beeped and displayed an unknown number in the Washington, DC, area code.

"Jason, it's Barry."

"Hey, how are you? You're not on your regular device?"

"No, I'm calling from one of those rare public phone booth dinosaurs downtown."

"Ah, I see. Didn't Superman change suits in those places?"

"Exactly, I got the information, but I hesitated to call from the office or my phone; it's touchy."

"Don't get in trouble over me, Barry. Let's forget this if it's improper."

"Not a problem, Jason. I'm sharing intelligence with a former FBI agent, not the Post or the Times. This is what I found so far on your man Mark Taylor. I first searched our main database and located records about Mister Taylor's disappearance reported by the Miami-Dade police. No other documents are available. I couldn't even discover a traffic ticket, no help there."

"OK."

"Later, I looked at our internal files and discovered a link to a Mark Taylor, uncertain if he was our man. When I tried to access these files, it advised me I needed a higher authorization code. We, IT specialists, get around this restriction in no time. I learned in this case, the Director of the FBI must consent. I have never come across this situation."

"The Director? Barry, you're sure?"

"Certain. The condition has been effective since last August, around the time your man vanished."

"Hum." I paused for a few seconds trying to figure out the reason behind this level of mystery.

Barry then explained how he got a computer operator to bring back an old database from almost a year ago. The team needed to verify if a new software could read older backups. Unclear what he meant, but the result is Barry restored files to a date in the past.

"Afterward, I pored over those documents before they altered Taylor's status and found interesting material. Mark Taylor was an informant for the famous Drug Enforcement Agency. And, to my surprise, they also paid him in cold cash, no checks, no payroll records."

Even the FBI moved away from such deals, I remembered, and the governance people hated it.

"Barry, what cases was he working on those days?"

"Can't say, case file data is near impossible to access, I must rethink my plan to reach the information. Maybe it's inaccessible."

"Don't get too sneaky and lose your job. I would never forgive myself for contacting you."

"Don't worry. I'll be cautious and drop the process if it's too risky."

"Good. Last question: do we know if Taylor is still alive?"

"I can't confirm nor deny, either way, Jason. With the status change in August, it could mean anything, including he is deceased, or he moved to Russia for all I know."

"I see. Thanks, Barry. Just so I don't call you on your cell phone and leave traces. If I text you with the word Florida, call me on a secure line."

"I will. Take care."

And I hung up and looked at Cynthia preparing dinner in the galley.

"What's up?" she says.

I resumed my conversation with Barry keeping silent about what risks he took to get the information.

"What does that mean, Dad?"

"Barry found a link between Mark's disappearance and his activities as a DEA informant. Someone sealed his records recently, and they gave no reasons. He'll try to uncover his assignment, but this will be difficult."

The Missing Taylor

After lunch, armed with my notebook, I started on a typical detective beat: walking and questioning. My first stop was to see Captain James. The administration office can entertain three people at most; it's tiny. I first talked about fishing the area to get the conversation going. After a while, I exhibited Mark's picture.

"This person came down to your hideaway in September. Do you remember him?"

"Do you recall what you did last September, Mister?"

"Can you at least check your reservations? I believe he arrived on September 10th of last year, Mark Taylor."

Captain James didn't move one bit. After a few awkward seconds, I pulled a twenty-dollar bill and gave it to an outstretched hand. He put it in his shirt pocket, turned around, and retrieved a well-used book.

"September 10th, you say?" as he flipped pages.

"Here we go... Taylor, Taylor," as he moved his finger down the page. "Yes, Taylor, on September 10th, stayed two days."

"Was he alone?"

"Is this a divorce case?" he asked, smiling.

"Just answer the question," I replied.

He looked at his book once more. "He was alone."

"Any other reservations that night?"

Without even looking, he answered, "No, he was my only guest. Thank you, Mister. I have to run."

The conversation ended on this note. I turned around and walked away. So the ledger confirmed Taylor's presence in Marathon, although we possessed that information from his credit card statements. It cost me twenty dollars to find out what I already knew.

It was only a short distance to Barnacle Barney, and I arrived in no time. The sun was high in the sky, but more than a dozen customers sat at the bar. I slipped onto a stool in a quiet corner. When the barmaid came around, I ordered another Sandbar Sunday, like when I dined with Cynthia yesterday. I liked that beer.

When she brought it, I said, "It's the first time I see you. Have you been working here for long?"

She looked at me.

"You must come at nights then. I've been working this bar for more than a year now."

"Then maybe you've seen this gentleman," as I showed her Taylor's picture on my notebook. While she looked at it, I added, "He may have been with a couple of Asiatic men back in mid-September, maybe two or three days in a row." She continued to look at the picture, but her memory failed her.

"I can't be sure, maybe. So many visitors come here once or twice that I can't remember everyone."

"I understand, thanks anyway."

I returned to the yacht and prepared to go out fishing with my daughter in the afternoon. I inquired what species swam around the Keys to other Marina residents. We aimed for African Pompano, and we tried in deep water and over the reefs. We were unsuccessful, but we caught a blackfin tuna, which I cleaned as Cynthia maneuvered us to port.

The Missing Taylor

After enjoying our grilled fish, we sat on the aft deck as we watched the sun go down over the sea. She asked about my theory on this puzzling case.

"You know," I began, "we have a well-educated young man working part-time only, at least that is clear. He disappeared six months ago, and the police could not find him. We discover evidence of fentanyl and cash in his possession. This has the makings of a young man selling drugs. How and from whom he gets the product is unclear. His target customers are other drugmakers who mix the product with cocaine or make fake pain-reducing opioids, possibly."

"But the DEA connexion?" she asks.

"It throws a wrench to my theory. Somehow I doubt Mark is on the good guy's side. The drug seller image may well be a front, a way to get closer to big players."

"Then, it's possible they eliminated him because they found out about his activities."

"Maybe, and it would explain why we can't find his body. They kill him, tie him down with heavyweights, and drop him in 500 feet of water. Fishes would handle the rest."

"But why come to Marathon? He works one evening in Miami and then runs down here the same night. There must be a pretty good reason."

"You are thinking like a real detective now, a good question. My theory is that someone summoned him here. He exited the bar, not even asking if he worked the next day. He left with two unidentified Asians, parked his car at home, and came down with his newfound friends right here."

"Why?"

"An important meeting, maybe?"

"Or an ambush?"

"Yes, possibly."

And we both fell silent. We were trying to imagine why this city was influential in the scheme of things.

# # #

The following morning after a refreshing sleep, I planned to visit local authorities. The station is near the tail end of a canal almost reaching Route 1, also named Overseas Highway.

I lowered the dinghy to the water and grabbed a lockable cable to secure the small boat while I visited the Monroe County Sheriff's Office. To reach there, I had to go west, round the tip of the island, and head back east into Boot Key Harbor until I reached the canal going inland. The rise lasted almost twenty minutes, but I had fun riding the tender and sightseeing at the same time. Much better than a taxi ride.

I walked toward the desk sergeant and asked to speak to the Sheriff; it was a courtesy visit. Directed to his third-floor suite, he was just stepping out as I arrived.

I used an old trick. "Sheriff, I bring you greetings from John Russell."

"Long time no see. And you are?"

"I lunched with John last week, and he said when you're in Marathon, salute Sheriff McBain for me." A small white lie! I got his credentials from a display panel when I entered the building.

"My name is Jason Tanner. I'm a private investigator and a former FBI agent. I am working on a missing person case from John's jurisdiction. We believe our absentee may have disappeared here, in Marathon."

"And how can I help you?"

"I would like to verify if the person I'm looking for matches any unsolved disappearance in the county?"

"Maybe, come with me."

I followed him down the stairs to the second floor, and he introduced me to an enormous man who looked like Sargent Schultz in the TV series Hogan's Heroes still in reruns. One thing was different: he was called Sargent Gomez. I saluted him politely, and after telling him what interested me, he invited me into a small room with a few screens and printers. He sat in front of a keyboard and asked me to come beside him.

"What are we looking for, sir?"

"Call me Jason, Sargent. We are digging for unsolved cases, filed on or after September 12 of last year, with an unidentified body."

Gomez typed something, and then a screen full of data appeared. "One-hundred-and-eighty-seven cases are still open in the Monroe County, sir."

"Could you sort them by the type of case?" I asked.

With just one click, the screen reshuffled. With the help of Sargent Gomez, we eliminated several cases such as property and statutory crimes, leaving us with personal offenses. We then removed felonies such as rape and sexual assault, leaving us with simple assault, battery, kidnapping, and homicide. With around a dozen investigations left on display, Sargent Gomez suggested we drill down into each. He highlighted one case at a time and double-clicked on it to have a full page of information.

After exploring the unsolved cases, only one got my serious attention. In August, a decomposed body washed ashore and is unclaimed yet. If I could get DNA samples for Mark, I could confirm or eliminate this particular case.

Gomez printed the summary with the name of the detective in charge, Roberto Angelillo. I informed the sergeant I would get some DNA from Mark's belongings and communicate with the detective. He said it was fine and would tell Lieutenant Angelillo the game plan.

"You understand, Sir, it's not because your missing person is not in our files they're alive. Water surrounds us, and there exist many ways to dump a body in the ocean and never see it again, ever."

"I have seen 'Dexter,' I understand, Sargent." I was referring to a popular TV series where a Miami Police blood-splatter analyst by day becomes a serial killer by night. He dumps his victim's body into the bay around Miami.

I exited the Sheriff's office and called Nadine. No answer, so I left a message. The phone rang a few seconds later, so I assumed Nadine was calling back.

"Hello."

"Jason, it's LeBron Jackson. Do you have a minute?"

"What's up?"

"We received the autopsy report for the man found on your boat. He did not die naturally. The medical examiner concluded drug overdose as the cause of death."

"No kidding. I knew William for a short period, but he's not a drug user."

"He doesn't fit the profile, that's certain. It looks like someone injected pure fentanyl into his neck. After the toxicology report came out, the medical examiner looked for needle marks in the usual places but found nothing. He inspected the body again and located a mark in his neck, in the jugular vein. He died right away."

My mind was racing now. The intended target wasn't William, it was me. I asked him to stay aboard while I searched for my daughter. They wanted to eliminate me, damn.

So much for a quiet pastime PI career; this is dangerous.

"Jason, did you find something on the camera recordings?"

"Gee LeBron, I completely forgot. I'm returning on the yacht now and get right to it."

"OK, let me know," and he ended the call.

Someone wished me dead, but why? Was I getting too close? To what? It baffled me. Cynthia was alone aboard PRIVATE EYE. My stomach clenched up in knots with the fear of what could happen to her; I had to warn her. I reached for my phone in its usual back pocket, empty! I either lost it, or I didn't bring it. I had to return right away. I ran to the dinghy, hopped in, started the engine, and pushed the power lever to the max. Blinded by the seawater splashing in my face as I raced back, I feared losing another loved one for a moment. The pain was excruciating. I didn't want to live the experience again. Every few seconds, I pushed the power lever to the max, again and again, hoping to find an extra bit of speed, to no avail.

In half the time I took to get to the Sheriff's office, I was back at the Marina and zigzagging my way toward her at full speed. Boat owners shot me dirty looks, but it did not affect my speed. I didn't intend to slow down.

As I approached, the rear door opened, and Cynthia showed up on the aft deck. "Are you OK?" I asked in a hurry.

"Fine, what's wrong?" she answered.

I tied up the tender and came on board. "I got a call from Detective Jackson in Miami," I said while we moved inside. Leaving no details untold, I repeated the conversation I had with Jackson.

"Noo… oo," she let out in her typical way. She pressed her hand to her chest, trying to catch her breath. She connected the dots without difficulty. My safety and hers, for the same reason, were on the line.

"We need to be careful going forward, darling."

"You can say that again, Dad."

"Let's stick together as much as we can, all right?"

"And when I go running?" she adds.

"I'll try to keep up."

# # #

I prepared a quick lunch for both of us, and after cleaning the galley, I got my laptop out and loaded the DVD with the Marina's recordings. A good ten minutes was necessary to locate my external DVD player well hidden in the storage area underneath my bed.

We set up the system on the dining table, closed a few curtains to get a better screen view, and sat together on the main sofa. A date and time stamp appeared on the screen's lower section.

The first images started at 7:03, Saturday morning, March 17. We could see the backside of the door used to access our dock with a security device on the other side to open it. The setup brought out my first reflection: to unlock the gate leading to the yachts, you need a proximity card delivered by the harbormaster. It's a procedure similar to when you rent a hotel room. They provide you with a personal card to unlock your door. At the Marina, it opens our gate, the one we're looking at on the screen.

"How would someone access the docks without an owner's card?" I asked.

"Don't know, Dad."

I adjusted the fast forward speed to three times normal so that we could review a half-hour of the video in ten minutes. Should we discover something interesting, we could go back and replay at regular speed.

At 8:05, we saw Cynthia's backside as she left dock H; I recall our berth was H9. I adjusted the speed as we watched her stretch her arms as she exited on the main walkway running along the Marina. At around five minutes to nine, she returned from her exercise, unlocking the door with one of the two cards they gave me when I registered at the Marina office.

Since it was a weekend, a lot of action occurred on multiple docks. People in beachwear attire brought in coolers and lunch boxes from the Marina's parking lot and went aboard their boats. Folks carrying lines with tackle boxes hurried along.

I skipped the DVD to around 10 am. A few minutes later, we both exited dock H, turned right toward the shore, and disappeared out of view a few seconds later. We were going onto our beach surveillance mission. I fast-forwarded to around 11:30, knowing I was back before noon. I set it at standard speed, wanting to see everything.

A young lady with blond hair and cut-off jean shorts turned onto our dock, approaching from the parking lot area. A few minutes later, William walked onto ours, probably coming from his dock, where his boat was moored. He exited a few minutes later, having found nobody aboard my yacht.

At 11:51, I reappeared with my backpack, unlocked the gate and walked past the camera. Now 11:54, William, who saw me arrive or observed a movement on my boat, returned to dock H. Four minutes later, at 11:58, I came out, turned left toward the city-side, walking fast in search of my daughter. This was when I asked William to stay and wait for my daughter's return. A simple omission with a terrible consequence.

At 12:04, someone exited my dock and turned left. The spring-loaded gate closed, but just before it locked, a hand stopped it. The visitor was sporting a broad Panama and waited near the entrance, still held open by his left hand. A few seconds passed, and another man arrived wearing a large hat with a shoulder bag. Both now walked onto the dock and disappeared from the video. They were going toward my boat possibly, but we couldn't know for sure. We're almost positive that they didn't have a proximity card with them. Therefore they shouldn't be on the docks.

At 12:11, both visitors passed under the camera again, this time leaving. They turned right and disappeared. They had my full attention: they were the only two visitors without shorts, swimwear, or jeans; they were donning dressed pants. The Panama hats were their only disguise, but the taller man was wearing big round sunglasses when he arrived. I have seen him before.

# # #

Sure to have seen the two Asians on the video, I headed to my cabin to retrieve my camera. I extracted the memory card and inserted it into my laptop. Several images appeared, and I located the one I wanted.

I zoomed in to find, in the middle of the screen, the same guys in discussion with Yang Nelson in South Point Park. The image showed Nelson clearly, but the two Asians were looking away, no face shot.

Still, they wore the same clothes as in the video. No doubt in my mind, these individuals had killed William Tudor. I needed to inform Freeman right away.

I extracted Freeman's business card from my pockets and got his email address, which I used to create a new message by attaching Nelson's picture with his friends. I noted time frames on the DVD he should watch. I hit send and called him. No answer, so I left a message.

"Wayne, it's Jason. I emailed a picture of two suspects found on the surveillance cameras. Look at it; these are the culprits. Picture and videos are only hours apart, and they're even dressed the same."

For the remainder of the day, Cynthia and I relaxed and spent happy moments on the beach, just enjoying the scenery and ourselves. Soon, we needed to return to Miami, where a plane would fly Cynthia to Denver, her vacation ending. A bit saddened by her departure but glad she'd be out of harm's way. While returning, we stopped at a fish market to grab a Pompano. The store provided better than the high seas!

Back on our yacht, while preparing dinner, Nadine returned my call. After a brief status of my investigation, I got to the essence behind my request.

"Nadine, I need you to produce DNA from Mark. They prefer a blood sample, but other options are available. I suggest you go back to the storage locker and retrieve either a toothbrush, a comb, or a hairbrush. We're looking for hair samples or something he put in his mouth. Can you do that for me?"

I wished I had thought about that when I visited the storage.

She agreed to my suggestion and promised a search by tomorrow. I gave her Lieutenant Angelillo's address and a case number to write on the package. I then called Angelillo to tell him he should expect the delivery of a DNA sample for his missing person case.

After an excellent dinner, we stepped up to the flybridge with our cup of green tea in hand. The salted smell of the ocean joined us, the humidity still present. The overhead canvas was a blessing; the sun was not my best friend. Blowing on the hot tea did nothing to cool it down; we both rested our cups on the table facing the L-shaped seating.

"You know, Dad, I have butterflies in my stomach now; I worry a lot about this case. Someone attacked you already, hit you on the head, and left you on the ground. It was only a warning. Someone does not want you investigating Mark Taylor's whereabouts. The FBI and the Chicago police department are big outfits, and you had colleagues, friends on the service, and support teams back then. Today, you have nobody around to make up the difference."

"I have you now," I said.

"Don't be silly. In 36 hours, I'm returning to Denver. I won't be of any help then. If thugs want to batter you, I cannot intervene."

"You can run and call the police."

"Don't be funny, Dad. The situation is serious. As an FBI agent, you would be fine. As a lonely private investigator, you face more trouble, in my humble opinion. You're good, but you're alone."

She was right — a single man against a gang was no contest.

"Do I need to remind you a man died on your yacht three days ago, and a murderer was looking for you?"

She was right again.

"I get the point, Cynthia. Let me see if I can hire temporary help. I have an idea; let me work on it."

The rest of the evening was especially enjoyable. My daughter talked about the new boyfriend again, a sure sign of a growing relationship. She apologized to return to her quarters, and I remained alone. I searched my contact list, looking for a name in particular. It was late, but I called her mobile number, anyway.

"Jennifer, it's Jason Tanner. How are you?"

"Jason, long time no see. Where have you been?"

"My days at the FBI are behind me now. I retired last year with a full pension, and with Laura's passing and a lot of time on my hand, I keep busy by impersonating a private investigator in South Florida."

"I am sorry about Laura, I could not attend the funerals, but I was present in thoughts with you."

"Thank you. It means a lot."

"What prompted a call today, Jason? Are you visiting the Miami Zoo? Are you looking for a personal guide or a pleasant company?"

Jennifer was a former FBI agent, like me, from Chicago. Pregnancy interrupted her career twice. After her second child, she called it quits. Her resignation coincided with her husband getting a promotion to head a branch of an investment bank in Miami.

"Well, Jennifer, my new part-time investigation activities are taking me in a direction where I should not work alone. I need help, someone to figure out this situation and watch my back. I was hoping we could work together again."

"Hum, maybe. You still have to fill me in, but I think I can arrange temporary employment. The boys are old enough and can manage by themselves. My husband can order out."

"Fine. I will drive my daughter Cynthia to Miami International Airport the day after tomorrow. She's flying back to Denver. We can get together then. Would that work for you?"

"Perfect," she answered.

# # #

A glowing sky had grown darker through an early evening, but still, the heat index made this period quite warm. The southbound winds helped cool the place, and I preferred this well-ventilated space to air-condition inside.

I switched off a few boats' lights and remained on the flybridge, enjoying the Marina's calmness.

A 90-foot Hatteras motor yacht had berthed late afternoon and settled alongside the entryway. This turned into the Marina's largest customer, and it's an impressive one. I just found it strange that such a large vessel came to a two-bit Marina.

From her aft deck came plenty of rock music and short laughs from what sounded like a group of around ten people. Another couple of young individuals, maybe crewmen, kept walking the yacht back and forth. Dress them in an official uniform, and they resembled prison guards, my fertile imagination at work. From my vantage point, I could only glimpse at the ship. So, curious, I went down to my cabin and snagged a broad brim hat and a paperback. I opened Cynthia's door. She raised her head. I told her I was going for a short stroll around in a low voice. I will lock the doors, she can sleep peacefully. "Be safe, Dad," she said to me before rolling over.

Nonchalantly, I walked toward the Marina office. An old bench sat alone just in front near a few flowers that had seen better days. A little light from the office allowed luminosity where I sat. From that position, I had a direct view of the latecomers. I pulled my hat over my eyes and grabbed my paperback, impersonating a tired sailor reading a nail-biting novel.

Though I looked concentrated on my book, my eyes scanned the surroundings, hidden by a large hat. The music stopped, and people moved around. Full lighting on the yacht made it simple to see. I was planning to report home when several lights were extinguished on the Hatteras, and I heard footsteps from the gangplank. A half-dozen people strolled down the ramp in my direction. I lowered my head and raised my book, still illuminated by the office lights.

The group wandered by while I peeked a fraction of a second only. To my surprise, leading the pack was Yang Nelson with a Chinese girl at his arm, followed by two other couples I did not recognize. My eyes moved back to my book as I tried to stay inconspicuous.

A few seconds later, I turned around and watched them walk away. They were leaving for dinner, drinks, or both. I was unprepared to follow them right now, but the Hatteras aroused my curiosity. What was Nelson doing aboard? Who owned this yacht? And more importantly, what was it doing here?

I turned my head toward the empty Marina office seeing a night light but nobody inside. Captain James maintained a ledger showing who had reservations, what berths, pricing, and dates. He wrote these details in his ledger. I observed him doing so when I registered. That document may have information for my investigation. My main question was: had this yacht been here on September 12 and 13 of last year when Mark Taylor disappeared?

But first, I needed to know the boat's name. With his nose pointed at me, it was impossible to see it. A simple walk would remedy my ignorance. I got up and ambled toward the Hatteras. When I reached its bow, I continued. The boat name typically appears on the transom.

I passed alongside the yacht like a tourist hearing a party aboard. The crew was checking out foot traffic around their floating castle.

I continued walking along, past the Hatteras, turned, and reversed course, making a note of the ship's name, Ocean Dancer. Crew members continued to look my way. They protected their ship from curious onlookers, so I tipped my hat and pursued my stroll.

When I returned near the office, I looked inside and confirmed it was empty. Way back, an FBI agent showed me a useful trick. I extracted a plastic card from my wallet and approached the office, turned around, my back to the door now. My heartbeat accelerated in anticipation of performing an illegal activity. Shaking it, the card found its way near the lock along the door jamb. It was a simple matter of pushing in, et voila!

I turned around, entered, and closed the door behind me. After a deep breath, I walked to the main counter, searching for the ledger, but it was nowhere to be seen; I concluded it was stored away. Behind the worktop were two more desks. While making as little noise as possible, I stepped over the counter and reached for a pile of documents lying there, no success either. I was getting nervous in a restricted space and in danger of being discovered. My Chicago police experience told me that I could be charged with breaking and entering if caught.

I pivoted and studied the space again. Below the counter, two doors protected some shelves probably. I opened the one on the right, nothing but forms and manuals. Behind the left door, a jackpot waited! I pulled out a ledger Captain James handled like a bible, and I crouched behind the counter. Nobody could see me from outside while I examined the large book.

I flipped pages up to the last registrations. The first few columns showed an arrival date, the vessel name, and probably the captain's name, a phone number, and other inscriptions I took to be the duration of the stay and the slip. I deduced this information from my PRIVATE EYE entry near the top of the page with my name beside it.

I did not see Ocean Dancer on the last page, so I flipped back. Nothing. But one entry appeared with just two letters O and D. For Ocean Dancer? And number 12. During my walk to learn the ship's name, I noted they used slip number 12. The inscription contained limited information for some reason.

Curious.

I flipped pages backward until I read another OD at slip 12 in January of this year. Back again, I noticed the same information for November last year. I flipped to September and discovered it arrived on the 13th, not a coincidence. Ocean Dancer was a regular visitor in the region. Not always on the same days, but once every month at least.

Before being a regular, I figured you needed to be a newcomer. I went back again until I located an entry with Ocean Dancer, written in full, with a name and a telephone number. I memorized both, closed the ledger, and placed it back underneath the counter. As I prepared to leave, I heard voices outside, my heart rate speeding up. I stayed put, hidden from view. My curiosity eclipsed my wish for safety, so I peeked out and observed two figures coming from the all-white yacht and walking toward the parking lot. I could bet anything these two guys were Nelson's friends at the beach in Miami and probably responsible for William's murder. After waiting until all was quiet, I crawled to the exit, pulled the handle with tenderness but like a typical old door, she let out a screeching noise. Holding my breath again, I got out and closed the door behind me, making sure I locked it.

I hurried to the parking lot and scanned up and down the street: nothing, vanished. Someone must have been waiting in a car to pick them up; that's the only explanation I could imagine. I raced back to my floating home, stepped in, and locked the back door in a hurry. I pushed a sigh of relief. What was this gang doing here?

# # #

At 5:30 in the morning, I got up wishing to sail out of Captain Pip's Marina today. I wanted an early start because I hoped the guests on Ocean Dancer were sleeping their booze off. I heard noises around 3 am. The Asians had stepped on my boat once and killed the wrong person. My plans did not include offering them a second opportunity.

The coffee brewing added a welcoming aroma, and I prepared a quick breakfast with yogurt, fruits, and toasts. I wished to be on my way soon. When the coffee was ready, I woke up Cynthia telling her why the plan changed since last night.

She joined me at the salon table. While enjoying our coffee, I went over last night's activities. My daughter understood we needed to be away when the folks aboard the visiting ship woke up, in case they remembered my yacht and the failed mission to eliminate me.

Cynthia helped me readied PRIVATE EYE for departure as I warmed up the engine. I hoped the diesel sound was not a wake-up signal for Ocean Dancer and their guests. To reach the sea, we needed to navigate past her. She blocked half of the channel by tying up right at the Marina's entrance. I wished I could have tiptoed by them, but that's impossible. I ran the yacht from the pilot station inside the boat and not on the flybridge, fewer chances of being seen. Cynthia made sure she turned her back to our unfriendly neighbors. Crew members were already busy on the deck of the Hatteras, but that's not surprising, given the small size of the crew quarters on most ships this size.

We exited the Marina at a snail pace, as every boater should do. Going out full speed would have raised suspicions. I headed east once out of the Marina, knowing we would get back on the Miami tack later. The rest of the voyage was uneventful. We arrived at the Miami Beach Marina around lunchtime.

Cynthia's flight home left the next day only, so we decided on an afternoon lunch in South Beach. When she got ready, I got a cab to drop us on Collins Avenue. Boaters around us recommended a great oyster and seafood restaurant, and we wished to end the week on a high note. It was a total success. The restaurant carried around ten types of oysters from different parts of the country and Canada. After the oysters, I ordered a grouper; she selected a red snapper, and we both appreciated the good times. She insisted I play it safe going forward, and I told her Jennifer could be my new sidekick now that Cynthia was returning to Denver.

"We will be careful, honey, don't worry," I said.

"What if things deteriorate, Dad?"

"I'll call in the cavalry, either the Miami police or at the Bureau where I still have contacts."

"Another thing that worries me," she said.

"What?"

"I see you popping the painkillers every day now since I've arrived. This opioid is addictive, and you know, Dad."

"Dr. Ferguson prescribed them for my back."

"No, Dad. He prescribed them for your pain. They'll do nothing for your back. You need help to solve your back problem or to manage your pain. These pills are just hiding the reality. Tell me you'll consult a doctor about your situation."

"I will, dear, I will." Happy this conversation was over.

We spent time on the beach and returned to the yacht around dinner time, but none of us were hungry. We skipped dinner and had a cup of tea while relaxing. Cynthia's words during our evening discussion kept turning around safety, backup, protection, and others of the same nature. It was clear the investigation worried her. My arguments included the fact that I was a trained FBI agent, a former police officer, and an armed marine. My claims seemed to have convinced her when we retired to our rooms.

Chapter 7

After driving my daughter to the airport in the middle of the afternoon, the cab dropped me off at the Hyatt Regency Hotel. Jennifer and I agreed to meet and discuss her possible involvement in the case. She arrived on time and in a quiet corner of the hotel bar; I ordered a beer while she had a glass of white wine.

Jennifer is in her early forties but does not show her age. She is five-foot-six-inches with short black hair. Her teeth are perfect, and her smile is contagious. But she can be all business when it's time. She had a great future at the FBI when she called it quits because of her long hours. She is talented and would help my investigation for sure.

We reminisced about our days at the FBI and remembered friends we both knew but ignored their whereabouts. If you don't work at friendship, it gets away from you.

"So you're now a private sailing investigator. How did that come about?"

"Well, first, after Laura's death, I wanted to spend more time under the sun, so I moved to Florida. The cold weather around Michigan Lake convinced me. Then, I always loved boats, but Laura appreciated terra firma. So, in her absence now, I indulged in this little pleasure."

"It explains the sailing part. How about the private investigator?"

"I wanted to keep my mind active in retirement, so I figured a few jobs here and there would keep me busy part-time. I could continue to use my expertise, my knowledge, and my contacts to help solve cases."

"And has it?"

"It's close to what I figured it would be except for the one case I am working on right now. So far, it has taken all of my time. And it's borderline dangerous. The gang which I believe is involved killed a man on my boat, and I suspect I was the intended target."

"Wow. Not trivial."

"Two thugs killed an unarmed, defenseless, 73-year-old man. I provided the police with information about the crime, hoping they arrest them soon. And don't worry, I would understand if you backed off."

"I'll decide when I have all the information, Jason, not before. Tell me how it started and how you got to this point."

I reported the story from the first footsteps at the Marina, meeting Nadine, and went all the way to locating Yang Nelson and, what appeared to be, his two bodyguards. I told her about my discussion with law enforcement, my private hacker, and my old FBI buddy, Barry Gilmore. She listened with interest, asked questions when it was not clear, and absorbed the essence of my adventure. She kept nodding as she learned more. When she stopped nodding, she asked a question, then listened again.

"And that's the story, Jennifer. My daughter suggested I reach out for some help and support, and here I am. I think two heads are better than one, and with your field experience, you can contribute a lot to resolving this disappearance. You have a sharp mind; you've done surveillance, that's an important part of our job."

"Compliments will get you nowhere, buddy."

"Oh no?"

She put her hand over her mouth and nodded, a sure sign she was deliberating internally.

"I have told you everything I know about the case. You are free to join me or not. We will not be worst friends if you decline the invitation, trust me."

She continued her reflection while I ordered another beer and a glass of wine from our idle waiter. I expected a polite refusal from Jennifer, so it surprised me when I heard her say, "All right, I'll help you, Jason, with one condition."

"And it would be..."

"I may call it quits any time, and no questions asked, OK?"

"Works for me. We should both quit if it becomes too dangerous. I'll drink to that."

And we toasted to the occasion.

"OK partner, now what's the plan?"

"Our bad guy at the top of our list is Yang Nelson, I believe. We need to figure out who this man is, what he does, where he lives, his background, his life. We know he surfs at South Point Beach; this could be our starting point."

"Do we have information on him so far?"

"We have a phone number and a license plate. He drives a jeep."

We continued to talk about Nelson and decided Jennifer would follow him. I would concentrate on digging into his past. She should watch out for the two Asians; they were dangerous. Her concealed carry license was still valid in Florida, and she would have her weapon at all times.

Another part of our investigation was Ocean Dancer. Why the regular trips to Marathon? Where else did it go? Since I was familiar with the marine business, I would look into this aspect. I also provided Jennifer with the phone number of Barry Gilmore. I would tell Barry that he may receive a call from her if she needed some background information.

On that note, I paid for our drinks and exited the hotel. Jennifer will be at the South Point beach tomorrow morning. I hailed a cab for Sea Isle Marina, where my yacht awaited me. Returning to the Miami Beach Marina was out of the question. Someone tried to kill me there and took the life of an innocent man instead. Somebody may recognize me or the yacht and alert our Asian friends to come back and finish what they started.

# # #

Back on board, I contacted Wayne Freeman to talk about the murder on my boat and my investigation into Mark Taylor's disappearance. I was lucky; I got Wayne after the second ring.

"Wayne, how are you?"

"I'm OK. I received your email and pictures. I did not locate these individuals in our files yet. They may be new to the territory and have no arrest record yet."

"Yeah, I see. These two are just executioners; the main guy is Yang Nelson, a friend of Mark Taylor. He's the third man in the picture I sent you. I believe the Asians take their orders from Nelson. You should look into him."

I gave Wayne the plate number I had written in my notebook. By consulting the Department of Motor Vehicles records, he could easily locate him.

"And Wayne, I saw Nelson with his two bodyguards in Marathon where Taylor disappeared. I don't know what they were doing there, but I'll find out. They appear to be regular visitors to the region. We need to discover why that is. I'm working on it."

"Good."

"One last thing, I drafted a new buddy on my PI team, another former FBI person. Her name is Jennifer Jones, and she's helping me with the case. I will give her your number if you don't mind."

"Jennifer, hey. Is she married?"

"Yes, and two kids at home. Don't go there."

"OK, OK, just checking. I need to follow every lead."

After hanging up, I sent a text message to my FBI buddy, Barry, saying, "Florida is fantastic this time of year. You should visit one day." I was expecting his call as soon as possible.

But when I woke up the following morning, nothing. I double-checked my phone to make sure I missed no calls. I had not. But when I put it down, it rang.

"Hello."

"Jason, it's Barry; you called?"

"Yes, I did; how are you?"

"I'm fine and still digging for information on the name you gave me; I'll need more time."

"Do nothing foolish and end up in the unemployment line."

"No, I won't. Don't worry."

"I gave your number to Jennifer Jones, an old FBI colleague. She may contact you as well for some information. She's working with me on the case now."

"Your friends are my friends."

"Thanks. Take care then. I just wanted to touch base."

I hung up and dialed my other faithful buddy Hank. He had access to information the FBI didn't have.

"How is your search of Mister Nelson going?" I asked.

"Almost done, boss. I should have something for you tomorrow. It's better to have a full report later than a small report earlier, don't you think?"

"I'll have to agree with you, Hank. I'll send some cash your way soon. Be careful."

The next thing on my mind was the large yacht, Ocean Dancer. It had made several voyages to Marathon according to the ledger I consulted in the small office. The trips were so frequent that captain James just wrote OD instead of the full name.

A thought came up, uncertain it would work out, but I had to verify it. A system called AIS for Automatic Identification System exists in the marine industry. It's a tracking apparatus used by ships to supplement the radar to avoid collisions. AIS combines GPS positioning, satellite operations, and VHF communications to track vessels. Like most large and mid-size boats, I have such a system on PRIVATE EYE. It may not be essential for small crafts sailing along the coast in the daytime, but it becomes critical if you go out at sea and even fundamental at night.

Users of the AIS can know about vessels in their area by having access to the ship name, unique identification, position, course, and speed. A website even provides the data online, so I looked it up.

I wanted to validate the information, so I searched for my ship, PRIVATE EYE. And there it was, on my screen, a map of the Miami area in the background with a small pink arrow showing my position at the Sea Isle Marina. If somebody wanted to locate me, they only needed a computer or even just a phone. My boat dealer had set up the system, but I had never looked deeper into its operation. I checked inside the main cabinet in the salon and found a pile of documentation. After a while, I located my AIS receiver/transmitter paperwork. I read through its features, benefits, and options until I got to a section entitled "Silent mode" and how to connect an external switch to operate in this mode. It got my attention.

I walked to the cockpit and discovered the AIS unit well hidden under the yacht's main controls. Looking closer, I found a small toggle switch without markings. Connected to the AIS, it could only have one function, the silent mode, so I flipped the switch.

I refreshed my computer screen, but it still showed my position, my last known position. Others could access this information as well, and it frightened me. I located my Glock 17 in my cabin and decided to carry it at all times from now on. I grabbed my binoculars and headed upstairs to the flybridge looking around for people who should not be there or suspicious characters. Nothing was out of the ordinary, but I remained on the flybridge for a while, observing folks walking up to my dock.

I had to get out of this Marina, find another local berth or return to my home port, and fast. It was Friday, and I had a full week; I decided to return home.

As I headed out at a slow speed, I did not see two guys looking in my direction on the shores of Biscayne Bay. One of them had a pair of binoculars.

# # #

On my way back to Pompano, I texted Jennifer to call me when she had a minute. I did not want to ring her while she was surveilling someone. Later my phone vibrated.

"Yes."

"It's Jennifer, you called O my partner."

"Yes, I did. I learned that just about any idiot can locate my yacht through a public website when my collision avoidance system is active. That is amazing but also problematic. If anybody can locate my yacht, so can our friends."

"Is that so?"

"Yes, so I'm currently sailing to Pompano. I don't like the idea they know where my boat is all the time. For now and for the foreseeable future, I have disabled the system, and my yacht is now invisible. I don't know if I will sail or drive back Monday. I will decide over the weekend. Anything new on your end?"

"I'm at the South Point beach watching a gang of surfers, but Nelson is not here. I'm going back home, and I'll return tomorrow, Saturday, my chances could be better."

"Alright, we'll keep in touch."

The Missing Taylor

The morning ride up the Intracoastal was better than perfect. The sun was warm but not too hot, no clouds around, the light winds not interfering with sailing yet providing comfortable well-being.

Feeling I acted like a deserter leaving my new partner on her own, the more I was sailing away from Miami, the worst I felt. I considered returning for a moment, but Jennifer said she was restarting her surveillance only tomorrow. So I cranked up the speed, but still within limits. I wanted to get to Pompano and immerse myself in more research to help forget my cowardliness. Once I arrived, I got busy: I filled up the gas tanks, cleaned the interior, and washed the exterior. I then hopped in my truck to replenish the yacht's cooler at my local market.

Once all these chores were behind me, I headed to my favorite German restaurant, where I sat alone at the bar and opened my MacBook to keep myself company. With an excellent German beer in front of me, I searched for more information on that mysterious ship. If the opposition observed my yacht using the AIS system, maybe I could do the same about theirs. I navigated to the website and keyed in "Ocean Dancer" in the search area. Its last known position was Miami Beach, but I also noticed more information was available for full members. I got out my Visa card, registered, paid the $29 fee, and accessed the ship's travel history. Ocean Dancer navigated only in and around Miami, the Keys, and the Bahamas during the last years. Mind you, in silent mode, they could go anywhere. I would be blind to those trips, so would the website.

But I had other questions like what kind of ship was Ocean Dancer? Single owner? Corporate ownership? Short or long-term rental? I doubted a bar owner could afford a boat like this full time. He could lease it on occasions, I suspected. While the waitress brought me a new German beer to try, I continued searching. After a good half-hour of looking around, I finally scored. Ocean Dancer was available for charter and offered by Yacht Charter of Miami, a corporation on Alton Road, close to the Miami Beach Marina.

The AIS system can be silent about a boat's destination, but the company's own records would say otherwise. The electronic or paper trail would show who chartered the yacht and where it went. To accounting services, precise travel information was mandatory. This charter company was now on my radar. I closed the laptop; my Schnitzel was arriving.

After a good night's sleep, I checked my emails while sipping my morning brew. Hank Hackman had come through again. His report on Yang Nelson was a few clicks away. Well structured, it covered his personal information, current address, family, education, employment, criminal or civil procedure implications, and financial profile. Since Hank and I exchanged confidential data, we agreed to use email encryption with a public key between us. I re-encrypted the entire message and sent it to Jennifer, knowing she would call me about the gibberish she received in her email program. I then would pass on the key to her over the phone giving her access.

Reading the report with more scrutiny, I discovered he had two prior assault charges brought a few years ago. In both cases, when the chief witness recanted his testimony, the prosecution dropped them. This guy had a bad temper but also an absolute power of conviction.

I scrolled down to his professional thumbnail, and a few words caught my attention right away: Black Cat. I read from the start and discovered Nelson owned a bar, but not any bar. It listed him as a partner of the Black Cat in Miami. I remembered my first conversation with Nadine; she mentioned this was the last place someone had seen Mark. It's quite a favorite spot on the beach, and Mark Taylor worked there occasionally. Someone called him to replace the regular bartender on that fateful Friday.

The Missing Taylor

Chances are, Nelson and Taylor knew one another because of the bar business. As co-owner, Nelson would be schooled about the man behind the bar; it requires only a small number of employees to run this kind of business. Pieces of the puzzle were coming together: interesting!

I continued my exploration of Hank's document down to the financial section. Nelson had a few credits cards listed but almost no usage. This was strange in today's world, where debit and credit card transactions are rising. The bar business being heavy on hard cash, it was not impossible portions of it found the owner's pockets. This could explain his reluctance to use plastic. From the list of his past transactions, I concluded his credit card usage was when he had no options, like online retail shops.

Early afternoon, Jennifer called, as expected. "What this garbage you sent me, Jason?"

"Hi Jennifer, how are you?"

"I'm fine and puzzled at the same time."

I explained to her about the encrypted message and gave her the key to decode her email and read Hank's report. She told me she had picked up Nelson at the beach this morning when he surfed until around eleven. She then followed him to a bar on the beach and stopped her surveillance there.

"The Black Cat?" I said.

"How did you know?" she replied.

"You will see in Hank's report. Nelson is a partner in that bar, the Black Cat."

"I see."

"It's also where Mark Taylor last worked before his disappearance. So Nelson was probably his boss back then."

"A partner, you said?"

"Yes, Nelson created an offshore company that owns the bar, but he's not alone. There is another mystery partner; we don't have his identity yet. I will ask Hank to continue digging."

"I'll read Hank's report now that the letters on the screen look like real words."

After she hung up, I read the Nelson report again, looking for other clues. He had a younger sister; I wondered if she was part of his business like the bar management. Information on his parents was missing. They may have remained in Singapore, where he was born. He immigrated on a student visa when he was 17 and received permanent status at 21. Hank found no marriage license either.

I wrote back to Hank to thank him and asked him to dig deeper into Nelson's business dealings, such as other company affiliations, and to perform the same research for his family. He also had an associate at the bar. Who was he?

Chapter 8

Monday morning at 7 o'clock found me in my car waiting in line for my medium black coffee to go, heading back to Miami. Yesterday I prepared two knapsacks, booked an apartment near South Beach on Airbnb, and sent Nadine a detailed invoice covering my last 15 days of work and expenses. A brief call informed Jennifer of my mid-morning arrival.

During the abominable drive on I-95 South, I reached out to Wayne Freeman; he was willing to meet with Jennifer and me for a short time. While on the phone, I suggested he look up two individuals, Eugene Byrd and Reginald Miranda, both from Miami. My researcher discovered these gentlemen registered an official complaint against Nelson for assault but rescinded it a few weeks later. I wanted to understand why. Freeman responded by suggesting I should hire my investigation team. Big help.

Both seated on one side of a dining booth at the Melting Pot, we expected Wayne any minute now. We looked foolish, but we both preferred to see Wayne's eyes, an FBI training remnant. He was on time, and when he arrived, he asked, "Expecting anyone?" as he slipped onto the worn plastic seat remaining and showcasing a broad smile.

"Thanks for coming, Wayne."

"Don't mention it. Detectives are always hoping for a free lunch. You served a fantastic dinner aboard your yacht last time. It was great. And this would be Jennifer?"

"Glad you enjoyed it. Yes, Jennifer Jones, she'll be working with me."

"Nice to see you, Wayne," as she extended her hand, Freeman did the same.

"I think you're in a hurry, so we'll get down to business. We learned the Black Cat bar's owner, where Mark Taylor was last seen on September 10th, is Yang Nelson. I read the case files you brought, and you interviewed somebody at the bar, the manager, I suppose, but not Nelson."

"Yes, I remember now. We talked to a guy, well dressed, polite, somewhat nervous, he said he was the owner, but we did not verify. We took his word for it."

Freeman's body language told me he was on the defensive. Was it the bar itself, its owner, or the fact we questioned his investigative actions?

"No reason to dig deeper," suggested Jennifer.

I knew Jennifer; she would not leave it there if this were her investigation. She would identify the final authority, the big boss. I figured she wanted to get on Freeman's side, at least initially, with her answer. So I continued.

"So, it's possible Nelson met Taylor as a staff member and then interested him in surfing with his friends. Or, the reverse is also possible, they bump into each other on the beach, and when Mark said he was a bartender, Nelson got him a temporary gig. But either way, it's not important. We now have a connection between these two gentlemen."

Wayne added, "Possible."

Jennifer looked at me for a fraction of a second, but I understood the subliminal message: is this guy for real? Freeman resisted getting involved in his original investigation, but why? He may harbor his reasons; however, he was not sharing them with us.

Our drinks arrived, and we placed our food order. The intermission allowed me to change the subject.

"As I told you this morning, the city dropped simple assault charges on Nelson before even reaching the courts. I wonder if the accusations pertain to his business operations, like throwing a loud customer out or from something else."

"No idea," Freeman said. The longer my queries were, the shorter were his answers.

"No problem, I'll follow up with John."

Never a good career move to have your boss reverse a decision you made. This would rattle his cage, possibly.

After a few seconds, he developed his answer. "Still, I dug up information on the two individuals involved in the assault charges," continued Wayne. "They have records of their own, suspected both of drug distribution in their neighborhood. They belong to a street gang. So far, we don't have enough probable cause to arrest them. As for why they dropped the charges, you must ask them."

After hearing Wayne talk about the two plaintiffs without offering to check it out himself, I brought up another concern. We needed to shake Nelson down by eliminating, at least for a while, his two bodyguards. I argued witnesses could identify the men at the bar, later leaving with Mark Taylor. But, more damaging still, video footage existed of these two idiots going onto my yacht and killing an honest man. Given William Tudor's time-of-death offered by the medical examiner and the time displayed on the videotape, was that enough to pick them up and question them? Could the Miami-Dade police get their fingerprints for comparison to any others found onboard?

"We have to charge them with an indictable offense to get their prints," Freeman answered.

"Murder is such an offense," said Jennifer.

"Yes, I realize," Freeman replied.

"Did you find any fingerprints on my boat besides mine and Cynthia's?" I asked.

"We did, but we can't match them to anyone."

"Why don't you pick them up, at least for questioning?"

"Miami is a big city. We have to find them first."

"Jennifer and I can help you locate them. If they cross our path, we'll call it in. Would that work for you?"

"Yes, that's fine."

Our food arrived, and we rushed our lunch as Wayne referred to a 1 pm meeting of importance. I thanked him for his help and promised him we'd be in touch.

With just Jennifer and I left, we made up our plans for the upcoming days. She will keep following Nelson. Should she spot the two Asians, she was to inform Wayne. From my point of view, I wanted to get more intelligence on Ocean Dancer's whereabouts. Without an FBI badge to ask questions, I needed new tricks.

"Something else troubles me, Jason," stated Jennifer.

"What?" I asked.

"You told me before, images from the dock showed a guy walk toward your boat, and then a second one follows him."

"Correct."

"How did they know which yacht you were on?"

"Search me. The guys followed me, I guess."

"Possible. Does your business card include your yacht's name?"

"No."

"The AIS system we discussed, can it locate with precision your boat inside the Marina?"

"No, the accuracy cannot show one specific boat when you have dozens in proximity, with tankers maybe, not with small crafts."

"Who knew your exact position at this Marina?"

I thought about it, and I only had one answer. "Wayne Freeman, we dined aboard the previous evening."

A heavy silence descended between both of us, lost in our reflections.

I placed a call to John Russell with Jennifer still by my side as we came out. I told him of our talks, and he agreed to discuss the prospect of bringing the two Asians in if they locate them. I promised him we would do our best to help him in that matter. We did not explain our doubts about Freeman.

Jennifer went her way. My next stop was on Alton Road, curious to learn why Ocean Dancer made these trips to the Marathon Marina so often. I located the offices of Yacht Charter of Miami inside a mini-business mart. Some advertising obscured its entrance.

My initial strategy involved trying to lure information from whoever I met inside. If I did not get sufficient data, I would need a different tactic. I noticed a common security alarm terminal near the front entrance as I walked in. Inside, a well-decorated space greeted the typically wealthy visitors who rented these big yachts. On the right, a waiting area offered four large white leather chairs, a glass coffee table in the middle, and a massive screen displaying, what else, large yachts in operation. On the left, two small semi-private offices with visitor chairs and a computer screen mounted on a tiny desk. A sales office, I assumed. When I looked forward, a large semicircular reception desk with a young lady busy on her keyboard. Behind her, a full-length opaque glass wall with a door on each side of the reception desk complemented the viewable office.

I did not think the receptionist would provide me with what I was looking for, so I used a different tactic.

"Pardon me, miss, my name is Jason Tanner, and I'm a private investigator. May I see your manager please?"

She looked me over and dialed a short extension number. "Mister Thompson, someone to see you in front, Mr. Tanner, a private investigator."

I examined the space, searching for window and door security apparatus as I waited. The ceiling edge revealed no movement detection sensor as I sat down and waited for the manager. Walls displayed promotions on huge posters. One of them attracted my attention; customers may reserve a three-day excursion to Nassau in the Bahamas for a mere three thousand dollars per person on a superyacht. Since I knew the cost of diesel and crew, I found it surprising such a crossing would be profitable. Unless it was a loss leader like a retail store's display when you walk in.

I was pondering this offer when a door opened, and a stocky bald man in a business suit came out. He looked around, and since I was the only visitor, he walked in my direction.

"Mr. Tanner, how can I help you?" he asked.

"Could we go somewhere private?" in the hope he brought me to his office to get a sense of the place.

"Let's go over here," he pointed to one of the small sales offices. As we sat down, I handed him a business card, and he reached inside his jacket for his, but he came out empty-handed. I extracted my notebook from my knapsack. "And your name is?" I asked.

"Thompson, Averell Thompson."

"And you are the office manager?"

"Yes. What is all this about?"

"Mr. Thompson, I represent a yacht owner involved in a collision while in a Marathon Marina. The other ship fled away, and I am trying to trace it."

"And you think it's one of our ships?"

"No, not at all. When the incident occurred, our guests and crew were dining in a local restaurant. It was only when they returned they noticed the scrape on the boat's port side. They examined all the vessels present at the Marina, and none had any sign of a collision. That's why we believe the culprit disappeared."

"And where do we come in?"

"A yacht sailed into this Marina, Ocean Dancer. It is one of yours?"

"Yes, it is."

"So I would like to talk to whoever was aboard to ask them if they noticed anything."

"I see. Wait here a minute." He returned with a large blue three-ring binder with Ocean Dancer written on the side.

"When was this mishap?"

I provided him with a date from the Marina ledger when his ship was on-site.

"Yes, our yacht was in that area on that date. Unfortunately, giving away contact information for our employees and our customers is out of the question."

"Ideally, I would like to speak with them but failing this approach, what if I communicate with them through e-mail?"

"The same answer, we don't give out our employee's e-mail information."

"I see. I will relay this information to our lawyers and let them sort this out."

"If the court orders us to identify them, we will but not otherwise. I hope you understand our point of view."

"I do, but I also have a job to do."

He closed the binder, showing this conversation was over.

"Thank you very much for your help, Mr. Thompson. I suppose, as a boat owner, you would also try to find the person accountable for an accident with one of your ships."

"Maybe, but we also carry maritime insurance."

"My customer does too, but I understand the deductible is important, and a small investigation may provide enough information to sue the offending party to recover it."

"Makes sense."

I thanked him again, and I left. I knew I would return.

# # #

It was only around 6 pm, and it wouldn't be dark until 8 pm this time of year. I watched Averell Thompson lock his office's front door from a safe distance. With time to spare, I drove away and looked for a quiet restaurant.

A little past midnight, I parked on a side street near Yacht Charter of Miami, grabbed my backpack, and walked behind the business mart. Earlier today, I had scouted the surroundings. On one side of the yacht rental agency, a clothing store, while a barbershop sat on the other side. The latter one was most likely unprotected; who stole gel or mousse these days?

Feeling nervous, I reached for my tools to pick locks, unused in quite a while. My hands were immobile when I looked down, but my active mind told me they shook. I worked on the barbershop back door, looked around often, and noticed no bizarre movement in my vicinity. I doubted anyone could see me in my black jeans and shirt at midnight, but you never know. Even rusted, I beat the lock in less than 30 seconds. With great care to keep quiet, I closed the door, still unlocked, and retreated to a hiding place, waiting for an alarm company to show up. After twenty minutes, I was sure nobody would come. I walked back, opened the door, and stepped right in. A backroom lunch area without windows greeted me; I was in luck. With my flashlight, I checked around and found only one area, under the door leading to the barber chairs, which presented a problem. I located a few towels and put them along the door's bottom. I switched the lights on with a long sigh of relief, but something interrupted me.

A chill ran down my spine as I heard a voice rising in the back alley. I turned off the light and moved behind the rear door, holding my breath. The sound diminished slowly as the late walker passed by position. After taking deep respiration, I flipped the lights back on.

Looking up, I found a typical false ceiling suspended from the roof structure as I expected. I put a chair on top of a table and manufactured a temporary but fragile ladder. I displaced a ceiling tile and directed my flashlight toward the wall separation between the barbershop and the rental agency. Luckily, it was a simple piece of drywall, possibly reinforced, dividing the neighbors. My heavy backpack was a testament I didn't know what to expect. I cut out a square hole large enough to get through with my knife and installed a portable cord ladder to go down in the office next door. I passed through the hole and descended, removed a ceiling tile on my way down, and set foot in the back office area of Yacht Charter of Miami. Somewhat relieved, I looked at my watch; it was 1 am; I used twenty minutes so far; it seemed like a few hours to me.

I dimmed my flashlight with a piece of cloth, not wanting light streaks showing through the front glass. I searched for the most prominent office, assuming it would be Averell Thompson's. It was right in the corner. I looked around his workplace, no sign of the blue binder. There were eight file cabinets in the back office space, each with three drawers. They were all closed with the standard locking mechanism, easy to pick. No labels indicated the file cabinet's content. I guess everyone knew what they contained. Good for them, not so for me.

I started on the first one, unlocked it, and searched for blue binders in each drawer. When I reached the sixth file cabinet, the top drawer finally contained what I was looking for. I imagined these were vessel names, in alphabetical order, written on the binder's edge. The middle drawer held the Ocean Dancer pedigree, the same document Thompson referred to in my presence this afternoon. I didn't want to remove it since the agency held my business card, and I inquired today about this yacht; too obvious. But I wanted the information it contained.

Lugging my backpack and the binder, I walked to one of the two bathrooms. I made sure no window would give me away, and I opened the light. With the book set on the washroom counter, I picked up my small camera and photographed all relevant pages. I was interested in the ship's destinations over the past year, customers, crew, and so on. I flipped a page, click, turned another page, click. When I wasn't sure, I clicked anyway. Altogether, I used more than twenty minutes to finish, I held more than a hundred images on my camera. Once my photography session was over, I looked at the ship's activities in September of last year, when it stopped in Marathon. It was that infamous weekend when Mark Taylor traveled to the Keys. I was looking for the ship's real customer name. BC International appeared in the schedule.

I returned the binder to its original location and hunted for customer records at full tilt. A bunch of company names showed up in the second cabinet, but they looked like maritime-related, maybe accounts payable. I continued and found another set of files arranged in alphabetical order. In the B section, I pulled up BC International, which was rather thick. I went back to the bathroom for another picture session. In no particular order were invoices, statements, requests to rent sent by email, and at the start of the file, a form to create a customer's account.

Having grabbed as much as I could, I turned the bathroom lights off, closed all cabinets securing them by pushing the lock-in, just like when I found them. I returned to my point of entry and looked around for debris I may have caused. I picked up drywall dust and climbed back the way I came. On my way out, I reinstalled the ceiling tile. I could not repair the hole tonight, but it would go unnoticed until someone looked into the false ceiling. I cleaned up on the barbershop side, replaced tables and chairs, turned off the light, and opened the rear door bit by bit. Not hearing anything suspicious, I locked it, walked back to my car, put my backpack in the trunk, and then took a long breath of air. I drove within the speed limit and headed for my temporary shelter near South Beach. Tomorrow promised to be another busy day.

# # #

I got up later than usual after my night out. Yesterday's operation tired my entire mind and body. But by 8 am, after a quick shower, I was out looking for breakfast, carrying my laptop and my camera's memory card safe in my pocket. The sun was already shining in Miami Beach as walkers and runners were out early. A French bistro crossed my path where I ordered a grilled cheese with bacon. When the lady refilled my latte with regular filtered coffee, I got my laptop out and connected to the restaurant's Wi-Fi guest network. Security was not an issue here.

I was now looking at a bunch of images, each one a page from Ocean Dancer's blue binder. I needed to analyze them all. Experience told me a second pair of eyes would be better, so I was thinking of reviewing the data with Jennifer's help. Therefore, I should get hard copies to work with. I searched for print shops in the area. I located a FedEx Office doing this kind of work, presented my memory card, and got two copies of 112 pages which I put into two separate brown envelopes.

I texted Jennifer hoping she was available.

"You know Jason, I am getting a fine tan while working with you."

"Part of the benefits package at Private Eye Investigations, darling."

"Benefits are better than wages."

"Wow, wow, now. Talk to your union guy about the compensation, not me."

"Sure, what's up, my leader?"

"A pile of documents needs our review, and I could use your help. My temporary quarters would provide a table and chairs to work on if you don't mind. Why don't you join me to peg away at this stuff?"

"What stuff?" she asked.

"I'll tell you later; it's a long story," I answered.

She agreed, so I asked her to meet me in 15 minutes. I picked up two mezzo coffees from my favorite shop on my way.

A few minutes after my return, I heard a discreet knock on the door. I walked over, opened with one hand, and presented a coffee with the other as a sign of gratitude. "Nice," she said. "Is this also part of the benefits package?"

"Yes, Mam."

She examined my temporary housing facilities and concluded it was OK. The location makes it great and expensive. I agreed. We sat at the main table, and I described my official encounter at Yacht Charter of Miami. I did not impress her. I mesmerized her when I told her about my unofficial visit to the same rental agency premise in the dark of night.

"You spent years in the Marines, the police, and the FBI, and then the first opportunity you come across, you break the law."

"Jennifer," I paused for a while, "Averell did not want to disclose the information."

"Averell? Like in Averell Dalton of the Dalton brothers?"

"Yes, just like that. You know, Jennifer, it's possible to get this information with a court order, but we can't waste time."

"OK, let's see what you got."

I pushed the envelope in front of her, and I opened mine, both of us scanning the documents at a rapid pace, curious. As I was reading, I scribbled notes, things to bring up and get her point of view. I finished reading my stack, so I leaned back and waited. She completed her first analysis just a few minutes later.

"So let's compare notes. Anything of interest you have spotted?"

"Well, for starters, they schedule one trip, every month, over the last year. You had hinted to that from the logs at Captain Pip's Marina. A bunch of people board in Miami, sail to Marathon, and return to Miami the following day, every time."

"Correct. But that is pretty much in line with the Black Cat's promotion going on."

"The what?"

"Well, yesterday, I drove by the Black Cat, and I stopped to check out the place. Inside, on the walls, posters were proposing a contest where two lucky winners, accompanied by a friend, get to sail to Marathon on a luxury yacht. That would explain why the Ocean Dancer sails there regularly."

"What do the participants have to accomplish?"

"Nothing. Fill in a coupon with your name and phone number. Anybody who orders a meal gets one. Not complicated."

I paused for a moment. A yacht like this was easily priced at $10,000 per day to rent. Add the diesel costs, the fees, some profit. The Black Cat was looking at a minimum $20,000 fee every trip. Could additional meals compensate for this expense? It seemed unlikely in my estimation.

"I doubt this promo would pay for itself given the huge costs involved. There has to be another reason for these trips. We haven't found it yet."

"Has to be drug-related, Jason."

"I would agree. But we need more information. Why did Mark Taylor come down here?" No response.

I re-examined my stack of papers trying to identify the captain and his team. By combining various trip reports, I concluded Captain Brad Scott was in charge of every outing. His crew was always the same group of three guys and one girl in a rotation. They could operate this ship with only two crewmates if needed.

"I also found an email in the file, a short communication from Nelson, he would cancel the expeditions if Scott was not captaining on the upcoming trip," Jennifer added.

"So he's an important piece of the puzzle."

"Affirmative, and you nailed it. I am looking at some monthly statements; the invoices are more than $25,000. Not cheap by any means."

"You know, Jennifer, the staging of these activities may be to hide that Nelson travels to Marathon regularly. The contest is just a cover for his excursions. Traveling by sea allows him to bypass any roadblock that the authorities may deploy on the single highway to and from the Keys; that's an advantage."

"And Jason, let's not forget, if he illegally transports anything, more hiding space exists in a 90-foot yacht than in a Jeep."

"That's true. And furthermore, because the trips occur in US waters, no need to register with Border Patrol and raise suspicion as well."

"When I saw them last time at the Marina in Marathon, Nelson went out with the so-called winners of his contest, and once they were off, his two buddies disappeared. It could be that they had a separate party or were on a mission. I think it's important to find out where these chaps are spending their evening. We must set up surveillance in Marathon next time around. We need to find out when."

"I already know?" answered Jennifer.

"How come?" I questioned.

"Intensive investigation and the fact that the poster on the wall of the Black Cat says the ship sails on April 7th in large characters," she joked.

"Well, April 7th is a date," I declared smiling; she did too.

Chapter 9

Back at my home base in Pompano, I woke up feeling happy the following morning, relaxed after a good night's sleep. I worked on this challenging case for almost three weeks straight. Now I ought to recharge my batteries, clear my mind, sit back, and return for a fresh start. A part-time investigation gig is what I wanted, not a full 24/7 operation.

After attending to my domestic chores, such as cleaning and saying hello to my few neighbors around the Marina, I made a quick trip to the Rusty Hook. I ordered a fresh Mahi-Mahi sandwich and a Corona after saluting my good buddy, Jeff, in his cuisine; just a fancy name he gave to his kitchen. That was a pleasant interruption and provided me the energy to finish my day.

At 5 pm, I mixed my usual martini, moved topside, and speed-dialed my daughter. "Hey gorgeous, sorry I did not call you before, but I have been busy. I verified that your flight, last Thursday, arrived on time, so I am not all that unthoughtful."

"You could have called earlier. It's been almost a week."

"I'm sorry, girl, you're right, my bad." By using a young person's expression, I thought I would win points and avoid her vexation.

"How is your investigation going?"

My quick reply seemed to have worked. She didn't sound mad.

"Well, I followed your guidance and brought in additional help. After dropping you off at the airport, I met Jennifer, and she agreed to help me. She can get out at any time, no questions asked; that's fine with me."

"That is excellent news, Dad. I suppose that's an upgrade, no?"

"Well trained, she possesses more insight and abilities in criminal investigations, she can stand up for herself, can carry a weapon, but she's not you."

"Nice of you to say, Dad. What else?"

I explained why I believed our adversaries knew about our movement using AIS technology and why my unplanned retreat to Pompano was necessary.

"Be careful. If they know where you're located, they can also figure out where you came from."

She was right, the marine traffic application would show Sands Harbor Marina as my usual parking spot. With already one attempt on my life, I would need to be alert at all times. Even running my AIS system in silent mode may not be enough. Some information was already out there.

"Careful is my middle name, dear. In other news, I received a report from my secret weapon, Hank the hacker Hackman, about our friend Yang Nelson. We'll see what he can come up with; he's meticulous."

She asked about Ocean Dancer, and I replied I had researched this vessel, but I did not mention that I escalated and cut a hole in a wall to obtain information. No need to get her excited. She updated me on events in Denver, and we promised to keep in touch more often. I hung up; I was most pleased.

The next few days were quiet, and I used the time to put my affairs in order, which I had neglected over the last three weeks. I had insurance to renew, bills to pay, that kind of exciting occupation.

Over that period, I debated Wayne Freeman's situation internally. Did he provide my location to the opposition? Was he aware of the endgame? Was it to get rid of me? It also occurred to me that Cynthia may have been on board at the time. Fate made it that William Tudor was on the yacht at that fateful moment. Poor William, life is not always fair.

I needed to know whose side Freeman belonged. I could confront him and ask him a terrible question. He would deny it without a doubt. As a detective, he would ask: do you have any proof? And I did not, at least not today.

Another option would be to bring up my suspicions with his boss, John Russell, head of detectives. I needed to convince him of my theory, unfounded so far, to start an Internal Affairs investigation. Would they find a link between Freeman and Nelson's organization? Phone calls between them, meetings, money exchange, whatever may provide a connection between Freeman and this gang. They orchestrated William's death, but in reality, they were looking to end my life. A friendly group of honest folks they were.

Another way to unmask Freeman existed: I could try to find some incriminating evidence myself before presenting it to JR. And for that, I needed Hank Hackman. I grabbed my phone and dialed Hank's number. I explained what I was looking for. If I could get Freeman's call logs between the time when I provided my yacht location and when they murdered William, maybe it would convince JR.

"A call log is easy to consult. From your guy's cell phone number, I can determine which carrier he's using. I can then send him a phishing email to get his user id and password to his carrier's website. From there, I'll extract his incoming and outgoing calls. As a bonus, Jason, I'll even tell you if he paid his account."

"Phone number and email; let me work on that. I have the first one already; I'll get the email tomorrow," as I looked at my watch. It was too late today. I slept better that night; at least a plan was shaping up about Freeman.

The next morning provided another sunny and windy day in Pompano with a high near 80 degrees. I was planning to go fishing and eat whatever I caught. But first, I had to call and obtain an email address as I promised Hank.

"Good morning LeBron, Jason Tanner here. How are you this morning?"

As Freeman's partner, I figured LeBron must have Wayne's email address.

"Fine, what can I do for you?"

"First, I wanted to thank you again for locating Mark Taylor's hideaway in Marathon. I visited the unusual combinations of luxury yachts, cheap rooms, and an ordinary restaurant. It's quite something. Our investigation is moving along. Nothing concrete yet, but it's progressing. The other reason for my call is that I would like to invite you and Wayne to a fishing day this summer. The last time I saw him, he mentioned you guys liked to fish. If you give me your email and Wayne's, I will send you the information in due time."

Holding my breath in silence, my bluff was out there. I hoped it added up. It took a little more time than expected, but LeBron gave me both addresses in the end. I updated my contact information on the two police officers and sent it to Hank for his research.

For a few days, I relaxed, happy to return to a quiet agenda: run in the morning, coffee after, some afternoon fishing. One day, upon my return from my morning occupations, walking in front of the Marina's management office, a door opened, and Rick, the lad who runs the place, stepped out.

"Mister Tanner, a package arrived for you this morning. The delivery guy left it beside your boat's door."

"That's fine, Rick. Thanks."

As I kept walking toward my home, I wondered what this package could be. I ordered nothing recently. Even then, the Marina's administration desk holds on to deliveries waiting for the owner's pickup. A gift? It's not my birthday yet. Documents Hank or Barry would send? Possible, but they would advise me first. Something puzzled me.

I turned on my dock, but a dozen feet out from my boat, I stopped. Rick was right; a package sat in front of my salon's doorway. Wrapped in a brown paper bag, it was a few feet long and roundish, something like a half-baseball bat. My sixth sense got the better of me, and I retreated toward the shore, dialed 911, and informed the operator I received a suspicious package. South Florida got its fair share of poisoned envelopes and pipe bombs in the past year. They reacted immediately, "Stay away. We're sending officers right now."

I kept watching my dock's entrance stopping anyone wishing to walk on. Only a few minutes elapsed before loud sirens disturbed the lunch hour. Two officers first walked to the administration desk and then, escorted by Rick, breezed in my direction.

"You called 911?" one officer asked.

"Yes, I did. My name is Jason Tanner, and I live aboard the yacht at the end of the walkway over there. Rick here tells me someone delivered a package this morning, but I'm not expecting anything. It's shaped strangely, and I don't feel good about this."

"Would anyone wish you harm?" an officer asked.

"It's possible." And I explained with few details my investigation. After a few questions, both officers walked toward my boat, looked around, and without boarding, turned, and now walked back at a quick pace. I heard one of them radio a request for the bomb squad. His suspicions equaled my own. One officer prevented anyone from accessing the dock. The other took me away for some additional questions. This time he wrote down notes.

Soon, a funny-looking truck bearing the Sheriff's department colors arrived. Three more SUVs followed; the bomb squad was rolling in. Another police officer cordoned off the entire Marina. From their vantage point on the Atlantic Bridge right beside the harbor, dozens of curious onlookers watched the scene, their phones recording hoping to win CNN's video of the day. Soon, the police closed the bridge to all traffic and evacuated the crowds to their great disappointment. A bomb the size of which we have seen on my boat could injure someone hundreds of feet away. Authorities took no chances.

A short policeman dressed in a strange suit transported a small mobile robot and left it on the aft deck of my boat, a dozen feet away from the package. He then returned to his truck to control the machine, an operation I witnessed several times in my career.

The same policeman returned to the yacht an hour later, picked up the package, and brought it back to his truck. He removed his stuffy protection gear. He emerged all sweaty, not sure if it was the tension or the suit. As he was toweling off, he walked in my direction and said, "False alarm. It's made to look like a bomb but is missing the essential ingredients for an explosion. There's no detonator nor C4 in the package."

"And you discovered all of that from your truck?"

"Yes, the robot has twin cameras, sensors, and a few hands we can use to open packages. Cool, hey."

"And now?"

"Safe to go back. I have the parcel, and we'll see if we can find clues on who may have done this, but I don't hold faith too much. These are amateurs."

"I may have a clue for you. Come with me." I walked to the Marina office and asked Rick to follow us. We all went aboard my yacht, and I pulled out my laptop, pressed a few keys, and located what I wanted Rick to see. A blown-up picture of the Asians on the beach with Nelson flashed on the screen.

"You know any of these guys?"

He sat down and got closer. He used arrow keys to view different pictures of the same moment. Suddenly he said, "This one. This is the guy who brought the package this morning." He pointed at a young Asian with blond hair, the shorter of the terrible duo.

The bomb squad officer asked some questions about who this man was, but I couldn't help him. I knew the faces, not the names. He gave me a business card to e-mail him the picture and any pertinent information about the stranger for his investigation.

On Saturday morning, I called Jennifer. I first reported on yesterday's activity around my Marina. She did not interrupt me, but her silence showed she worried even more. She did not like what she heard. I restated my advice to be careful and offered her to withdraw from the investigation. She had no such intention, she answered after a short silence.

Moving to another subject, I wanted to get updated on Nelson's stakeout. She had nothing new to report. Nelson spent his time between the surf, his bar, and his girlfriend in Miami, what looked like a luxury apartment near Biscayne Bay. But the night before, Jennifer had offered her husband to dine out downtown, and she brought him to the Black Cat! Some nerve, this Jennifer. She even entered her name in the ballot box to win a cruise to Marathon.

"And why did you do that?" I asked.

"I figured that if I needed to follow the creep to Marathon, I might as well do it in style aboard a fabulous yacht you told me about." The draw was this coming Tuesday, sailing the following Saturday.

I concluded our conversation by asking Jennifer to stop tailing Nelson for now. Let's not gamble and raise his suspicion. We know pretty much where he will be next Saturday if he's consistent with his schedule.

# # #

On Tuesday morning, five days after asking Hank to explore Freeman's call log, my Inbox alerted me. Hoping to break this case wide open, I frantically pressed on my phone's email icon.

As I read the message, disappointment replaced my earlier enthusiasm. Hank got the job done all right. He snatched up Freeman's user identification, accessed his cell phone account, copied and attached his call log to the message, and after further analysis, concluded no smoking gun existed. Three days were of interest: on Thursday morning, Freeman called me while sailing to Miami, that's when I invited him for dinner. When he confirmed his presence in the afternoon, I gave him the directions to my yacht. On Friday, Cynthia arrived; that night, they attacked me near the Marina. And, on Saturday, they murdered William. Therefore, these three days were crucial. Freeman got the information late on Thursday; William was dead on Saturday. If he passed intelligence along, it would be one of these three days.

Hank associated my phone number with calls Freeman made in the morning and another one late Thursday to receive and then confirm my dining invitation. A dozen other calls were listed in the log, and Hank had scribbled names and some addresses when he found the information. Half of them were to his partner LeBron Jackson, one to John Russell, and the rest to various commercial entities. None at the Black Cat, nor to Yang Nelson or unidentified parties.

When I closed my mail, I tried to come up with a sensible conclusion, but my mind wrestled with two options: either Freeman was not the crook I believed him to be, or he owned a second phone, a throwaway phone.

# # #

The days kept rolling on, one long day after another. I briefed Jennifer Wednesday about our weekend plans and adjusted a few details with her. I would drive down to Miami Friday morning and pick her up. Afraid some complacency existed between the crew and guests of Ocean Dancer and the Marina management, I had reserved two rooms in a local motel, but not Captain Pip's. No need to return there; I broke into their offices last time around.

Both Jennifer and I were on the same wavelength. Nelson was there for the show, the Asian guys, their names unknown to us, would be present, we hoped, for the business side. These two were our real targets. We both would carry weapons, and Jennifer would get a separate rental car so we could follow our marks with multiple vehicles to avoid suspicion and detection. I had gotten a pair of walkie-talkies for our direct communications, and I would bring my backpack with tools of the trade if we needed to enter somewhere uninvited.

We settled on Porky's, the closest restaurant, with a view of the Marina. It would allow us to hang around and keep an eye on Ocean Dancer from a dining table. Marathon is the opposite of a typical South Florida neighborhood in terms of design and architecture. The pavement is rare; cement sidewalks don't exist, street lamps are few. Beautiful houses surrounded by green grass, flowers, and trees exist but are scarce except in newly developed communities. In its defense, hurricane Irma ravaged the area in September 2017, about twenty months ago. Since then, tax dollars went to rebuild the necessary infrastructure. While I think about it, I realize it was approximately the time Ocean Dancer first came to Marathon. I wondered if it was a coincidence. In the aftermath of such a terrible situation, sometimes opportunities develop. Did the Nelson gang profit from this? Hum.

Jennifer and I spent the afternoon chatting, eating like birds, and drinking ice tea. We wanted to be sharp tonight and avoided too much food and drinks. At around 5:30 pm, the large mass of the Ocean Dancer came into view. With our binoculars, we could observe some people dancing, flirting, or just milling around. Yang Nelson looked at ease right in the middle of all the excitement.

An hour later, Yang, a girl at his arm, and two couples disembarked, crossed the parking lot, and walked east on the bike trail toward Barnacle Barney's, their hangout for tonight, we assumed. That was our signal to get into our vehicles. Jennifer covered one end of the parking lot, me, the other. We were expecting the two Asians at any moment, but 7, 8, and 9 o'clock came around without them showing up. We kept the discussion going on our expensive but safe walkie-talkie units.

The Missing Taylor

At around 9:30 pm, a cab entered the parking area and stopped, lights on, waiting. I hit the push-to-talk button and said, "Heads up, this could be it." Two Asians, well dressed, walked out of the Marina and entered the cab. Within a few seconds, they were off, and the chase was on.

In my big black FBI-looking SUV, I was the first to follow the cab with a car in-between. Jennifer, in her rented small pickup truck, was trailing. Her choice of transportation fitted right in the neighborhood. Mine would be suitable in the Presidential caravan. Having examined the city map during our ice tea period, I turned onto a side street, Jennifer's pickup just one car off the target. I turned left twice, and I was back on A1A, the main highway linking all the keys together, right down to Key West.

Half a mile later, it was her turn to bear left, leaving me four cars behind the cab. She rejoined the procession not long after. A few minutes later, the taxi signaled and turned right into a shopping mall occupied by a dozen small businesses. A huge sign read Big Whale Plaza. I kept going up to the next street while Jennifer stopped in a parking lot opposite the plaza. She radioed the information, and I made a U-turn and picked a spot across the street, unseen from the people in the cab. The driver brought them to the far end of the lot, in front of a single white one-story building. The two passengers exited the cab and stood around waiting for the driver to leave, which he did soon after. A minute later, a small red convertible car arrived, a tall man got out, and all three stood around talking.

It was dark now, and no lights were shining at the far end of the parking lot where our guys were standing. From my point of view, the building carried no identification; at least, I could see no sign. I asked Jennifer if she could still see any activity, and she replied, "None, they're just standing there." I wished I had infrared binoculars but my days in the FBI were over. So I told Jennifer I was going in for closer observation. Without waiting for a response, I got out of the SUV, crossed the street and ran behind the business center, to the far end, sure they couldn't see me. I left the comfort of my car with only a gun in my back holster.

I ran to the end of the shopping mall from the backside and looked around the corner. I could still observe the building's front side from my vantage point. I now realized our quarry had disappeared. Are they inside? They must be. Asking Jennifer was out of the question. I didn't bring the walkie-talkie with me, damn. I believed my inner voice told me my spoken words would reveal my position; that's why it still sat on the passenger front seat.

A row of shrubs separated the mall from its neighbor on my left, and I planned to use it as a cover. Since no one was outside the building now, and I couldn't knock on the front door, maybe I could glean some information from the backside. Hidden by the plaza, I walked toward the shrubs, found a hole, and crossed over to the other side. Half-crouched now, I ran along the natural fence and tried to get a sighting toward the back of the property. Through the shrubs, I saw light coming from a window. Because the building was dark from the street, I assumed the light must have originated from a back room. Curious by nature, I wanted to peek inside.

I found another opening to cross back through the shrubs and moved in silence toward the nearest building corner. Still half-crouched, I got to the window. I looked around; it was eerie quiet. I deployed my body to its full length and looked inside from the corner of the window. A wall of tablets filled with small boxes appeared on either side of the room. It was unclear what these boxes contained. In the middle, I saw three regular-size tables, a few chairs, and nothing else. The neon lights inside were all on, but I still couldn't see anybody. I bent down and moved to the other end of the window; the same result, I saw no living creature inside.

I was about to turn around and go back to the safety of my SUV when I heard the words, "Hold it right there" as my heart skipped a beat.

# # #

"Put your hands in the air and turn around, no sudden moves."

Stunned, I raised my hands and did as ordered. My eyes were drawn to a big gun in the man's hand. Shining a flashlight on me, the voice disappeared into the darkness, without a glimpse of the person behind the weapon.

"Mr. Tanner, the man with all the questions. Well, well, what a surprise."

"And you are?"

"Quiet, turn around, and put your hands on the wall, spread your feet." This guy must have watched a lot of police movies, or he was a retired cop himself, or someone gave him these instructions before.

He frisked me and removed my gun.

"Stay there!" he told me as he moved to the rear door past the window I was peering into a moment ago. I turned my head a fraction, and I still saw the gun pointed in my direction. He knocked three times and then twice again with a long beat. Got to be their secret code.

The door opened, and my captor signaled I should follow him inside. I looked around and did not see any cavalry arriving to rescue my butt from this awkward position. I walked toward him, as instructed, my hands still above my head. What did he have in mind for me? I didn't have a clue, but it wasn't anything nice, I presumed. I thought about Jennifer coming to my rescue, but I left my post so quickly that we didn't prepare any significant plan. That should be a lesson for me.

The light inside blinded me for a few seconds. When I peered from outside a few minutes ago, I detected no human presence. Now, I recognized my two Asian friends smiling. Another individual studied me from a distance, his face was familiar, but I couldn't remember where I had seen him.

Someone pulled a chair and my captor, signaling with his gun again, hinted I should sit on it. After I obliged, he asked that I put my hand behind my back. When I did so, my two Asian captors came behind me and locked my hands with zip ties.

Someone walked behind me and pulled down the rear window blinds. The silent period was stretching. Finally, the man who held the gun outside now stood right in front of me, empty-handed, his two colleagues on each side of me.

He walked away and returned with a chair which he placed right in front of me. He straddled it and leaned his arms on the backrest. He looked me in the eye but was silent. I was about to open the discussion myself when he finally spoke.

"Let's start with a simple question. Why were you following my two buddies tonight?"

"I am under orders from my client to locate her missing brother. He was last seen in this area; it's why I'm here. Now it's my turn; what are you guys doing here?" I was not expecting fair play, but I tried anyway.

"I ask the questions, shut up."

He continued. "Who would that client be?"

"Sorry, I am not at liberty to share this information. I signed a non-disclosure."

"Tanner, once again, let me remind you, I ask questions, and you better answer them; that's quite a simple process. Otherwise, I will leave you to the professional hands of my two Asian brothers here. They can make you suffer a long time until you die, or they can kill you right away. I know they enjoy the first option better."

In my opinion, the two heartless idiots killed William Tudor with a fentanyl-loaded injection to his neck. I didn't want to go through the same fatal experience. I needed to play along until I could find a way out.

"I will respond to your boss, Yang Nelson, only," I answered.

A big laugh erupted all around. I turned my head, and they were all smiling.

"What was so funny?" I demanded.

"Well, Tanner, if you want to know, I may have to kill you after I tell you."

I thought about their reaction and their response, and I came to a new conclusion. "Nelson is just a pawn. You're the brain of this operation?"

A smirk appeared on his face; the big laugh was over. The cat was out of the bag.

"Nelson is a part of our business and a minority owner of the Black Cat, but in reality, it's just a gimmick. We need him in that position as it legitimizes our trips down here. But we have to get moving. Nelson is about to return to the ship, but we need to be there before his guests arrive. As the captain, I'm always in charge. And the second thing is I don't want to have your body discovered in this neighborhood; it will be bad for business, so let's move out."

One Asian helped me out of the chair with my hands still tied behind me. The other one disappeared through the door leading upfront. A minute later, he returned. The captain turned his head toward his colleague coming back, and that's when I saw it. On his right temple, I observed a tattoo. It was at a fair distance, but I could distinguish several dots and a small animal. I had seen this image before, and my memory returned on the double. The morning of our failed raid in Chicago some seven years ago, we were looking to apprehend this asshole. He set up a bomb, a booby trap, to protect his business and harm anyone who would breach the entry. This was a monster quite comfortable killing to protect his assets. Suddenly, I knew I was in all over my head. If the entire FBI couldn't apprehend him, what was I doing all by myself against this man?

We all moved to the back door and waited. A few minutes later, a vehicle arrived. A black panel truck stopped in front of us, and we all boarded; the captain in front, me, and my two gorillas entered through the back door. I looked at the driver; it was the individual I couldn't place yet. Instructed to sit on the floor, facing away, I hoped Jennifer was still around and would follow me. But deep down, I didn't believe it.

After a short drive, we turned into the sandy parking lot at Captain Pip's Marina, which I recognized as soon as they extricated me from the panel truck. It was dark, past midnight, and we walked toward the docks leading to the only large yacht moored on site. A few lights illuminated the Ocean Dancer, but only a minimum. One Asian was leading the way, the other still holding my arm like a father escorting his daughter to the chapel. Steiner, the captain, a name I would never forget, was tailing the procession. The black panel had vanished by now.

The Missing Taylor

We reached the ship's bow and walked toward the stern. Someone got onto the transom platform and opened a door leading, I knew, to the ship's crew quarters at the back of the boat. Isolated from the guest area, it ensured the separation of masters and slaves. The crew quarters on this ship included a captain's suite with a full-size bed and a shower. For the crew, a separate room with two basic bunk beds and a live-in area including a tiny table, a microwave, a TV, and that was just about it. The captain enjoyed a small porthole; the crew lacked this luxury.

Pushed inside, I bumped into a wall in the dark and stopped. A few seconds later, someone turned a light on in the cramped space. My guide reached for my arm again and pushed me onto the bottom berth of the bunk beds, my hands still tied behind my back. I rested on my right side, silent, waiting for their next move, no other options evident to me.

Steiner walked in and said, "We will finish our conversation later, Tanner. For now, we have to start our return trip to Miami." I heard him move upstairs to the galley, leaving a single guard with me. The door was then closed, and calm returned to our intimate space.

My situation was less than enviable, their options multiple. They could kill me right here with a fentanyl injection like William and dump my body in the Atlantic. Or they could transport me to Miami and take care of business when everybody left. None of these options appealed to me.

Some fifteen minutes later, I heard footsteps topside, guests returning from their outing, I assumed. A few minutes later, the engines fired up, the superyacht came alive and departed on what I imagined was my last trip. My logical mind told me nothing would happen until the guests were out of view. A little time lay ahead.

Despite my uncomfortable position, I tried to relax. My daughter entered my thoughts, I then fell into a deep state of sleep.

Chapter 10

I woke up from the sounds of a door opening above me. A voice was calling my captor, who seemed to have fallen asleep while watching me. He slid from behind the table and went upstairs, leaving me alone, still tied up. The captain required more hands atop, a sign we were arriving at our destination.

A few minutes later, engine revolutions slowed down, and the ship started a turn to port. I figured we were coming into either south or north of Fisher Island heading into Miami or the Miami Beach area. In both cases, we were getting closer to land, enough to attempt a swim to shore if I could find a way out of my shackles. The sounds of footsteps aboard showed either the crew preparing for arrival or guests waking up, maybe both. I estimated the time to be around 9 am, unable to see my watch in my back.

It was time to leave such a nice ride, but first, I had to get rid of these zip ties holding my hands. An excellent swimmer would still drown without using his arms in a coastal sea. I got up and, as I was alone, looked around for a tool or a sharp edge to cut into my plastic handcuffs. I first thought about the table only to discover its edges were round, for safety precautions, I presumed. Next, I reached for the kitchen drawers looking for a knife. I only found a bunch of white plastic utensils. I then remembered a former FBI colleague who told me that you could break these ties in your back by hitting them on your rear end. Not having seen the trick, I had to guess how it worked. I found a spot where I could maneuver and bent down from my waist. As much as possible, I raised my arms and then came down hard on the lower portion of my back, to no avail. A second attempt failed as well. On my third try, I added a movement to open my arms as I smashed them on my back. To my amazement, it worked, and my hands were free. I could now move around in the crew compartment. I picked up the zip ties and examined the clean break, fabulous, so I tossed them on the bunk.

Going upstairs was nonsense. My abductors had guns; they confiscated mine. In front of the guests, they would argue I was a stowaway and tie me up again. The compartment's rear door would take me outside, on the transom platform hidden from the folks above. I would then look for the closest land and make a run for it... or rather make a swim for it. I removed my shoes and shoved them under the table. I wanted to avoid any unnecessary noises and also facilitate my swim.

Would the captain or the crew be aware if I opened the transom door? These luxury yachts harbored all kinds of electronic sensors and indicators ready to give me away. Would a light blink in the cockpit to show an opened door? I figured it was most probable. As the captain, I would want to know of any abnormal situation aboard, especially one where water could flow in.

I rushed to the captain's room and peaked at the only porthole. As I figured, the sun was out already; the swell was minimal, and I was looking south of the entrance between Fisher Island and Miami Beach. I recognized the area. A mile and a half down this way is the Miami Beach, where I stayed just a few weeks ago. I remembered a jetty protruding to the North and one to the South. We were just coming right in between them. If I swam to either one, I would escape. The distance between the two jetties was only a thousand feet. If the ship traveled in the middle, I would have five hundred feet to swim equivalent to three lengths of an Olympic pool. Not much of a challenge.

Just as I decided on my next move, I heard noise originating from above the steps leading to the upstairs galley. Someone was coming down. I rushed back to the bunk and positioned myself as they left me, on my side, hands in the back; except now, they were free. A few seconds later, the big Asian peaked into my room. I spotted my old zip ties just resting on the bed at the same moment. If my guard looked that way, he would discover the truth. I moved my legs to block his view of the evidence in slow motion. Would he notice I was shoeless now?

I think he spotted my move and came toward the bed to check on me. As he bent to verify what was behind my legs, I reached up, grabbed his dress shirt, and pulled as hard as I could. When he felt my hands on him, he straightened up, but the pulling force I exerted was stronger and brought his face right on the metal railing of the bed just above me. His nose exploded with blood while his legs disappeared from below him, and he fell to the floor, unconscious. The bigger they are, the harder they fall.

Worried the noise would bring others to my quarters, I moved to the only door leading to safety and, without hesitation, opened it. Even if the captain notices the breach, he will discover it too late to react. I moved onto the rear platform and looked left, then right; the jetty was closer on the Northside because the yacht held a starboard course in case of crossing another vessel's path. This would give me a shorter swim to shore. Also, coming toward us was a large cruise ship leaving Miami on its way to some fancy destination. But one thing I knew for sure, it would cross our path soon, and I did not want to get caught in its wake.

I filled my lungs with air, dived in the warm waters, and headed toward shore, away from the cruise ship. I stayed underwater as long as I could. When I emerged, I retook another deep breath and returned immediately under. When I surfaced next, I turned around to look at the Ocean Dancer. The sound of its engines and the water movement at the rear told me the captain had put the ship in full reverse. He could not catch up as I was already in shallow waters and out of reach of the big yacht. I aimed for the jetty and swam as fast as possible in my best high school freestyle stroke.

Once at the jetty, I climbed the large rocks and looked back at the yacht, now idle in the canal. A bunch of people gazed my way; some knew why I had done this, others were clueless.

# # #

I traveled to the mainland after walking the uneven jetty and its large rocks, still shoeless. I reached the South Point pier where I met Jeff Mason some time ago. I now needed a few things; a pair of shoes, a phone to contact Jennifer, and a new plan. In my pockets, some wet paper money and dryer credit cards along with my car keys, I could manage.

I walked toward a street with plenty of commercial businesses, oblivious to the onlookers smiling at my passage. I entered a small bicycle shop and asked if I could use their phone. The owner observed me from head to toe, especially the toes, and asked what happened.

"My friends threw me in the water and disappeared. I need to call someone to come and get me." My explanation seemed probable. He directed me to the end of the counter where a phone sat. I dialed Jennifer's number from memory.

"Hello."

"Jennifer, it's me, Jason."

"Oh my God, where are you?"

"In Miami Beach now, abducted in Marathon, and they brought me back here aboard the yacht, but I escaped. I'll tell you all about it when I see you. Here's what you should do."

I suggested she returns her rental and go to my SUV. A man with foresight like me hid a spare key in a magnetic holder under the right front wheel space. We could meet at a restaurant in Miami Beach around 2 pm, almost a three-hour drive ahead of her. I would use the time to get dry, buy a new pair of shoes, eat something, and plan our next move.

Jennifer arrived a little earlier than predicted, but so did I. She must have driven fast to get the news, motivated by her curiosity. Sipping a nice cold beer, I saw her looking for me. She trotted toward the table, and even before being seated, she asked, "What happened? Tell me everything."

"Sit down; we've got plenty of time. Do you want something to drink?"

"I'll have what you're having."

I asked our waiter to bring two more beers.

"Well, I got out of my car and ran behind the shopping mall to the other end where the taxi dropped the two Asian guys. The building is strange, with no signs, just a single door upfront. No activity there, so I moved to the backside. A light appeared from a window, and I peeked inside: just an empty room. Anyway, as I turned around to leave, someone stood there, a gun in his hand."

"And?"

"They brought me inside, asked a few questions, and then transported me aboard the yacht, in the crew quarters, tied up."

"And you escaped?"

"Yes. As we entered the canal at South Point pier, I jumped into the water and swam ashore. Then I called you."

"As I watched the building last night, a panel truck went behind it and drove off a few minutes later. I hesitated to follow it but decided against it and awaited your return. I waited and waited. Your car didn't move, and I checked it a few times to no avail. I rang your cell but heard it inside your car."

"And then?"

"I found a spot where I could see your car, parked the rental, and watched. I think I fell asleep a few times."

"And there's more bad news, in this case, Jennifer."

"What?"

"I think the gang leader is Bruce Steiner."

"Who?"

I explained how I came to know Steiner and the actions the FBI deployed to catch him. I left no parts untold, including the bomb and the death of a respectable FBI agent. The whole time I narrated the bizarre story, her eyebrows drew closer and closer. When I stopped, she expelled a long breath of air and sat back.

After ordering sandwiches and a shared salad, we talked about the evolving case and how we were getting way over our heads. We'd gone from a simple missing person's situation to a full-fledged battle against a criminal organization. Mark Taylor's disappearance made us discover this gang. Now, we still ignored what happened to him, like if he disappeared into thin air or into the deep sea.

"I think it's time we saw the authorities about this situation. At least, report your own kidnapping Jason."

"Maybe, let me think about it. You know what, Jennifer; it's Sunday, be with your family. I'll drive you home. I'll try to get a hold of John Russell and seek his guidance. If we're lucky, we could meet him tomorrow. Then we'll decide."

"It's not that I don't want to help Jason..."

"I know you do, so do I. But the case has escalated big time, not quite what I expected in the beginning either. Let's see what John recommends, and we'll take it from there."

Jennifer agreed, and after our light lunch, I drove her back to her place and then booked a small hotel near the beach. From my returned SUV, I recovered my backpack with my laptop inside and reclaimed my cell phone with a dead battery. I recharged it during my trip to Jennifer's place and back. When I looked at it inside the hotel's parking lot, I had several missed calls, the majority from Jennifer looking for me but also one from an unknown number. A voice mail was present, and I retrieved it while waiting for the elevator in the garage. It was Angelillo from the Marathon police. He wanted me to call him back, and he left his number. It was still Sunday; I would wait until tomorrow.

At the hotel, I watched professional golf from the comfort of my king-size bed. I closed my eyes during the first commercial, and when I woke up, the Sunday edition of the news was on. I had slept over two hours, and now I was hungry. But first, I called Cynthia. She had asked me to keep her informed, and it was time to do so. But she

159

would get my personal version of the news. To worry her was my last intention.

I gave her the highlights but skipped details I preferred to keep to myself. I told her Jennifer and I went back to Marathon. We followed the bad guys to a building and both of us returned to Miami today. These were all truths. I then told her I was going out for dinner, and I planned to return to the oysters and seafood place she had liked so much. She envied me and wished she was here with me. So did I. I left her on that note with a promise to send her information on what I had for dinner. She asked me to be careful. I replied I always do. In my mind, I regretted going in alone looking for the Asians without the help of Jennifer. It was my mistake, and I made myself a promise not to repeat it.

I grabbed my backpack, knowing my laptop was inside. I would enjoy time on my hands to update the little social media I used and clean out my Inbox. The restaurant was within walking distance, and the retreating sun provided lower temperatures which I enjoyed.

# # #

I picked a quiet area of the restaurant, ordered a martini, and opened my computer. But first, I needed to verify if Jennifer and I could talk to JR soon. I texted him this message, "Any possibility I see you tomorrow, lunch or otherwise?"

Even on a quiet Sunday evening, JR answered a minute later. "11 am, Monday, my office?" My reply was as brief, "10-4" used by all policemen to mean OK or understood. I then confirmed with Jennifer, telling her we would meet in the lobby of the Miami-Dade Police Department building on SW 117th Avenue. She replied she was OK and would see me there.

When I launched my email program, my inbox had a dozen unread messages, two-thirds I could dismiss at once, and a few I moved to my to-do folder. One of them caught my attention from Hank Hackman titled FYI and contained another of his famous encrypted file.

Once extracted with my secret password, the first page showed an image of a company database service about Black Cat Management Corporation. The report provided information such as registration in Delaware and ownership split between Yang Nelson and another entity named Sailing the Atlantic LLC, owning 85% of the 1,000 shares issued. They still listed Yang as the president of the company. Nelson's home address was the same as the famous bar in South Beach. I guess this was standard practice.

The next page showed information about Sailing the Atlantic LLC, but no ownership data appeared. The LLC was also registered in Delaware. If I were the IRS, I would know the people behind this company, but I was neither the Internal Revenue Service nor the Justice Department. Which reminded me I still had friends at Justice; I made a mental note to reach out to Barry Gilmore.

Another page to Hank's email included information about a company named Vitamin World of China. Only a single owner existed, Sun My. The main business address was in Miami. On the double, I launched Google Maps and located 460 NE 28th Street on the mainland, just across Biscayne Bay. This was a million-dollar condo unit with a fantastic view of Miami Beach across the bay. The vitamin business must be booming.

My oysters arrived, but I could not put the laptop down. Hank had provided me with a lot of information. I search the Miami-Dade property appraiser website hoping to see the real owner of the condo. The corporation name was the official title-holder of the unit, and no other owner information was present. Also provided on the appraiser site were past buy and sell transactions. The last purchase was recent, about a year ago. And the price paid was $950,000. Having a condo near the water must be nice.

I finished my oysters, enjoying each one. Near the water. Someone used that expression around me in the last few days. Who was it? My daughter? Maybe. Then I remembered a talk with Jennifer on the Nelson tail she performed. I grabbed my phone and dialed her number.

"Sorry to bother you, Jennifer, but I have a pressing question."

"No problem, Jason. My husband and I were just cleaning the kitchen waiting to watch a romantic movie on TV."

"Good for you, Jennifer. Some days ago, I believe you mentioned going by a condo near the water. Do you remember the context and where it was?"

"Yes, one day, I followed Yang Nelson after his surfing to a condo building downtown. He stayed there for a while, and I got bored. I returned home."

"And where was this?"

After asking me to hold a minute to get her notes, she returned and said, "460 NE 28th Street in Miami."

"How interesting. I received information from my friend Hank about Nelson and his business connections. I will mail you the documents. Looks like the location Nelson entered is the business address of a company named Vitamin World of China owned by a Sun My; she may be his girlfriend."

"Possible."

"The other news is two entities own the Black Cat Bar: a company called Sailing the Atlantic with 85% ownership, Nelson, the rest."

The Missing Taylor

"And?"

"It sort of confirms Nelson is the number two in the organization. Whoever is behind Sailing the Atlantic owns a larger share of the business. If Hank didn't name the real owner, it's because he couldn't. It's probably because it's registered in Delaware or something. It would not surprise me if we find Steiner behind this front, but I have no proof. Anyway, I'll see you tomorrow."

As I hung up, I remembered this data I was looking at was from a request made to Hank about Nelson. I returned to the first email. Had I missed something? My fish arrived, and I ate while reading files on my laptop. This time I checked each page and every written line. And then I found it. One document I got from my favorite hacker listed the 28th Street address as Yang Nelson's home. Sun My could be his current girlfriend.

I was not a DEA expert by any means, but the story was forming like this: a bar that distributes drugs, a company importing and selling vitamins in tablet form used as a front, and a large cruising yacht able to transport people and things all over South Florida.

# # #

The following morning, I had wandered to a neighborhood Starbuck examining the crowd in and around the renowned coffee supplier. My phone then complained about receiving an email from Lieutenant Angelillo of the Marathon police. The DNA delivered by Nadine did not match the individual discovered back in August. I responded with my thanks for informing me. I called Nadine Taylor right away. The good news was they had not found Mark's body, but it was also bad for the same reason. I told Nadine I was meeting John Russell this morning but gave no details.

At a quarter to eleven, in the hall of the Miami-Dale Police Administration, I was awaiting Jennifer for our session with JR. When

163

she strolled in, I joined her, and we both approached the security desk to obtain our visitor passes. With time before our appointment, we rested near a large window waiting for our host to sign us in.

Jennifer looked up the Vitamin World of China business this morning before arriving. Her research showed a company importing rare herbs and supplements from China and manufacturing vitamins which they move on the Internet all over Florida. They even run an excellent website where you can choose either prepared vitamins or ingredients, creating your personalized concoction. The company ships orders to your home and accepts payment by credit card or PayPal. The website's news section promised deliveries in other states soon. The look was sharp, not a low-budget operation. She wondered if a link existed to the drug business, but we held no proof yet.

I asked her, when she could, to deliver Hank a message. We needed him to dig into this website to determine if it's legit and give us an idea of its popularity and sales levels for a typical month. We would also welcome any other pertinent information.

From our vantage point, we observed police officers, detectives, and various species of the human race enter or exit the Miami-Dade headquarters for multiple reasons. Some folks worked at this location, others didn't want to be here, even less be seen. But when JR showed up with his towering height and perfect blue striped banker's suit with an immaculate white shirt, most heads spun in his direction. Jennifer's jaw was dropping to the floor when I told her, "You're a married woman, slow down."

"It's not because I'm on a diet that I can't look at the menu," she whispered under her breath.

As John strolled toward us, he extended his right arm for a handshake in Jennifer's direction, completely neglecting me.

"This must be Jennifer; I am delighted to meet you," he announced as they both peered into their eyes for an awkward moment that looked like a minute.

"Yes, and I'm Jason, we're both glad you could find the time to see us," trying to regain control of this scene. "If you'd let go of her hand, we could move on to a spot where we can talk."

"Please follow me," as he finally pulled his hand out and showed the way to Jennifer, moving by her side leaving me to trail behind like her assistant. After a quick ride up the elevator where my two partners continued their social acquaintance, we entered a tiny but comfortable meeting space. A single window provided most of the lighting, and a whiteboard decorated the area, the only object on the walls.

"Sorry, the boardroom was not available this morning," JR admitted with his perfect smile.

"I prefer it cozy anyway," replied her new admirer.

"OK kids, can we get down to business?" I asked.

As we all sat around the small table with cushion chairs, JR asked if we wanted a coffee, but we all passed. I wished to get the ball rolling.

"Thanks for seeing us on such short notice, JR. I asked Jennifer to give me a hand on my investigation. She's a former FBI colleague. We have discovered new information over and above what the existing police investigation uncovered."

"Should I invite Freeman and Jackson in here?" JR asked.

"First, let me tell you what we have found. Afterward, if you want to, I can brief them," I suggested, wishing to bring up Freeman's situation later on.

"Fine."

"The police investigation showed Taylor left the Black Cat bar after his shift with two individuals. It's the last time they saw him in Miami, Friday, September 10th, of last year. Freeman could not locate the two guys in question, but we found them, although we still don't have their identities. We know that they're friends or work with Yang Nelson, the official owner of the bar. Nelson is also a surfing buddy of Mark Taylor."

"Are these oriental gentlemen the ones we're looking for in the old man's death on your boat?"

"I see you follow your investigations; yes, they are."

"Thank you, that's my job over here," he said, looking at me, but the information was for Jennifer, who returned another perfect smile.

"So Taylor, the two individuals, Asians, by the way, and Yang Nelson landed in Marathon, where our search continued. We identified lots of trips to Marathon by a large yacht carrying Nelson and his bodyguards, all this happening at regular intervals. Nelson's job is to entertain his guests while the two guys and the captain have other duties."

"What kinds of duties?" John asked.

"Well, they could be drug-related. Taylor talked about fentanyl to his friends in Miami, and William Tudor died on my boat from a pure fentanyl injection given by the two Asians. It's not a coincidence, and we have video surveillance tapes of their arrival and departure at the time of the crime."

"Hold on a second. Taylor was inquiring about fentanyl. Was he a user?"

"No, he was a DEA informant." A long silence followed. This was news to John.

"How are you aware of this? Your FBI connexions?"

"From reliable sources, let's say."

"OK."

Jennifer, quiet until then, continued our story. "In Marathon, we tried to understand what the gang was doing there, so we organized surveillance. Nelson was off with his customers as usual as soon as the yacht arrived. His guests are winners of a phony contest at his bar. The two Asians were of interest, so we followed them to a location where they kidnapped Jason."

"Kidnapped?"

"Yes, I was snooping around a building where our guys had stopped when their boss saw me, held me against my will, and questioned me."

"Did they hurt you?" asked John.

"No, they brought me back on the yacht returning to Miami, but I jumped ship and swam to shore, no harm done. I have a good memory; I'll find them, for sure."

"Will you want to press charges?" asked JR.

"No, I'll pass."

"Well, so far, it's quite a tale," said JR.

"And my kidnapper is a man I crossed paths with some years ago, Bruce Steiner. Back then, we executed a search warrant, but he escaped. I'll have to check with the Bureau what his status is today. We believed then he operated a drug manufacturing plant; he may be doing the same thing today."

"And it's not over yet," continued Jennifer. "We believe there's a link between the yacht's captain, Steiner, Yang Nelson running the

Black Cat bar, and his girlfriend involved in the import and distribution of vitamins. We must look at her website, her place of business, and the relationship with the captain, maybe even the yacht rental company. Something illegal is in play here. We need to identify it. Then we'll know what happened to Mark Taylor."

"We are still searching for the two Asians to question them on the incident on your boat. This inquiry is not over," stated John.

I added, "When you have some spare time, hang around the Black Cat. You'll find them there. Or, another option, the Ocean Dancer's next trip could see them aboard if they sail again."

"I'll check with Freeman if he has these two leads on file. Anything else I can do?" asked John.

"Yes, and this is my central question, John. Do you think we should involve the DEA? I believe Taylor worked for them, or they used him. As Jennifer said, this smells like a drug case for several reasons. What do you think?"

"Yes. Contact the DEA sooner than later. They may already have Nelson or the Black Cat on their books. You should work with them, or at least advise them you're in the neighborhood. I can introduce you to the DEA region manager. His office is in Fort Lauderdale."

"That would be perfect, John. Thank you."

After a pause, I looked at Jennifer and nodded, a sign we had agreed upon earlier.

"Gentlemen, it was a pleasure to meet you, but I have other business. If you'll excuse me," she said.

She got up to leave, and I motioned JR. I had one more thing to discuss. He got up to open the door. "I hope you'll find your way out,

Jennifer. Just turn left at the corner, you'll reach the elevators. And I hope you'll find your way back," he said with his best smile.

He closed the door, and now we were one-on-one.

"Nice lady you have working with you, mate."

"I noticed you liked her. Married with two kids."

"That's unfortunate, for me at least."

"I have one last subject I want to bring up: the murder on my boat."

"Yes."

"Over one hundred ships were in the Miami Beach Marina on that day. How did the perps discover which boat I was on? Answer that one, John. The Marina's video was clear. The first man walked without hesitation or looking around to my boat. I questioned surfers the previous day and provided them with my business card with my phone number only. Nowhere does it say I have a boat and that it's parked at the Marina next door."

"What's the name of your yacht?"

"PRIVATE EYE."

"Not very undercover, one would say. If I were searching for an investigator, that's the first place I would look."

"Seriously."

"Were you followed?" he asked.

"Unlikely, I know how to pick a tail. No, only one person knew of my boat's location because I told him when I invited him over for dinner."

"Who's that?"

"Wayne Freeman."

"And you think Freeman passed the information to the suspects so they could hurt you? Why would he do that?"

"Uncertain, but when he got dispatched to my location, he seemed surprised to see me. It's just a feeling, but it's strong."

"What do you recommend I do, Jason?"

"Launch an Internal Affairs investigation into his external associations."

After a long pause, JR continued. "It takes more than a feeling, even a strong one, to launch an IA investigation. You should know that."

"I know. But I was still hoping you could."

"I will if you bring me some proof of wrongdoing."

"OK, I'll dig and get back to you."

"Fine. Let me contact the DEA region manager and get back to you, all right?"

"That's fine, JR. I'll wait for your call. I'm returning this afternoon. Take care."

# # #

I took the elevator and back to the reception desk. I asked if Wayne Freeman was in the building. Might as well strike while the iron is hot. The policeman on duty consulted the directory and placed a call.

"Mr. Freeman, someone to see you at the front desk."

"The name is Jason Tanner," I whispered.

"It's Mr. Jason Tanner. OK, thanks."

"Detective Freeman is coming down, have a seat."

The Missing Taylor

A few minutes later, Freeman arrived in the lobby, and after we shook hands, we walked to a quieter space.

"Thanks for seeing me. I was in the neighborhood and curious about the murder investigation aboard my yacht."

"Well, as you know, the autopsy report confirmed a drug overdose, given by lethal injection. LeBron and I studied the Marina video files, and although we see two men walking toward your boat and coming back, it does not convince us of their involvement."

"Did you at least talk to them?"

"Not yet; we must locate them first."

"I believe the two gentlemen on the video and the Asians that left the Black Cat bar with Mark Taylor are the same people."

"You think so. I must review the Taylor casebook, I don't remember this testimony, but I'll verify it."

"These two gentlemen crossed my path on a few occasions. If I point them to you, can you at least bring them in for questioning? I can suggest a couple of good reasons to talk to them. How about putting a warrant out for their arrest?"

"Too early. We don't even know their names. But we can chat with them if you point us in their direction," Freeman said.

"Did you look at a Yang Nelson during the Taylor investigation?" Freeman was staring, figuring out his reply. The case files never mentioned Nelson, even if his name shows up as a bar's part-owner. A basic search on the Internet could provide this information.

"Not that I can remember, no."

"Well, Nelson was a friend of Mark Taylor, a surfing buddy; he may have information."

Freeman got his notepad out and wrote the name down. "Where can we find him, any idea?"

Reaching for my notepad, I gave him the address on NE 28th Street, careful not to mention the link between Nelson and the Black Cat.

"The apartment may be under his girlfriend's name. At least, it's a good starting point. Otherwise, he surfs most mornings at South Point beach. You could find him there."

"Excellent, thank you for the information. We'll get on it."

"Fantastic then; keep me updated if you can."

"I will. What's on your agenda now?" Freeman inquired. The last time I provided information to him, a friend got killed. I'll be damn if I tell him the truth this time around.

"Chicago, I have family matters to attend to and cannot postpone them. I'm flying tomorrow and should be in the windy city for at least a week, maybe more, some legal issues with my wife's succession. I'm not sure if I have enough warm clothing for this time of year."

"Yeah, it can get cold up there. Have a good trip. I'll call you if something turns up."

# # #

On my way back from Miami, I called Nadine with an update. I provided Freeman with a new person of interest, Nelson, and where to look for two Asians connected to Mark's disappearance. We would sort this out; I told her not to despair.

I again reached out to Jennifer about my solo conversation with JR and the brief encounter with Freeman. She was my partner, and I needed to share the information and not keep her ignorant. She confirmed emailing Hank about the Vitamin World of China website to dig out numbers on sales volume or any other pertinent information. Hank had said he would give a 24-hour turnaround.

Late afternoon, I arrived in Pompano and avoided most of the heavy traffic this Monday. I rejoiced to find my yacht again after spending time in my car and on a bunk of crew quarters. I loved my new living quarters and was happy to see my bed. The sound of cars crossing Atlantic Bridge did not prevent me from falling asleep as soon as my head hit the pillow.

The next morning, with a clear sky promising a warm day, I put on my sneakers, shorts, and headed toward the recent North Pompano Beach Boulevard for a morning jog. This renovated area presents a pleasant separation between the beach and Ocean Boulevard. It displays a large grassy area for sporting activities, family BBQ parties, training equipment, restaurants, and a room for small concerts. It's common to see folks exercise or take yoga classes along the small strip. The wide sidewalk allowed residents and vacationers to view and enjoy a sight of the ocean and the beach. Other than strolling, you could see all kinds of activities like running, cycling, and roller boarding. Kids, adults, and many pets visited the site. The best times were on weekends when groups arrived early to get the right BBQ spot and set up tables for a beach dinner. The aroma coming from the site was enticing.

After my 45-minute jog, I stopped at the training area where a dozen exercise equipment was waiting to hurt your muscles if running did not get it done yet. I returned aboard for a quick shower. Life was great.

My phone's message light was flashing. JR had come through again and scheduled a get-together with the DEA regional manager day after tomorrow, 10 am, in his office. I was to call JR back only if I couldn't attend. I sent JR a quick text message to thank him.

Mid-afternoon, my phone vibrated in my back pocket due to an email from Hank addressed to both Jennifer and me. Hank would be available at 7 pm if we're interested in discussing the website. I verified with Jennifer and confirmed she and I would be on the early evening call.

I spent the rest of the day fishing waters off Deerfield Beach, looking for my dinner on the reefs. During these quiet times, I reflected on the strange Mark Taylor case. They never recovered his body. What was the purpose of his trip to Marathon with the Asians? How close was he to Yang Nelson? We knew he was a DEA informant from Barry Gilmore's research into Government files, and that could explain the cash found in his safe-deposit box. But Fentanyl? Why did he have that?

And then, sighting Bruce Steiner. What was his role in all this? He ordered people around and described Nelson as a minor player. Was he leading the pack? Would those trips to Marathon persist? If he continued to captain Ocean Dancer, authorities would easily pick him up, assuming they still looked for him.

I walked inside, grabbed my phone, and dialed Barry Gilmore's number.

"Barry, I am reporting a sighting. Can you verify if any warrants are outstanding for Bruce Steiner? I ran into him, and I have an idea where he hangs out."

"Bruce Steiner, you say? Let me verify right away."

It only took a few seconds before Barry returned.

"We have a Bruce Steiner on our most-wanted list for several criminal offenses, including drug possession, distribution, and manufacturing. He has evaded capture in multiple states. He's a slippery person. Add to this possession and use of explosive materials linked to the bust that went boom in your days, Jason."

"Nice way to put in Barry. What else?"

"He is armed and dangerous."

"I can confirm that. Take notes, Barry. I came across Steiner, but I believe he goes under the name Brad Scott and captains Ocean Dancer, a large boat, in South Florida. Yacht Charter of Miami rents the ship out. This would be his current employer. If you start there, see a man named Averell Thompson, he's the manager. I presume they would have all his contact data."

"There's a reward for information leading to his capture, you know."

"Excellent, send the tip in my name, you're not eligible, and we'll share the reward if the FBI catches him."

"Will do, Jason. Talk to you soon."

I walked back to the aft deck to see my fishing cane agitated and bent in a half moon's position, to the point of breaking. I grabbed it and reeled in whatever was on the other end. After a short but epic battle, I pulled in a rare red grouper around two pounds. My dinner had arrived. I raised anchor and headed home.

After a delicious meal, I sat at the salon table with my laptop, a notepad, and my cell phone. I first dialed Jennifer's number and then added Hank to the conversation.

"We're all present, Hank. Thanks for your time. As you know, we are interested in ascertaining if the website is related to our missing person and how. Is there a connection between the vitamin and the drug distribution businesses? We know both principals live together; it's natural. Did you find anything else?"

"The vitamin website is a full-fledged transactional site with sales and orders. It includes a product list and functions to set up a user account, consult the products, place orders, and go to the checkout function. You have run into dozens of similar sites for clothes, jewels, auto parts, and others. It's like an Amazon but on a smaller scale."

"That seems elaborated for a mom and pop operation, no?" asked Jennifer.

"Years ago, yes, but now, all kinds of providers offer these services in your company's colors and brand name. They call it white labeling. They offer all the technology, and you manage a catalog. You create it with descriptions, images, pricing, and a few more information. Then, bingo, you have a machine that sends the owner its daily sales figures and the money posted to his bank account."

"So, all Sun My has to do is prepare her catalog of vitamins, specify her bank accounts, and she's in operation," I said.

"That's it in a nutshell. Orders come into the system, the payment received, and products shipped. So the website will direct every order as they arrive, by email, for example, to a location that will match the order with the inventory. Someone would pick the merchandise, package it, and ship it by postal service or private delivery firms like FedEx or UPS. And that's about the entire cycle; it's not very complicated."

"Do we know where these operations are located?" asked Jennifer.

"Well, the website itself runs on virtual servers in Seattle, but business operations can be anywhere. It's typically sent by email, remember."

"I see, but it would have to be close to the business manager who needs staff for administration and production. It could be in Miami or somewhere close by," I added.

"My research started with creating a user account to look at the product list and buy some vitamins. My doctor recommends it anyway. But then I dug deeper. I connected to the Seattle servers and poked around databases and files of the site. At first, everything looked normal. But then, I found a series of web pages displayed just like the regular product catalog but inaccessible under my user account."

"Meaning," both Jennifer and I asked in unison.

"I presume only selected customers have access to the secret part of the website, and it's not available to the common buyer. Or they have their private catalog."

"And how different are these pages?" I asked.

"Well, the catalog included products like oxycodone, hydrocodone, and buprenorphine, not your common vitamins."

An ominous silence arrived as we tried to understand this curious information.

"And you don't see these products as a regular customer?" Jennifer asked.

"No, I did not. A site manager has various means to associate a different catalog to a specific user, and it's easy. It could be a simple code in the customer account indicating a 'special' customer. He would then access the specific files."

I presented my theory to get comments from the team. "So, if I understand well, she sells vitamins, he peddles drugs or opioids or even both, she presents the regular products, he tags his 'special' customers for a separate listing. Orders come in, are prepared, and shipped from whatever secret location they use, probably around Miami. Does that make sense?"

"It does, and do you know the beauty of it, Jason?" Hank continued. "Payment arrives with the order, before delivery. It's excellent for the company's cash flow and its legitimate money, coming in small amounts and not $10,000 installments that trigger an investigation from banks. The other advantage is that cash is king on the street, but credit cards dominate on the web. They'll get orders from drug users paying with their credit cards or most likely, stolen."

"Do we have any idea about transaction volumes, Hank?" I asked.

"That's hard to say. I got a look at yesterday's orders, over a hundred. If the average size is $50, then we're talking about a $2-million-dollar business with few expenses and not more than two employees."

"OK, great Hank, thanks for the information. Back to your computer games now."

"Yes, you're welcome. I have an epic Battle royal going on, bye."

While I still had Jennifer online, I wanted to continue the discussion. "Your thoughts, Jennifer?"

"It looks smart. A vitamin store fronts a drug store, like a magician, a feat of the hands."

"I'm trying to figure out the delivery aspect, Jennifer. If Hank is right and they ship a hundred orders daily, they must work with a delivery service. Either a pickup occurs where they produce the orders, or they transport them to a delivery office. It's 100 little or medium-size boxes, just about every day."

"What if the trips to Marathon were to pick up or drop ingredients or products, Jason? Things they don't want in a car for obvious reasons such as interception by cops or being involved in an accident. The water has always lacked police enforcement."

"Possible."

"In that case, they are working with a local delivery service. If we find who, we can locate where the gang operates from."

"To ship all over Florida, they'll use a major carrier, not a local delivery boy. Only a handful of majors operate in the state."

"Here's what I suggest, Jason. I can go to Marathon and visit each available delivery service. I can be someone looking to ship multiple boxes every day, and I'm trying to decide if their service can do the job. Perhaps I could ask for similar companies in the area who are doing it as I'm looking for references. What do you think?"

"That works. But be careful."

We discussed details and agreed Jennifer would head to Marathon tomorrow while I meet the DEA. We would exchange notes on Thursday.

Chapter 11

April in South Florida kicks off the warmer season and today was a perfect example. If you needed to get work done outside, you'd better start early because, by mid-morning, it will be just impossible.

DEA Administrative offices occupy a large space on West Cypress Creek Road in Fort Lauderdale, a 15-minute drive from my port of call. It's a grayish building, three stories high, protected by tall trees and fronted by a conventional parking lot with no apparent security. Ten minutes ahead of my appointment time, I walked to the reception desk and asked for Mr. Donavan Baker, the name JR had provided. Shortly after, a trim woman wearing a red blouse with gray slacks came in my direction, a firearm on her right hip.

"Mister Tanner?"

"Yes."

"Tianna Hester, nice to meet you. Please follow me."

She turned around, and I tagged behind her up the staircase to the third floor. Elevators were available, but she bypassed them, part of her daily exercise plan, I assumed. Amid several cubicles, we walked toward a large corner office. She knocked on the open door, "Mister Tanner is here, sir."

Three separate zones came into view as I entered the expansive room: a large wooden desk near the corner windows, a three-place sofa, matching chairs, and a rectangular coffee table for an intimate conversation on the right and an oval conference table on the left. The walls bore classic fake paintings, flower pots divided sections, the lighting was discreet but darker than usual. FBI offices would defer this kind of opulence for top brass alone. This was only a local civil servant.

The occupant of the large office got up and, smiling, walked toward us. "Please come in, Mister Tanner," as he pointed toward the conference table. I stepped inside and shook his hand. "Thank you." I walked to the table, pulled a chair, and got comfortable.

On the wall behind the conference table, a kid drawing hung in a frame. It pictured a small person, sex was not discernible, standing on a surfboard over a large wave. The drawing was in sharp contrast to the traditional paintings surrounding it. Baker noticed my curiosity.

"My daughter, when she was only six years old, she adored surfing. She started with a small board. Today, she contends with the best. She'll be competing at the Miami Beach Regional Surf Championships this coming weekend. The best surfers should be on site."

"How nice," I commented. "You must be proud."

"Very."

After a pause, Baker continued, "I asked Tianna to join us. She's one of our most experienced agents in the region." I looked in her direction. A tiny smile appeared on her face, shy maybe.

"John Russell called saying you have tips for us? What's up?"

"I retired from the FBI recently and now run a private investigation practice. Over six months ago, one of your informants, Mark Taylor, disappeared in Miami. The police have not located him so far. After a while, his family contacted me for help."

"Hold on, an informant? Who told you that?" I noticed Baker did not deny my statement. He wondered how I knew that.

"Sources."

I couldn't disclose the information came from an IT genius at FBI headquarters.

"Don't get me wrong, Mister Tanner, but does the family believe a private investigator can locate someone the well-equipped Miami-Dade police can't?"

"Valid argument; for one, I can invest more time on the problem than the police. Next, they juggle multiple cases simultaneously; I concentrate on only one. Jennifer, my partner, is also a former FBI agent. The FBI performs best during a manhunt; it's a well-known fact," I answered with a smile, proud of my former organization.

After a brief pause again and a severe look on his face, he continued. "And what else did your investigation uncover, Mister Tanner?"

"Well, I'm willing to share information with the DEA if we work together. We discovered illicit activities you may find of interest."

"Depends on what you have," Baker declared. I paused, trying to decide how much to tell him. Too little will not excite him, too much will give away our secrets.

"OK, first, we believe Taylor moved his way up the echelons of a drug gang in South Florida. One of the big boys is a Yang Nelson from Miami, owner of the Black Cat bar. Second, an opioid manufacturing operation is active in the Florida Keys, and finally, the group uses a simple transactional website for orders and delivery. For now, that's what we have."

Baker nodded affirmatively, but no words came out of his mouth.

"Do you have any proof?" asked Tianna.

"Yes, we have. We're ready to open the books if you are too."

"And Taylor?" asked the manager.

"We have no information yet on his whereabouts. He could be dead, or he could still be alive. We don't know. For now, he's a missing link."

One could sense from Baker's eyebrow movement he was skeptical. "Fine, this is what we'll do, Mister Tanner. We will review our own case files and see what we have on this gang. After the review, we'll get back to you," he then stood up. "Tianna will escort you."

He abruptly ended our meeting for a reason I ignored. He either didn't believe me or correctly understood what I was talking about, and Taylor was a subject not to be discussed. I wasn't sure which one yet.

Again, we used the stairs, and I followed Tianna. When we reached the reception desk, she turned around and asked how they could get in touch with me. I handed her a business card from my shirt pocket and grabbed one of hers.

"Were you acquainted with Mark?" I asked.

Tianna's eyes looked into mine for a few seconds, and she finally said, "We'll be in touch, thank you." She couldn't or wouldn't answer my simple question.

Disappointed, I drove back to the Marina. I now regretted having offered so many of our discoveries in the quest of getting their interest. I was uncertain if they had prior knowledge of my statements. One thing was sure, they showed no surprise at the people or the bar's name. As a DEA informant, Mark would keep his management posted on his activities. But did he tell them the entire story? I couldn't be sure.

I was hoping Jennifer would have more success. Back aboard, preparing to grab dinner at the Rusty Hook, my cell phone chimed Jennifer's unique ringtone.

"Yes, Jennie."

"FedEx, the organization ships through the FedEx Office in Marathon."

"And how did you find that out?" I asked.

"Just my super investigation skills at work, Jason. Listen and learn; I first checked the local post office, then UPS and FedEx. The scenario was always the same: I would ask about business rates to ship small boxes from Marathon to Orlando. They all gave me pricing for different levels of service. Are you aware a $9 shipment can become $90 for the same box if you want it overnight? Amazing."

"No, I didn't know that. But then?"

"The FedEx Office is operating from a temporary trailer since hurricane Irma hit the Keys in August of last year. They expect a new compound to replace the temporary one, eventually. It could explain why the gang uses this transporter. No high-tech scanners are present in the temporary office. Some of these latest scanners can detect cocaine and even explosives like Semtex. By using this location, they avoid the equipment, making it easier to ship their crap."

"That makes sense, Jennifer. And the source of these shipments?"

"The cute young man at the FedEx counter was most forthcoming and informed me a local company ships hundreds of small boxes every day just about. They seemed to appreciate the service, and they've been doing it for over a year."

"How impressive, you're a sharp investigator, Jennifer. Don't tell me you also located the source of these shipments?"

"Not yet, but I will. I waited in the FedEx parking lot and screened customers. A black panel truck arrived late afternoon. The driver got as close as possible to the entrance. He opened the truck's rear door, and I saw three good-sized plastic cases containing smaller boxes. After he carried the first one inside, I waited. He returned a few minutes later for the second trip. I dashed to the truck, sneaked inside, snapped a box, and ran away."

"And then?"

"I hopped in the car and followed the black panel truck when it left to a large private residence still in Marathon. I figured the driver was finishing his day with the delivery. I plan to follow him tomorrow when he drives to where he works and the boxes prepared."

"Sure you want to do this? The last time we followed these individuals, we ran into problems."

"You got into problems, mister, not me. Don't worry Jason; I'll be careful. It's a simple tailing activity. I have performed dozens in my days."

"Are you going back home tonight?"

"I don't think so. I have a travel bag in the car; I'll find a place to crash tonight and be on site bright and early. Don't worry about me. I will be all right."

"And the box you picked up?"

"The markings show Vitamin World of Asia, with a Jacksonville delivery address."

"And inside?"

"I think we should hold on to it as evidence if we need it."

"Yes, an excellent idea Jennifer."

"And the DEA meeting?" she inquired.

I reported the conversation and the reply from the regional manager. "I asked Tianna when I left if she knew of Mark Taylor. Her silence was eloquent. I'll bet she knows more of what happened to him."

# # #

When I came back from the Rusty Hook last night, I called Cynthia to update her on the case and my DEA meeting as she asked. Just the mention of their name excited her. She concluded that the backing of a reputable federal organization would better serve my search for Mark Taylor. I wasn't sure of that but didn't mention it.

Already a month old, my missing person investigation had transformed into a drug case and a quest for an opioid manufacturing alliance. Not convinced the Taylors would have moved ahead in such a project knowing what we know now. The billing issue was also ambiguous. I devoted hours on the case, and the customer would not resent paying the invoice if I located Mark. It could be another story if we still don't know his fate. I told Nadine about the job parameters before commencing. I should not have any guilt in presenting my fees.

The telephone rang mid-morning, an unknown number. I expected a call from Jennifer, so I answered, anyway.

"Jason Tanner, how can I be of help?"

"Mister Tanner, Tianna Hester from the DEA, we need a talk."

"I'm listening."

"Not on the phone. Can you meet me at the Jet Runway Cafe? It's a small restaurant right beside the Fort Lauderdale Executive Airport. Shall we say 4 o'clock?"

"See you then," and I hung up. The DEA wanted a talk, surprise! From my days at the FBI, if a PI wished to participate in a case, we pushed him aside; we didn't share investigations with anyone. The agency was in a bind and curious about the information I could provide. Even a teaser thrilled them. I could not stop smiling and shouted, "Wow!" This discussion and the following steps will be crucial to my investigation. I sent Jennifer a text message with the happy news but got no reply.

Before my late afternoon meeting, I decided to go shopping. I purchased a new Glock and got in some practice at the local gun store harboring a professional range. Confiscated by my abductors in Marathon, my earlier firearm had disappeared, and I didn't stay around asking for its return. At first, I was all over the target. My lack of recent training showed right away. I decided to put in more practice time today. I may need it before this case is over. This later version of the Glock, lighter than its predecessor, called for every bit of my attention. After a hundred rounds or so, I could now see most of my shots in the inner circle. After I had purchased a holster and plenty of ammunition, I gazed at my watch and headed for my talk.

Tianna picked a restaurant right on the edge of a small airfield, its two runways busy with flight training and private jets. Fort Lauderdale's international airport, less than ten miles away, caters to the regular carriers who fly tourists all year long to South Florida.

The public enters the well-decorated restaurant from the non-secure sector of the airport. If a door existed on the opposite side, you'd walk right onto the tarmac. But access is impossible, and only large windows provide a superb view of the runways. Aviation buffs, like me, just love it.

Tianna was easy to spot from the few patrons inside. I shuffled across the room in the belief of my tardiness, but once there, I was 10 minutes early by my watch. Most people would get a seat near the airstrip to appreciate planes landing or departing. She had elected the opposite, away from it. With her back to the wall, I sat right in front of her, blind to the activities I like seeing on the runways.

"Thanks for coming, Mister Tanner." She wore the same slacks as yesterday but a discrete color blouse, her firearm not in plain sight. Unlike yesterday, she was wearing her black hair combed back in a ponytail high on her head. A notebook emerged from her purse, ready for action.

Like her, mine came out as well, showing Mark Taylor's picture on its cover. After a second, she noticed, and a somber expression appeared briefly, but she soon regained her composure.

"Come here often?" I asked.

"On occasions, the office is close by, and the food's decent."

After we both ordered a black coffee, I shot the first salvo. "What's on your mind?"

"Mr. Baker and I discussed the situation after our meeting yesterday. He thanks you for coming to see him. You presented some interesting intelligence. At his suggestion, he asks you to provide details of your findings to the department."

Looking straight into her eyes, "Sure, I'm willing to contribute. How about doing your part?"

"The agency hopes to collaborate as much as possible, but some data is not for public consumption, and unless I'm mistaking, you're public, not FBI."

"Not the best start of our relationship if you ask me. I tell you what I know while you decide what I need to know."

A grimace appeared for a fraction of a second, a sure sign she did not appreciate my answer. I kept a straight face. After a few seconds, she shifted into a wry smile. "Now, mister Tanner, you must understand, as an FBI Special Agent, some information must remain confidential during an investigation. It's common sense, don't show your hand."

She looked up my records because I did not mention I was a Special Agent. I said I was an FBI retiree during the meeting. I paused, thinking about her reply, but I decided on my approach a while ago. "OK then, let's test our future collaboration: does the DEA have an active investigation on a drug ring operating from the Black Cat? Simple question."

She hesitated, looking for a smart answer.

"Can't say. It's on a need-to-know basis."

I leaned forward and slammed my hand on the table. "What? Can't say? Why bring me here if you can't say?"

She pushed back from the table suddenly, surprised by my reaction. If her eyes could fire a gun, I would be dead. But after a few seconds, she continued, "It's confidential. You should understand that; you've been in the business."

"I'll tell you what I believe, Mrs. Hester. The agency lost track of an informant. He disconnected and disappeared. Even possible he has turned coats on you. For all we know, he could have joined the other side now if he's not already at the bottom of the ocean. That's what I believe."

"Impossible," she said.

"OK, if he's your informant, when was the last time you two talked?"

She lowered her head like a Christian in a confessional. "Almost a year now."

"What does the DEA workbook recommend as a frequency of contact for your informant?"

She lowered her head even more. "Two or three weeks, less if possible."

In a louder voice than I intended, I said, "When you're ready to share intelligence, Mrs. Hester, you have my number." I got up and dashed toward the exit hoping my theatrics would sway her and her boss.

Driving back, some arm muscles were still quivering with my hands on the steering wheel. The exchange of information with the agency was a one-way street. Sorry, not my cup of tea. Still, all worked up, my phone rang.

It could be Tianna wishing to continue the so-called discussion. "Yes," I was responding in my best impolite voice.

"Mr. Tanner, it's Damien Jones, Jennifer's husband."

In a more pleasant tone now, "Yes, Mr. Jones."

"Any news from Jennifer? We expected her after lunch, but she has not arrived yet. She doesn't answer her phone."

"I have no information either. I sent Jennifer a message earlier today but got no reply."

After a few seconds, with a raised voice, he added, "I hope she's not in any trouble because of you, mister."

"Jennifer is a big girl, able to handle herself. She wouldn't take any unnecessary risks. What is she driving today?"

"The red Subaru."

After obtaining her license plate number, I told him I would get someone to search for her and keep him informed. Sargent Gomez from the Marathon police was my next call, and I pleaded to locate my partner's red car. He promised to tell his officers in the region. I thanked him and left a number where he could reach me, no matter the time of day.

I rushed home and sat inside, trying to decide what to do next. Could Jennifer have suffered the same fate I did? If she waited in her car observing a black panel truck at a distance, it's not impossible someone noticed. Should I rush to Marathon to find her? Where would I look? The city is small, but still. She hadn't provided a location during our last conversation.

An inspiration.

I grabbed my phone, searched for a recent call, and hit dial.

"Mr. Jones, Jennifer carries an Android phone, does she not?"

"Yes, she has an Android unit."

"You'll need her account password, but if you get Google Maps going on her laptop, you can see information about her itinerary unless she turned the option off."

"Yes, I see what you're getting at. Hold on for a second."

Different sounds came over the line as he put the phone on a table and a computer started up. After a minute, I heard Jones's voice again.

"Here it is. The last location shows up near the Marathon airport. I have an address on 92nd Street, 2900."

"Any time on this sighting?"

"16:24 to 17:20, it's the last entry, nothing else. That was yesterday!"

I thanked him and returned to my dark thoughts. If I put myself in a bad situation, I deal with it. When I put someone else, it's uncomfortable. I walked the small space, back and forth, inside the yacht, trying to decide on a course of action. Wait for the police or a call from Jennifer? Not for me. Lack of action is not my style.

I elaborated a plan to drive down tonight and be there around 9 pm. Go to the location shown on her Google Map history and knock on doors in the area, check with the Marathon police as well. I prepared a backpack with the tools of my trade and some fresh clothing, not forgetting my new Glock.

My phone rang as I stepped out of the yacht, another unrecognized number.

"Hello!"

"Jason, it's Jennifer."

"Jennifer! Where have you been? Your family and I worried about you."

"I know. I just arrived home and talked to Damien. He said he raised his voice to you, and he regrets it now."

"It's OK. I was testy myself. It's all forgotten. What happened?"

"You will not believe it. I neglected to bring my charger with me. I called Damien last night from the phone inside the motel room, and before going to bed, when I wanted to recharge my phone, I discovered it was not in my bag, I left it at home."

"Don't you carry a cable inside your car? You can recharge it while driving."

"I don't, but I will next time."

"But you were missing all day. What did you do?"

"This morning, I took my post off 92nd Street. The black panel truck was still there, parked where I saw it last yesterday. People moved from the neighbor's house into the home I was checking. Somehow, Jason, I think both properties are connected. My guess is they live in one house and work in the other. A metallic gate protects access to both buildings. The houses are typical stilt construction, the ground floor empty, the entire home on the second level. I'm no expert, but I'd say the construction is recent, a year or two at the most."

"How interesting. I'll get Hank on it to see who owns these properties."

"What's also interesting, Jason, one house is directly at the edge of the ocean with a canal right behind it. A good spot for a quick getaway, or to pick up and deliver stuff, if you see what I mean."

"Do you have the address of both houses, Jennifer?"

"Yes, 2800 and 2810 92nd Street."

"Noted."

"Before my phone went dark, I shot images of the houses and the surroundings. I'll send them over later."

"Fine. You gave us a scare, you know. Damien was expecting you early today, though."

The answer was slow to come out. "Well, I passed in front of a large mall in Homestead on my way back, and I couldn't resist. I wanted to call Damien, but, as you know, my cellphone was dead."

"Public phone?"

"Have you seen one recently?"

"Hum..." And I left it at that.

"I'm grateful everything turned out OK today. Relax, I'll call you in the morning to plan our next steps."

"Fine. I'm sorry for the trouble Jason. Be good."

I hung up, happy the whole situation was under control but annoyed a simple phone charger led to this situation.

# # #

My next move was to call Hank and give him the addresses of the homes identified by Jennifer. While on the phone, he connected to the tax appraiser database for Monroe County. In no time, he had a result. Surprise! Both houses belonged to Sailing the Atlantic LLC, the same company that owned the Black Cat bar. As Hank had discovered earlier, this firm, registered in Delaware, can hide the real owners. Impossible to find out who operated the LLC. I suspected someone but had no tangible evidence yet.

That night, while watching television but not concentrating on the program, I reached for my notebook. Writing memos is a new habit of mine to compensate for small but expected memory losses caused by aging. In the hope something jumped off the sheet of paper, I flipped pages. The first encounter with Nadine, drinks with JR in Miami, the deposit box, the surfers. I placed my hand to the back of my head, and

I could still sense the abrasion from meeting a baseball bat near the shore. Suddenly, an idea popped, and I located Jeff Mason's contact information in no time.

"Hello."

"Jeff, Jason Tanner, I'm the person you met at South Point Park Pier, the investigator looking for Mark Taylor."

"Yes, I remember you, Mister Tanner. How can I help?"

"Just a few questions, Jeff. Your buddies Nelson and Taylor, did they compete in surfing contests?"

"They loved it."

"This weekend, one is happening in Miami Beach. Is it possible they'll be part of it?"

"Yes, and they do well. The Miami surf familiarity grants them an edge."

"I see; thanks for the intelligence."

I needed to think offense now. If I wanted to cut the beast's head, I needed to catch it first. The beast was running, I had to cut the legs off, and that meant the two Asian legs.

# # #

Early Saturday, I came back to the Miami Beach Marina in time for the Surfing Championships organized by a national association. It attracted local talent and others from the coastline. Held at the South Point Beach, right beside the Marina, I believed the competition would appeal to Nelson due to the familiar conditions, a site where he often practiced. My objective was to start shaking them in any way I could.

The event debuted yesterday as a warm-up to the weekend action. Multiple categories compete based on sex, age, and gear; my interest was for the men's longboard. If I remember correctly, that's what Nelson hoisted on his jeep when I saw him the first time.

So I dressed for the occasion, resembling a person with a skin disorder afraid of the sun. A wide hat with a back flap covered the side and the back of my head. A white linen shirt with full sleeves and beige pants completed my disguise, along with an oversized pair of sunglasses. Water, snacks, a long-range binocular, and a Glock, in the event of trouble, went into my backpack.

With the schedule in hand, I strolled to the contest site when the first of four elimination runs were starting. I walked the limit of the beach, needing to be discreet, trying to fade in the crowd. Thousands of individuals were on-site. Not only competitors, friends, and family but officials and regular beachgoers who had now become spectators. A group of surfers was honing their skills and testing the waters. Waves were large, crowds anxious, and the weather cooperating.

Around the 11th hour, officials called the practicing surfers from the water and replaced them with the first wave of real competition. On my way over, I grabbed a paper listing the day's participants. Everyone was wearing three-digit numbers on their chest and back for identification by the judges.

Each wave of competitors included roughly fifteen names. The committee had scheduled four sessions for this class of surfers. The third flight included a name I recognized immediately, Yang Nelson, number 254. I was happy to have followed my instinct. But I found no trace of Mark Taylor. Without a body to confirm Taylor's fate, I still believed he either infiltrated the gang or joined based on personal interest. I did not see his name on the roster. But another one intrigued me, Mark Patry, from Miami. Where had I heard this name?

The Missing Taylor

As I moved around in my head-to-toe gear, I scanned the competitors looking for number 254. From the beach's edge, I gazed through my binoculars toward the sea, but in reality, I was looking for a single person. Without success, I moved to a new location and repeated my scenario. The second wave of competitors entered the waters, and I expected Nelson in the next one.

Just then, I saw a strange trio. A person in a black wetsuit, hurrying, followed by a big man carrying a longboard, a third one, smaller, trying hard to keep pace in the sand. I moved closer and came to rest near a large palm tree. The two Asians still looked out of place with their pressed-down trousers, dressed shoes, and a white shirt.

At once, I reached in my back pocket for my phone and dialed LeBron Jackson, Freeman's partner; I tried keeping away from Freeman for now.

"LeBron, Jason Tanner. I know it's Saturday, but I have two guys in my sights you need to talk to. They're the ones who visited my yacht and killed Tudor, I believe."

"Where are you?" he asked.

"South Point Beach."

"Let me get patrolmen on-site. I'll be right over. Wait for us. Do nothing stupid."

I turned my attention to Nelson again as he strapped on his 254 identification, walked toward the big waves, and jumped in the water. When I looked back for his entourage, they walked away in the city's direction. I put my backpack down, stored my binoculars, and kept the duo under discrete observation.

LeBron said he was sending some patrolmen; I checked, not seeing them yet. With a thin cover, the Asians could maybe see me, but my disguise should be good enough. A bar and restaurant looked to be their target. Close to midday, the big man's stomach was trying to get his attention while his boss was playing in the water. I kept a hundred feet behind them. They turned into a restaurant's entrance and spoke a few words to a young girl at the front desk. The hostess called someone over to accompany the customers to a table where they could keep an eye on the event and their upcoming lunch.

Oblivious to the stakeout, they ordered from the menu and waited for their meal while I kept looking out for the patrolmen or a call from LeBron. The car arrived first. I walked in its direction and waived, keeping an eye on the restaurant's entrance. I informed the two police officers I was expecting detective LeBron. A few minutes later, a white Honda arrived and parked alongside the patroller. LeBron got out.

"Where are they?" he asked.

I pointed to the restaurant. We all walked in that direction, LeBron and I in front. As we approached the main door, LeBron asked the police officers to wait a second. He and I moved forward until we saw our two lads enjoying a drink, waiting for food. LeBron signaled the officers to join him, and all three entered the premises. A few minutes later, the police officers led the individuals to the patrol car. They passed right beside me, not even looking.

As LeBron trailed, he stopped by my side.

"We'll talk to them, but on the Taylor situation, I don't know if I can bring charges. What offenses can they have committed by leaving with Taylor? On the Tudor murder, we may have more. The video, we'll get fingerprints, we'll work the case. Thanks for the tip."

He turned around, walked to his car, and drove away.

The competition had switched to smaller boards now. I tried locating Nelson, but to no avail, I couldn't find him. I imagined him calling his two bodyguards who were not answering, hands behind their back in a police car. It was my time to be hungry, so I returned aboard and made myself a quick lunch with a beer.

It was Saturday; I hesitated to call Jennifer, giving her some family time. The same thing with JR, I wanted to inform him about the lukewarm reception I got from the DEA. I put aside the case for now and thought about fishing techniques and locations William Tudor had shown me. It was still early, and I could be onto his fishing spot within an hour, so I prepared to sail off in search of my dinner. Tomorrow I would look for Yang Nelson, uncertain if he had reached the next level. But for now, fishing was my priority.

# # #

On Sunday, they scheduled afternoon finals. Donned with my fancy outfit again, I walked to the competition site, where I grabbed a flyer listing the participants in today's action. In no time, I located Yang Nelson's name. I was wondering who would carry his board today. LeBron had not informed me yet of his conversations with the suspects.

I looked for another name that intrigued me yesterday: Mark Patry. After careful examination, I didn't find him. Maybe his results did not carry him into the finals. Where did I hear this name? Then, I remembered: Patry is the last name of Nadine's husband. She told me when we met for the first time. Could Mark Taylor use the name Mark Patry? It was a stretch but not impossible. The terrible news was if Patry was the man I was looking for, I just missed him yesterday on this beach. If my memory had served me better, I might have seen Taylor on his surfboard and at least approached him, talked to him. Instead, I concentrated on Laurel and Hardy. It disappointed me, but I still had no tangible evidence Mark Patry was, in fact, Mark Taylor.

That's when they arrived: the famous trio. Nelson was leading the group, empty-handed, the big one carrying the board, and the little one trailing the pack. I did not expect them on the street today. It was a complete surprise. For first-degree murder, anyone arrested would be behind bars waiting for a bail hearing. What happened? I looked for a quiet spot; I had a call to make.

"LeBron, it's Tanner. I saw the two men you arrested yesterday. How can they be out on the street already?"

"Hold on, Tanner, let me go outside."

He returned half a minute later.

"It's complicated. I brought the two guys to the police station and into an interrogation room yesterday. I called Freeman, my partner, but he was not available, so I worked with another detective. We showed them the pictures and the videos, but they denied everything. It's not them, they said. I didn't believe them, so I read them their rights, arrested them, got their fingerprints, and put them in our local jail."

"But they're out today?"

"Yes, I know. Freeman called later, and when I told him about the arrest, he went berserk. He rushed to the station, and we argued for a while. He's saying we don't have probable cause to arrest them. Since he's the senior detective, he released them."

"He what?"

"He let them go."

"You had the individuals in custody, booked, and he let them out?"

"That's his prerogative."

"Bullshit. Go over your partner's head on this. If you don't, I will."

The Missing Taylor

The line went dead all of a sudden. LeBron was angry, but so was I. A lone detective released two murder suspects on his authority after his partner booked them. This was unheard of. My suspicion of Freeman's association with the gang grew a fraction more. First, the inefficient investigation when Mark disappeared, then pointing my yacht to the Asians and now, releasing the same guys out on the street. Although I had no proof for any of his actions, my investigating experience from the Marines, the Chicago Police, and the FBI pointed me in that direction.

I was still boiling inside when I returned aboard, and I took a while to cool off. While in this frame of mind, I resisted the urge to call John Russell right away. Tomorrow would do. Later, after cooling down, I contacted Jennifer to invite her and her husband on a boat tour around Miami Beach to view the sun going down. I would have something simple to eat and expected them around five.

I tried to relax in the afternoon but was anxious because of the proximity of the Asian trio. When I tried to get a half-hour snooze, I locked the doors and had my gun close by.

When my guests arrived, I greeted them from the aft deck. Jennifer stepped aboard first, with her husband Damien following. He offered me a bottle of wine while saying he was sorry to have lost his cool on our call earlier.

"Understandable, Damien. In a similar case, it would upset me too. Let's forget it, make yourself comfortable. Or rather, let me give you a rapid tour of the place, and then we can get underway."

We cruised inside Biscayne Bay and picked a beautiful location where we could observe the MacArthur Causeway and the city of Miami in the backdrop with the setting sun. The colors were amazing, reflecting on the calm waters of the bay. After dropping the anchor and serving drinks all around, we discussed a few mundane issues before I addressed the subject I wanted to talk to Jennifer about. Her husband's presence did not bother me. He could even spawn a different point of view.

When the discussion slowed down, I brought up the subject. "I'm glad you guys were available today because I needed to review our case and examine our options going forward. And Damien, your input is welcome." I looked at them, and they were waiting for the follow-up.

"Yesterday, LeBron Jackson arrested Nelson's partners, Laurel and Hardy, on the beach for what I believed would be a slam dunk case for the murder of William Tudor. When LeBron later informed his partner, Freeman rushed to the station and released them."

"Why?" Jennifer asked.

"Probable cause, he says. Still, I must conclude at least one detective on the Taylor investigation does not want to see it through and is no help to us."

"Why would they do that?" Damian asked.

"I'm not sure at this point. For multiple reasons, I don't think Freeman is playing on our team." I let the message sink before continuing.

"Despite this situation, our job is to find Taylor if he's alive. I have an idea, and I'll need your help."

Before going over my plan, I listed who, in my humble opinion, we could count on and who caused problems. The DEA was not on my favorite list. When we tried to implicate them, they only wanted to siphon our information. They offered no collaboration. The DEA lost an informant and since then have slept on the case. All the people we talked to know drugs infested the Black Cat Bar, yet the DEA did nothing, just sat there. The bar was still in operation, the owners the same, the activities the same. Nothing had changed.

The Miami-Dade police were a toss-up. Some individuals should not be privy to our actions, Freeman and Jackson at least. I still believed John Russell could help, but his implication should remain confidential and not be discussed with his detectives. On the other hand, we had several people who would support our initiative; Hank Hackman for sure, Barry Gilmore too. The Marathon Sheriff's office collaborated when they were asked.

I then suggested playing the gang and delivering them to the authorities. The plan surprised my guests initially. It involved some technical aspects which they were unfamiliar with. At first, they hesitated, but they believed it would work after further discussions. Now we only had to put it into action.

Chapter 12

After my guests left last night, I cleaned up the yacht and reached for my OXY 40, the street name for Oxycontin 40 mg. Having no official prescription and having avoided the pain management sessions, illegal drugs were the answer to my problem, at least for now. I wished it was temporary, but I wasn't sure. I knew my back was still hurting, and I needed medication to help me through the pain.

Sleep did not come easy, but the Oxycontin helped again. Both Jennifer and Damien questioned my strategy, assumptions, and predictions, and raised concerns that I had not thought about. These matters were turning in my head, unable to sleep. I got up, boiled a cup of tea, and rechecked the information I had discovered before our get-together. Everything was a green light still, and I retired back to bed, feeling relieved, and after a while fell asleep.

I woke up around seven, and with fresh coffee in hand, prepared my day ahead. After breakfast, I listed activities and calls needed to get going. Events could not happen before others, and some had dependents. My project planning 101 courses would help; happy I did not skip these classes.

The Missing Taylor

One of my plan's key ingredients involved stopping orders coming into the gang's website, cutting their source of revenue. If no orders came in, no money flowed in either. Hank would know tricks on how to achieve this venture. He was my first contact today. Once I explained what I was looking for, he said, "Easy." My next question was: how much time until they felt the impact of the site not being operational? "At once," was his response. I told him to prepare and wait for my signal. I would give him one hour's notice.

The plan consisted of attracting all significant players to one place. If the drug orders stopped coming in, I hoped top management would step in and rush to their primary operation site to the rescue, like the cavalry. Nelson would precipitate himself at the first sign of trouble. But the main catch would be Steiner. The man I believed ran the entire operation had another outstanding quality: the FBI wanted him.

To organize an assault on their operation in Marathon, I needed eyes-on-target. Jennifer had singled out two houses on 92nd Street. While I examined satellite imagery of the area, I noticed they were sitting on land extending into the sea, resulting in both houses being surrounded by water on three sides. The fourth side was the street itself providing access. A brick wall and a metallic fence further isolated its inhabitants. It reminded me of medieval castles with a moat all around and a single drawbridge to access well-protected grounds.

Another decision had to be taken: should we observe them from the land or the sea? To keep an eye on the ins and outs of the 92nd Street property, I could station my yacht on the water, far enough, and watch with binoculars. Close to the city, my phone and Internet access would still work. A second choice was to park a vehicle on the street behind the houses and watch from that viewpoint. Positioned there, I would be a sitting duck. This option was not tempting. The sea won the debate.

Steiner was the unknown in my plan. Pretty confident Nelson and his bodyguards would show up when the website stopped its operations, Steiner remained a complete mystery to me. His captain's job could take him anywhere, far from Marathon. We should spring the trap when we have a high certitude he'll be around. And to do that, we had to follow Ocean Dancer and hope he was on it.

Confident the ship's AIS system was in operation, I connected to the website and entered "Ocean Dancer" in the search field. A few seconds later, a new page appeared. Based on the map, the ship navigated in the Bahamas region. Another field showed the destination to be "BS NAS," which I decoded as Nassau, Bahamas. Before triggering the plan, I must have Steiner in Marathon, or at least in South Florida. But was Steiner on that vessel? How could I make sure?

One way was to repeat the intrusion at Yacht Charter of Miami a few weeks ago and find his current and future assignments. But that included a real element of risk. It worked once. Would it work again? For all I know, a new security system could have been installed if my illegal entry had been discovered. No, I needed a different way to get Steiner's position.

An idea slowly developed, and I speed-dialed Jennifer. After thanking me again for a great evening last night, I countered, "I need a female assistant to make an inquiry."

After spelling out the reasons for my call, I presented her with a general scenario in which she could make adaptations. Later, when she called back, she described her intervention in detail.

"Good morning, Yacht Charter of Miami. How can I assist you?"

"Good morning, my name is Susan Moody, I'm Mr. Nelson's new assistant from the Black Cat bar. Mr. Nelson would like to book Ocean Dancer with Mr. Scott at the helm for a two days' sail to Marathon on April 18 and 19th of this week."

"Let me check the calendar, hum, that yacht is not available on those days, I'm sorry."

"Can we get Mr. Scott with a different yacht? Is it possible?"

"Mr. Scott is leaving with Ocean Dancer today and won't be available until next week."

"That is unfortunate. We may have to change the dates. I will have to call you again."

Bingo. She located both the famous yacht and Steiner himself with a single telephone call.

My next call was to Barry Gilmore at FBI headquarters.

"Hello."

"Barry, it's Jason. I believe I will be able to deliver Bruce Steiner's location in a few days."

"No kidding, where?"

"I don't know today, but soon I'll know. I expect Steiner to show up in one of three places."

"In Florida?"

"I believe so."

"You know the drill, Jason. You have to notify the local office first. If they need to intervene quickly, only our local boys could do it. Let me get you a contact name and a number; start there."

207

"Fine, one more thing. The gang I'm following operates an electronic commerce system. It would be helpful to determine where the revenues are going. Do you think you can help me?"

"That's probably embedded into their own systems; I doubt I can help with this. I am also pretty busy in Washington these days, Jason. I would love to go down and help, the warmer weather would be good as well, but I can't."

"It's OK, don't worry about it, buddy, maybe some other time," I answered.

"I may not be able to help you, but I know who could. The FBI field office near Miami now has a new digital forensic team, and the leader is a good friend of mine. I'll send you his contact information later today, but first, I will tell him to expect a call from you on this case. How is that?"

"That's perfect, my friend. I can't thank you enough." I set my phone on the table. Pieces of the puzzle were slowly falling in place.

Over the next few days, the maritime traffic application ran continuously on my laptop. I followed Ocean Dancer, first sailing to Nassau, staying in port awhile, and then eventually getting underway, I was hoping, toward Miami Beach, or better even, Marathon.

On Thursday morning, when I verified the status of Steiner's ship, I discovered it left for Miami at 7:24 that morning. With a reasonable cruising speed, we could expect an arrival around 7 pm tonight. I prepared PRIVATE EYE and set sail for Marathon once more.

# # #

On my way down to the Keys, I called Jennifer and recommended to once again get a tail on Yang Nelson and to be careful. Thursday, she would undoubtedly find him at the Black Cat, usually an active day. In my estimate, Steiner should arrive early evening, but I intended to bring down the drug website way before. This way, their technical crews would have time to study the situation and signal the problem to their bosses. Jennifer planned to go by the beach first to locate Nelson. Otherwise, she would just walk into Nelson's bar. She was a stranger to him at this point.

Around 11 am, I instructed Hank to stop all website operations. No more orders placed, no vitamins, or painkillers. No payments would flow in either; the flow of money had to stop. The site should be inoperable as of that time and for the foreseeable future, pending further instructions. He was ready to proceed.

My floating journey should have me arriving in Marathon close to 3 pm. Their moneymaking machine would have been down for a few hours with their technical team working hard to locate the problem's cause. Hank had informed me people trying to access the site would not receive any response. Restarting either the user's computer or the website would not resolve the issue. The affected customers would have to turn to other procurement sources, but the Nelson website would not supply them today.

During my six-hour trip, I had plenty of time to study maritime maps of the area. Between the houses sitting at the end of 92nd Street and the ocean were the muddy and shallow waters of Marathon Shores. PRIVATE EYE couldn't maneuver in all safety in this environment with its almost four-foot draft. But the maps also showed private channels created to allow boats to reach the ocean from canals on the island.

Once in Marathon, I navigated through one of these channels and positioned my yacht about half a mile away from the two houses. It was tight, but I made it without scraping the bottom. I set up a few rods for effects, showing that I was here for the sport to anyone looking my way. A few fishing boats were already floating around. I then installed long-range binoculars on a tripod near the flybridge's pilot station. The rented equipment provided a clear frontal view of both houses and the main gate, where I now noticed a man walking close to the front entrance. Was he guarding the place? Quite possible.

My phone rang, I recognized Jennifer's number.

"Yes."

"Hi Jason, I'm having a drink with Damien at the Black Cat. I stepped out to give you an update."

"So."

"Nelson was behind the bar when we arrived this afternoon. Someone called him in the back office later, and another gentleman replaced him upfront. It's been a while now. He's stuck in there, maybe."

"Someone must have informed Nelson of the situation, it's obvious. As of one o'clock today, no new orders are coming through."

"What do you think he'll do?"

"Not understanding the technology behind his website operation, Jennifer, he will argue with his technician on why they have not solved the problem yet. I can imagine him saying: don't let me come down there, it will not be pretty."

"It's possible. Hold on."

The phone went silent for about 10 seconds.

"He just passed in front of me, Jason. Nelson came out with a young lady I'd never seen. He didn't even look at me. They're walking down the street. Wait, they're getting into a white Mercedes convertible. And now they're gone."

"That's fine, and we expected that. Could the young lady be Nelson's girlfriend, Sun My?"

"Possible, I never saw her."

"If the drug orders are not coming in, neither are the vitamins. It preoccupies both of them. It sort of confirms the drug and vitamin businesses are pretty much connected, no?"

"Makes sense. What shall I do now?"

"OK. Drive Damien home and then come to Marathon with your equipment. Move to the south end of 96th Street and then call me back. You should be here between 5 and 6 pm according to my calculations. I will pick you up with the dinghy. Park your car close by. We may need it later."

"Fine, captain. You have something to eat on your tub?"

"Yes, plenty of food, and you'll have your private VIP suite."

"Fine, see you in a few."

I observed the compound once again. No changes were visible. The guard was still on duty. If my calculations were right, Nelson would arrive around 5 pm, Jennifer about 30 minutes later. The timing was perfect; I needed to prepare a few phone calls until then. In anticipation of Jennifer's arrival, I lowered the tender from the flybridge and tied it to the back, ready to go operational when needed.

Back at my post, I continued to scrutinize the compound. According to Jennifer, the complex looked to have one house for operations, by the sea, while the second one was the living quarters, and in between them a parking space with two small trucks. Besides the guard, no movement was visible from either house. All doors were closed, no personnel outside except the lone guard who kept walking back and forth, at speed better suited for a funeral.

He suddenly turned his head toward the main entrance and hurried over; a white Mercedes arrived. Next, the dual swing driveway gate opened, and the white car sped up toward the operation center. I zoomed in on the new arrival just in time to watch two car doors fly open. I recognized the driver as no other than Yang Nelson, and I assumed his girlfriend was the passenger, although I had never seen her. Someone had locked the front door because Nelson's group had to wait a good minute before it opened, and the couple rushed in.

I could imagine the shouting occurring inside. The money machine had stopped working.

Someone came out of the same house with a plastic container in hand. He walked to the black panel truck and left with the few orders the gang received this morning, I assumed. I backed up from the binoculars, happy the plan was moving along.

# # #

When my phone vibrated later, I recognized Jennifer's number.

"Just in time," I said.

"Hi Jason, just arrived. Do I need to swim out to reach you?"

"Hold on. Your carriage is on its way."

When we returned, I directed Jennifer to her quarters. She had a small bag with her, perfect; it was a small cabin. I maneuvered our floating house to another location, further away but within range for my binoculars. Rods still in place, I wanted to look like a regular fishing vessel, although my yacht was pretty big for this area.

"Nelson is still on-site?" she asked.

"Yes, nobody left this afternoon. His white Mercedes is still in the courtyard."

"And our plans for tomorrow?"

"We meet at 8 am with Sheriff McBain of the Monroe Sheriff's office. Our job will be to convince him this group represents a real threat to his region, and he needs to move right now to raid the property while Nelson and his girlfriend are still there, and catch them with their hands in the jar. You brought the evidence as I asked you?"

"In my travel bag."

"Perfect, let me get you a drink first. I will serve dinner in only an hour. Let's try to get a good night's sleep. We'll need all our full energy."

During the evening, we reviewed our presentation to McBain developed to convince him. We needed to show enough reasons for the Sheriff's office to raid and search the premises. It would not be easy. I had to ask JR to put up a good word for me to arrange the meeting.

# # #

Jennifer and I were up early, a good breakfast already in our stomach, the second cup of coffee in hand. After a good night's sleep, my back did not hurt this morning, so I skipped my daily medication, but I put a pill in my pocket, just in case.

We waited outside Monroe's Sheriff's office for a crucial meeting about our investigation. The weather promised to be below average as dark clouds rolled over the seven small islands forming the city of Marathon. At our appointed time, we entered and asked to see the Sheriff. We walked up to his third-floor office, and an elderly assistant asked us to wait; the Sheriff would be with us in a minute.

McBain's office door opened, and he came out, wearing a somber face. An 8 o'clock meeting with a pair of private investigators was not on top of his fun list of activities. He looked like a Christian being led to the arena.

He walked right in front of us, and we assumed we had to follow. He led us to a small conference room. His assistant trailed behind and asked if we wanted coffee or water. We already had a cup in hand, so we thanked her. The Sheriff requested nothing, a man in a hurry, I concluded.

I took to the floor, not wanting him to tell me he only had a few minutes to spare.

"Thanks for seeing us, Sheriff McBain. We'll be as quick as possible; we're aware you have an important department to run."

Not wanting him to interrupt me, I continued.

"Jennifer Jones is like me, a former FBI agent, and together, we have been searching for a missing person by the name of Mark Taylor, as I informed you before. Your staff helped locate possible missing person cases in the area, but none matched our subject."

The Sheriff leaned his head on his left hand, his elbow supported by his chair. He already looked bored. I had to revive his interest not to lose his attention.

"We believe there is a drug manufacturing and distribution business right here in Marathon."

He leaned in and asked, "Are you positive?"

"Let me fill you in on the details first. Mark Taylor's last workday occurred on a night shift at the Black Cat bar in Miami Beach. In Miami, it's a well-known fact that this bar is involved in drug distribution. Afterward, he traveled south with two Asians. We call them Laurel and Hardy, a big one, a small one, and they're always seen together."

"Taylor stayed in a local motel and drank at a nearby bar. His credit card transactions prove it. We detected no more financial activities after that weekend. Our search for clues had us locate Mark's friends in Miami Beach, where Laurel and Hardy murdered an old man on my yacht. I was the intended target, but they made a deadly mistake. The Miami police are working on the murder case. They informed me the suspects injected pure fentanyl into the victim. He had no chance."

"So far, I see no criminal activities in Monroe County."

"We're getting there, sir. The Asians and their boss travel to Marathon regularly. We believe it's to both deliver manufacturing ingredients and pick up finished goods. When we tailed them one night, they captured me, but I escaped while they brought me back to Miami."

"You want me to arrest them for kidnapping you?"

"No, I'm not done. Because it's a well-organized gang, it operates out of a location on 92nd Street, right here in Marathon. We tailed them, and we now know where they operate from. That's their base camp."

"And you want us to run there and arrest them? On what grounds?"

"Drug manufacturing, sale, and distribution."

"Do you have any proof?"

I turned to Jennifer, who brought out an evidence bag containing a small box with a delivery address and a sender identification. She handed it over to him.

"Vitamin World of China has a website where people can order either vitamins or opioids." I pulled out a stack of papers Hank had provided me before leaving with screenshots from the compromising website. It was clear, and I highlighted that users could order hard drugs.

"What you have in your hands is a shipment we believe comes from the production site, here in Marathon."

"How did the shipment land in your hands?" he asked.

"It fell from their delivery truck," Jennifer answered. The Sheriff looked at her. He did not believe a word she said.

"I suggest you get your lab to verify its content. If you're satisfied, the bad guys are on 92nd Street. A few of the leaders are still there. That's what I ask of the Sheriff's office, sir. Get a warrant and search that location."

"If what you say is true, Mister Tanner, we'll look into the situation. If not, you must bring your problem elsewhere."

"I understand."

"We can't send this box to the lab. It will take days to get results. Barbara!" he shouted suddenly. The door opened, and the elderly assistant walked in. "Get me, Gomez, right now." She left on her mission, closing the door behind her. He then leaned back and waited, looking at both Jennifer and me. He got up abruptly and walked out of the conference room, closing the door and leaving us alone.

"You know Jason, the box could have vitamins and no hard drugs."

"I took a chance. If we can't get his support, we must resort to plan B."

"Which is..."

"I don't know yet."

The door flew open, and McBain appeared, followed by Sargent Gomez. The sheriff carried a utility knife in hand. He took his former chair, Gomez stayed standing.

"Gomez, get your immense talent over here and tell us what's in the box?" the sheriff asked.

"Without opening it, sir?" I liked him the first time I met him, but now I appreciated his dry humor.

The sheriff handed him the knife while making a smirk and shaking his head, not believing what he heard.

"I'm good, boss, but not that good." He smiled, so did Jennifer and I. The sheriff kept his game face on.

Gomez pulled a chair and sat down while putting on a pair of plastic gloves and reaching for the package under investigation. He looked at me, "Nice to see you again, Mister Tanner." He remembered my name, another good mark for him.

Sargent Gomez rotated the box looking for a way in. He understood he needed to preserve the evidence and wanted to destroy as little as possible. After turning the container in his hands, he slipped the sharp knife on one edge and cut through the paper glued over the cardboard. He repeated his incisions on two other sides and opened the box.

After looking inside and concluding on its safety, he reached in and pulled a plastic pillbox. He showed it to everyone around the table. Receiving a go-ahead sign from his leader, he unscrewed the box, reached in, and extracted one small blue pill which he deposited in front of us.

He looked at the all-white pillbox with a simple company sticker with a logo and a name, "Asian collagen extra vitamin." He looked at the label, then at the pill, and repeated his movement once more.

"Typically, collagen products are presented in a translucent gel capsule. What I'm looking at here is a solid tablet with markings. It reads Oxycodone 215, that's not a vitamin."

It looked very much like what I had in my pocket.

The sheriff's shoulder seemed to drop, his mood changed, and his smile returned.

"Well, folks, we seem to have a case here."

# # #

The sheriff got up and said, "Wait here." Gomez followed him.

"Our point came across, didn't it?" Jennifer asked.

"Maybe. I reported our information rather quickly because I didn't think the Sheriff had a lot of time nor interest at the beginning."

"Yes, that looked obvious."

We waited in silence now, uncertain of the results.

The conference room door burst open, and both the Sheriff and Gomez returned, the latter with a rather serious-looking expression, the Sheriff, a mad look on his face. They both sat down. McBain spoke first.

"The DEA informs me an operation is happening on my turf. It's the first time I find out about it. So much for inter-agency cooperation. But this does not implicate you."

I understood him; the FBI operated the same way. They talk about sharing information and keeping everyone in the loop, but they work from their silo in reality.

"Something also happened that increased the urgency of their operation, I am told. Would you guys know what they're talking about?"

I looked at Jennifer; she returned my stare, we both shook our heads, and our raised shoulders indicated we were clueless. McBaine's facial expression showed he did not believe us one bit. Hank's intervention on the website was a good reason, but we remained silent.

McBain continued. "They're arriving this afternoon to review the situation. They are bringing firepower in case we need to go in. I order you, folks, to sit in the conference room this afternoon. You know more than you're willing to bring up. We need to resolve the entire situation today, understood?"

This time, Jennifer and I both nodded our agreement.

"Be back at one o'clock. Is that clear?"

"Yes, sir," Jennifer and I said in unison, happy to leave the small conference room with a plan in the making.

As it was still early, we walked around Marathon, making sure not to step on 92nd Street. The sun was out, but a northwestern breeze provided cooler air, comfortable for walking around. I called Hank and asked him to let the website run for thirty minutes, then stop it again to make them believe they were getting closer to the answer. He replied he would oblige right now.

Following an early lunch, we walked to the Sheriff's office in time for our afternoon meeting. Once on the third floor, Barbara walked us

219

over to a larger conference room. We could hear voices from the corridor. Jennifer entered and I followed her in.

Several people were standing or already sitting around the large table in the room. Some wore police uniforms, others in plain clothes. It was men for the majority. But then, another face turned around to catch the new arrivals, Tianna Hester, my surprising DEA contact.

Chapter 13

My favorite DEA agent moved toward me with her hand stretched out.

"Mister Tanner, nice to see you again," she said. A polite smile appeared on her lips, and it was all business.

"Nice to see you too. May I present Jennifer Jones? She's working with me."

Jennifer moved forward and also shook her hand.

"Ladies and gentlemen, if you'll please take place, we have work to do," McBain's voice transcended all others. Soon, all the group sat in silence. He asked for a quick go-around to identify each participant and their function. Overall, four people were from DEA, four from the Sheriff's office, plus Jennifer and myself.

"I was not a happy camper this morning when I was informed a drug gang was operating on my territory. That this gang exists should not surprise me. That a private investigator from Pompano Beach informs me is difficult to accept. Is he right? I wanted to verify, and I called Donavan Baker, the DEA regional manager which you all know. Not only does he confirm Tanner's statement, but he tells me you're planning an operation on my island, and soon."

McBain stopped for effect and examined the faces around; no one was smiling. He turned to Tianna and looked directly at her before continuing.

"Ms. Hester, Baker says it's your case. Can you brief us on what is happening, what the operation will look like so we can protect our citizens?"

"Thank you, Sheriff. First, I wanted to inform you the DEA was in the process of contacting you this morning when you reached us. You called just before we did," Tianna opened with.

"Yes, sure, continue please," McBain added, everyone aware he didn't believe her one bit.

"Yes, our team has been following a Miami Beach gang involved in selling narcotics and opioids. Over the past year, they have grown and now have set up a manufacturing arm that also feeds their local market. Our indications are they operate from right here, in Marathon."

"How long have you known Ms. Hester?" the Sheriff asked.

"Just a few days only."

McBain was looking at her, uncertain to believe her. This statement also surprised me, for one.

"My colleague Chris, right here, manages our informant network in the region. Chris, maybe you can explain how we got the information."

Chris eyed Tianna, then looked at the others around the table.

"Well, seven or eight months ago, we had an informant in Miami who disappeared. The Miami police and the DEA independently tried but could not trace him. The family hired Mister Tanner to locate a Mark Taylor. Yesterday, we received an anonymous tip showing the drug ring was about to pack up and leave the region. If that happened, our year-long investigation would go down the drain. We don't know who provided the information, no way to trace it."

Tianna raised her hand, and Chris stopped right there, and she continued the story.

"Although we cannot identify the source, we feel the intelligence is credible. The informant indicates two locations are involved with the drug manufacturing, one here in Marathon. It also talks about a bar in Miami Beach that sells drugs, and it names a person on the FBI's most-wanted list as the main character behind the operation. Because of the urgency, we planned an intervention for tomorrow, at dawn, and here we are."

The audience sat in stunned silence as all participants tried to grasp the situation. The Sheriff looked at me.

"Mister Tanner, were you the one who contacted the DEA and spread this information? It's close to what you told me this morning."

"No way, Sheriff. I don't operate that way. I came to you, not the DEA. A man cannot serve two masters."

"Hum... any bright idea on who provided this anonymous tip?"

Someone offered, "Could it be the missing informant?"

Tianna answered, "It's a possibility, but we have had no communication with him in the last eight months, maybe more. I would be surprised if that were the case."

"I have no idea either, Sheriff, but I can confirm the information. The gang gathered in Marathon yesterday. If the government wants to stop these criminals, they need to pick them up as soon as possible, if not earlier. They are ripe," I told him.

McBain stood up, his two hands resting on the table, leaned in, and said, "This is what we'll do. The DEA and the Sheriff's office will continue to plan the operation. We have all the right folks around the table to proceed, except for you, Mister Tanner, and your associate. We will contact you on your phone if we need additional information. Are we good?"

On that day, some seven years ago, I remembered our assault team had no sign the opposition would use such a radical protection mechanism, a powerful bomb, to defend its territory. A close friend died in that blast. I did not want to see a repeat. I had to relay the message to the team.

"Just two items, Sheriff, if you don't mind. For one, the last time we tried to catch Steiner during my FBI days, a booby trap exploded at his place of business. A brave agent had his life taken away. Be aware of his tactics."

"And the second item?"

"For your evidence gathering, the local FBI field office now has a new digital forensic team. They are willing and able to help if you call them."

"Well, thanks for reminding us anyway. That will be all. Sargent Gomez here will coordinate our participation. I leave you folks to review the operation. I suggest 6 am tomorrow as the moment we move in. Questions?"

With full silence inside the room now, I got up, followed by Jennifer, and we left the meeting.

# # #

The Missing Taylor

Jennifer and I retreated to my yacht, still at a fair distance from the authorities' target. When I took the long-range binoculars, everything looked quiet. Nelson's car was still present, the guard walking around. No new vehicle was visible, and Steiner's yacht was in Miami. Would he show up?

We were debating dining aboard or going out when my phone rang.

"Mister Tanner, it's Tianna. Can we talk?"

"Sure."

"Where?"

"Why don't you come aboard? Jennifer and I will be here; I'll prepare something simple."

She agreed, and after giving her some directions, Jennifer and I prepared dinner. It's fun to carry your whole kitchen with you when traveling. Later on, when my phone rang, it signaled Tianna had arrived at the rendezvous point. I jumped into the dinghy and headed toward shore to get her and bring her aboard the yacht.

"Welcome aboard, Tianna. Can I offer you a drink?"

"White wine, if you have any?"

"I always do." I walked to the cooler while Jennifer entertained our guest. The group had worked all afternoon preparing tomorrow's raid, not including the time also spent yesterday.

"Are we ready?" I asked.

"I think we are. The Sheriff's office will provide security by blocking sensitive streets and displacing close neighbors. I hope it's done as quietly as possible. We have the Coast Guards, who will have two ships at proximity ready to intercept any escapee. The DEA assault team is on its way. That's about two dozen well-trained and equipped specialists who will enter the grounds. I think we're ready."

"What can we do?" pointing to Jennifer and myself.

"I convinced the sheriff you should be on-site, in a backup role, you and Jennifer. Once we secure the grounds, we may need you for identification. You're not on the assault team."

"I understand. Those days are behind me. But I want to be close by. Where do we meet?"

"Sheriff's office, 5 am tomorrow."

Gathered around the main dining table, the only one, by the way, we ate some fried shrimps in a tangy lemon sauce as an appetizer and then chicken over lettuce. It was a light dinner to benefit from a good night's rest.

In the evening, we chitchatted about all kinds of subjects except the case at hand. Tianna left an hour after dinner, pretending an early wake-up. Jennifer and I didn't object either; tomorrow would be a big day.

# # #

My alarm sounded at four o'clock, and I dressed in a hurry to prepare the morning coffee. Jennifer was up five minutes later; the noise may have woken her. We had something to eat and left in Jennifer's car driving in silence for five minutes. Marathon is not an enormous place.

The people involved in the assault were milling around in the parking lot, behind the Sheriff's office, checking their gear, verifying their firearm, anything to chase the nervousness. Over seven years ago, an FBI operation concluded on a terrible note with a dear friend dying in my arms. Keeping it out of my mind was impossible. I observed Jennifer, and she also looked preoccupied. Not having followed her career, I didn't know if she had similar memories, but I suspect any FBI agent has some. Flashbacks when events did not go as planned, sometimes with deadly conclusions.

Lost in our thoughts, Sargent Gomez arrived to inform us we were riding with him. It was not a long drive, so I suspected he wanted to have a close eye on us. He pointed to his car, and we sat in the back.

The stark and bare interior of a police car's back seat is not a pleasant sight. Cheap seats offer little leg room, the doors' handles don't work, and a metal mesh divider separates the bad guys from the good guys upfront. They can clean the plastic or smooth vinyl seats with a simple hose when required. Just thinking about this brought memories of very offensive odors. Back there, we were prisoners and suspected this was McBain's idea out for an act of little revenge.

At the agreed-upon time, Gomez signaled and shouted to the attendance to mount up, an expression dating from cowboy days. He sat in the passenger side of his car, and the driver then joined us.

An assault vehicle first rolled out of the lot, followed by five large black DEA trucks. A half-dozen police cars trailed, including ours, right behind the last black truck. Two ambulances followed the convoy at a safe distance. As we rolled out, Gomez received a radio call. The surveillance teams from the DEA on the target houses since last night reported everything was quiet, everyone sleeping. They had not seen the outside guard for a while either.

As the assault truck turned onto 92nd Street, it rolled midway down and stopped. This allowed the local police to block the street behind them, although the traffic was light at this time of the day. They would let no one onto the street while the operation was happening. Over the radio channel monitored by all participants, Gomez gave the go-ahead with a medieval expression: CHARGE!

The assault vehicle sped up toward the end of the street, still obstructed by the property gate, which afforded little resistance to the pressure applied. With a massive bang, it broke into multiple pieces flying in the air while the black SUVs followed behind. Like a rehearsed ballet, the first assault truck and two SUVs pulled up in front of the furthest house. The others stopped at the closest one, right after the broken gate. The group had projected to invade both places but believed people would be in higher numbers in the last house.

Our car blocked the street just at the gate, stopping anybody from entering or leaving the compound. We were the new gatekeepers. Gomez exited the vehicle, and I knocked on the window asking to open the rear door. He smiled, waited a few seconds just to tease me, and then opened it. Jennifer also slid out, and we all got behind the police car for protection. The DEA agents had broken in from the backside, a good strategy in case the main entrance was booby-trapped. A few agents stayed up front, near their trucks, but most ran behind the houses. A loud bang showed they had breached the door, and we heard voices shouting orders.

That's when all hell broke loose as the gunfire started. The radio erupted with, "Mask on, mask on" while the agents in front of the house shot gas canisters through the windows of the building under attack. Masks would allow the agents to breathe normally in a home full of tear gas, a definite advantage. The gunfire continued for a while, but as they injected more and more gas into the building, the guns became silent.

The agents went inside over the furthest house, but no gunfire erupted. It was empty, or the residents didn't fight much. Not long after, they declared, "House 1 secured" over the airwaves. In the other house where all the gunfights occurred, we waited for the same message. White smoke escaped through the broken front windows. A few minutes later, we received the message, "House 2 secured."

Soon after, the same voice announced, "We need an ambulance, two people injured in house 2." The yellow box trucks positioned one street over rolled with all lights flashing. One police car at the end of the road moved over to let the emergency vehicles through. The police car returned to its original position right away. Gomez's driver also moved the car back from the gate.

As this was occurring, armed agents were bringing people out of the smoked house, coughing, and spitting. They placed them on their stomach on the front lawn, several rifles trained on them. Four people were now lying on the grass, their hands tied with plastic strips. Four ambulance personnel with two stretchers moved toward the back of the smoked house, the front door still unopened at this point. A few minutes later, we understood why. "Gomez, we'll need the bomb squad over here. The front door has a curious package taped to it."

"Roger that," Gomez replied. He used the car's radio to have the bomb squad brought in.

Gomez walked toward the group of DEA agents standing over the figures on their stomachs. Without asking, I followed him, Jennifer, right behind me.

We trotted to the group arrested and lying on the ground. I bent down and looked at their faces. I recognized no one except for the tall one at the end, which I saw before. The last time was when Steiner surprised me behind the building. This man was present. Then I remembered: the bartender at Barnacle Barney's, Tony with the neck tattoo. Cynthia and I dined there on our first day in Marathon. I observed the other three men, two of them Asians, but not Laurel and Hardy.

"Coming through." The ambulance attendants were returning. The DEA agents moved away to let them through while I inched closer.

"What have we here?" I recognized Laurel in the first stretcher while Hardy followed close behind as usual. They were not smiling for a comic team, just grimacing. A bullet hurts, and they found out the hard way. I watched as they rolled the two men toward the waiting ambulances and loaded them on. Police officers also stepped in and would now accompany them until they faced justice. I remembered William Tudor, and my eyelids became gummy. I turned away for a few seconds, wiped my eyes with my sleeve, and took a deep breath.

At the furthest house, agents brought three people out and had them on their stomachs, hands tied behind their backs. A DEA agent walked over to Gomez, and I approached the small group.

"Sargent, we have a big catch here. Inside we discovered a sophisticated laboratory. I have called our technical team; they're on their way. They should be able to tell us what magic powder these guys were making. We found several tablet presses inside. The capacity is impressive, it's a substantial production site. Bags of opioids, different colors, different flavors are everywhere. They must have had a large market. The basement has packaging equipment. This was quite an operation."

Everything I heard so far confirmed what the gang's operation was all about. I was eager to know what the investigation would conclude on Taylor's disappearance. Would they find the people responsible? The future would tell us. The ambulances left on their way to prolong the life of the comic duo. Thinking about it now, they're not funny at all.

Gomez, the DEA agent, Jennifer, and I walked toward the furthest house. Three figures were lying on their stomach. The head of the organization, I hoped. As we approached, a female Asian still dressed in her pajamas with bare feet moved about, trying to get comfortable.

"This could be Sun My, Nelson's girlfriend. Jennifer followed them to this location yesterday."

The DEA agent asked, "What's her role in this?"

"I believe she runs a vitamin business that fronts drug delivery through her website. It seems the site has technical issues these days; that's why the top management dropped by."

Both the DEA agent and Gomez turned toward me, and before they could speak a word, I raised my two hands and said, "I had nothing to do with this." I was telling the truth; Hank did it.

A female agent helped Sun My up, her tiny eyes wide open now and her jaw clenched. The agent had to pull her forcefully toward a police van brought in for the occasion.

On the ground, the second suspect, in a daze, trained his eyes on the women walking away. He shouted something in a language I didn't understand, and I recognized Yang Nelson.

"This, my friends, is someone the Miami-Dade police have been trying to catch for a while. Mister Nelson here operates not only a popular bar in Miami involved in the drug distribution business, but he seems to have expanded his operations to manufacturing and online sales. It's a new organization trying to answer all the needs of their buying customers." Nelson was not looking at his girlfriend leaving but at me now.

"Go fuck yourself, Tanner."

"I think they got you now. You wanted to take matters into your own hands, and look what happened," I teased.

"You have nothing against me," he rattled on.

"I hate to disagree," the DEA agent interrupted. "From what I see there, it's an operation that will land you in prison for the rest of your life. Take him away."

While a police officer led Nelson into custody, I directed my attention to the last suspect, immobile and looking away from us. My heart was pounding as I walked closer to get a better look, anticipating discovering a tattoo with a cat on the man's temple. The organization's leader, the monster who wanted to eliminate me on the return trip to Miami, and most importantly, the man who got away in Chicago and killed one of my best friends.

He looked at me, but it wasn't Steiner. This face was familiar nonetheless, having been in my notebook for a while now: Mark Taylor.

Chapter 14

After the raid, the police evidence squad arrived and combed through both houses to collect fingerprints and other items to build a case against the traffickers. The DEA lab also showed up with a small convoy of vans. Once the police arrested the principals, they brought them to the local detention center for processing.

I walked away from the crowds to place a call to Nadine. I wanted the news to come from me and not the media. Although no media were present now, some would make their way over in a short time, I guessed. It was early in the morning to reach out to her, but it was the thing to do. I paused for a minute, thinking about how I will address the subject.

"Hello," she answered with a low moaning voice.

"Nadine, it's Jason. Sorry to bother you at this time of the day; it's important." I paused, waiting for a reaction, but all I got was a simple yes.

"We have found Mark, and he's alive."

"Wow, that is great news, Jason. Where?"

"In Marathon, finally."

"Are you going to take him back to Miami, or can I come down to see him? I'm so excited. Daddy will be pleased. Can I pick him up myself? I can be there in a few hours?"

She sounded so excited. It was a shame I had to bring her back to earth.

"Not so fast, Nadine; here's the situation. Mark was picked up in a raid on a drug gang. I know he worked with the DEA over the past few years, so he was likely on-site as an undercover agent. That's one possibility," I replied.

"What else could it be, Jason?" This time her voice trembled. Her mind was racing, thinking she received the good news, now the bad one was coming.

"He could have been kidnapped, or he was working for them. I don't know, Nadine. The police will interrogate him later, and if everything checks out, they'll release him. But that's not going to happen today, maybe not even the day after. As soon as I have some developments, I'll call you. If you want to pick him up, that can be arranged. I can return him to Miami by sea if need be, or my partner can drive him back too. So be patient, wait for my call, and let's hope for the best outcome."

"All right, Jason, but I'm certain he's a good man, and he'll return to his family."

"Let's hope so, thanks Nadine,"

Jennifer and I came back to the Sheriff's office and examined samples of the evidence collected inside a war room-like environment. The Sheriff made it clear he charged detective Roberto Angelillo with the investigation. The DEA should collaborate if called upon. Jennifer and I were just onlookers. They would solicit our input as needed.

The Missing Taylor

I contacted Angelillo once before. He worked on a missing person's case last summer. I believed then a link existed with Mark Taylor's case. He was the detective of record in that case; he seemed like a decent man.

I looked at stacks of photographs from both houses raided; It appeared like a real professional operation. They neglected no details: automated machines, pill presses, stainless steel works tables, and computers. But from all this material, my particular interest rested on Taylor's phone. Who was he in contact with? Not his family for sure.

Roberto asked a technician to process Taylor's phone in priority. Less than an hour later, we received a standard report which included all the calls in and out of Taylor's phone. Where the information was available, the contact name appeared. Since a name was present on most calls, I presumed he dialed mainly from his contact list.

The vast majority of calls were to or from Yang Nelson or Sun My, no surprise there. A few were from Brad Scott, a.k.a. Bruce Steiner. Nelson may have known Steiner only under his new alias. The First State Bank of the Florida Keys received a few calls too. Was this relative to the drug business? I walked over to Roberto, showed him the entry, and suggested they make further inquiries. He agreed and called in a detective. After brief instructions, he was on his way out a few minutes later to grab a warrant and visit the bank.

The calls listed on Mark's phone included entries starting in October 2017, just a few weeks after his disappearance. He probably got rid of his previous mobile to cut any ties to his life before Marathon. This new phone only presented the current Mark Taylor.

The last page included all the entries in his contact list. Less than a dozen appeared. Most memorable absent: Tianna Hester, from the DEA. Jeff Mason, his friend from Miami, was also absent. No ties with the past. It looked improbable he intended to return to his old lifestyle.

Our day had started early, and we were tired; we elected to leave the station. Dinner aboard was not practical tonight, so Jennifer and I planned to eat out. When we crossed Tianna in the corridor, we asked if she wanted to join us for dinner. She accepted, to our amazement.

Angelillo recommended an Italian restaurant, what else, and the three of us found our way to the well-hidden place. We ordered drinks and our dinner together; we were hungry.

"You know Jason, the intervention yesterday may well prove to be a major achievement for our war against drugs," Tianna said. "We have shut down several fentanyl routes coming into the country. At first, everything was arriving from China, but the Chinese asked the Mexican cartels to bring the dope into the country with our increased seizures. And even on that front, we had remarkable success. But looking at the numbers, something didn't add up."

"And what was that?" Jennifer asked.

"We closed a good number of routes, but in recent months, fentanyl made a strong return. Even though we disturbed the traffic from China and Mexico, fentanyl overdoses after a dip kept going up. I spoke to Mr. Baker back at the office today. He concludes that remote traffic did not increase; they elected to manufacture Fentanyl right here in the US. They monitor the basic ingredients at the border, but we can't stop everything. With a good chemist supervising the operations and people who are not afraid to take risks, you're in business."

"Isn't it dangerous?" I asked.

"Sure is, and the folks working the labs on 92nd Street were professional or lucky, maybe both. It's a poison that can kill by just touching it. The intervention today will make our country safer. Thank you both for your implication."

When our meal arrived, we jumped right in, hungry as we were. In a sense, we were proud our investigation brought tangible benefits to our country on the war on drugs.

"One more thing is puzzling Mr. Baker," said Tianna.

"What is it?" I asked.

"We still don't know who provided that anonymous tip."

"That's why they call it anonymous," I replied.

Tianna looked at me with a wry smile, I think she guessed I was the author of the tip, but I will never admit it.

Jennifer and I were back at the Sheriff's office in the morning. Around the conference table in total silence sat McBain, Gomez, Tianna, Jennifer, and I. We were waiting for detective Roberto Angelillo who would lead the first interrogation of Mark Taylor.

The door opened, and Angelillo walked to an empty chair and sat down, a signal for McBain to start the meeting.

"Ladies and gentlemen, we have a dilemma here. The DEA and the Sheriff's office have picked up an individual yesterday who is a missing person, a DEA informant, or a drug trafficker. He cannot be all of those." He stopped talking, everyone else also silent.

Turning to the DEA agent, he said, "Ms. Hester, why don't you start?"

"Sir, after discussion with my superior, Mr. Baker, the regional manager, he has instructed me not to discuss the Taylor case until we complete an internal inquiry about the subject."

"I smell a cover-up in here. Anybody else has this impression?" the Sheriff added.

Silence again.

"Sheriff, if I may," I said as I raised a finger to get his attention.

"Yes, Mister Tanner."

"From our investigation, I suggest Taylor, if he was an informant, either infiltrated the gang or they pulled him in, and he yielded to the temptation of easy profits. These two behaviors are different, but we need to identify which one is true."

McBain looked at Tianna and said, "Anything to add, Ms. Hester?"

"No sir," she replied.

The Sheriff kept himself silent; he was thinking about the situation and how to resolve the dilemma. He must have reflected on the issue before because he decided in a short time.

"Alright, here's the plan. Mister Tanner, you have a lot of facts about Taylor. You will first bring up to speed detective Angelillo here. Then, as you probably took part in several interrogations before, you will go in with the detective for a talk with Taylor. The aim is simple: if he's a deep cover for the DEA, we must release him. Otherwise, we need to charge him with a crime. Are we all good with the strategy?"

Tianna moved her hand to show she wanted to speak up. "Except you, Ms. Hester," the Sheriff added as he got up and exited the conference room, leaving all participants speechless. After a minute of silence, the detective got up and motioned me to follow him. We entered a tiny room nearby, a round table, and two chairs only. He let me in and closed the door behind him.

"It looks like we have a job to do here, Mister Tanner. I wanted to get things straight before we enter the interrogation room. From what

238

my boss told us, you may have the experience, but you have no authority. Are we clear on that point?"

Angelillo wanted to mark his territory. I didn't mind the conditions.

"No problem, Roberto. I'll fill you in as much as I can about the case before we go in. You lead the interrogation; I may have a few questions as we go along, but you're the ringmaster." He smiled.

"Have you used the Reid technique for interrogation before?" I asked.

"Yes, on certain occasions. This case fits the bill, probably."

"Yes, it would. I am comfortable with the process but rusty. If you handle the initial interview, I will take notes to develop the baseline. Are you good with that?"

We planned to use a well-known law enforcement technique that gives good results in interrogations like what we had before us. It may be marginal when examining young teenagers, but this was not our situation.

"Yes, I'm fine," he answered.

We talked for a good thirty minutes as I brought him on board with the missing Taylor. From Nadine's visit, Mark's disappearance, and his revival in Marathon. He asked a few questions as we were going along. Once I emptied my bag of information, we agreed on our future strategy.

He called the detention center and asked the officer to bring Mark Taylor to interrogation room # 1. We left the cramped space and walked toward Sheriff McBain's office to inform him of our readiness. Outside his door, Tianna and Jennifer were chatting. Both turned in our direction when we approached.

Looking at me, Tianna spoke first. "So…?"

"We're ready," I replied in all simplicity. Tianna was curious; you could see it from the looks in her eyes. But when she noticed no more information was forthcoming, she reddened, a sign I interpreted she was getting mad. I was preparing a smart remark, but for a second, I hesitated: should I?

After that brief pause, I continued, "We're not supposed to discuss the Taylor case until after the inquiry." These were her own words, almost exactly.

She had a reddish tint on her face before. Now it was approaching firetruck red. Jennifer looked at me with a face that says, "Don't push your luck, buddy." I understood the message, and I entered McBain's office, not looking back, and joined Angelillo, leaving the two girls with different emotions.

"Which room have you reserved, Roberto?" asked McBain.

"Room 1."

"Perfect. Next question: I'll attend with Gomez behind the observation mirror. Anybody else we need there?"

I looked at Roberto; he turned toward me at the same time. Each one of us hoped the other one would answer the question.

"I see no problem in having Jennifer and Tianna present," I said. "Strictly as observers," I added.

McBain turned to Angelillo, who raised his shoulders to show he didn't mind or didn't care.

"Then let's go," said McBain.

The Missing Taylor

We left the office with McBain leading the march. As we walked past the girls, McBain just said, "Fall in." It must have come from his military days. As I walked past the girls, none of them were smiling.

All five of us descended the main stairs, and through a meander of offices and desks, we reached a wall with multiple doors; we stopped in front of Interrogation # 1. Gomez was waiting for us, the prisoner already seated and handcuffed inside. As Angelillo and I entered the room, Gomez led the rest of the assembly to the observation area.

I would finally meet the man eluding me for so long.

# # #

Lieutenant Angelillo led the way into the small interrogation room, I followed. The place has no windows, just a giant mirror adorned one wall. Everybody knows someone is behind it, looking and listening to the conversation. Otherwise, why have a mirror in the interrogation room? Wouldn't it fit better in a bathroom?

A table sat in the center, two chairs on one side, a single one on the other. Those were the only pieces of furniture. I moved to the single chair and Angelillo sat beside Taylor. We both put our files on the table. Mine was thin, his looked more massive.

"Mark, I'm Lieutenant Angelillo. This is Jason Tanner, and he's also an investigator."

The choice of words is excellent. I am an investigator, but not with the Sheriff's office. As Angelillo introduced us, he stood up and removed Taylor's handcuffs. It was only to make him feel comfortable so he could open up with us.

"Cameras are present in the room, and they record this session. They're located there and over here," Angelillo pointed toward the ceiling on both occasions. He returned to his seat and consulted his file folder.

"For the records, it is April 21st, it's 10:35 am, I'm Lieutenant Roberto Angelillo, we have Jason Tanner in here, and the suspect's name is…?"

"Mark Taylor."

"Good, before we start, Mark, I want to inform you of your rights: you have the right to remain silent. Anything you say will be used against you in a court of law. You have the right to have an attorney. If you cannot afford one, one will be appointed to you by the court. With these rights in mind, are you still willing to talk with us?"

"I don't need a lawyer," Mark responded in a hurry. Like 80% of the people arrested in the country, he chose not to have representation by counsel. A bad move already.

"Fine, let's begin then. The Miami-Dade police are looking for you, Mark. Your sister reported you missing. What's her name?"

"Nadine."

"You were last seen working in a Miami Beach bar. Do you remember what day it was?"

"I believe it was in September last year, maybe around the 9th or the 10th."

Angelillo was following the game plan. To have the suspect use the "memory" side of his brain to answer, Angelillo presented an innocent question first. And in both cases, I observed Mark's eyes shift to the right. When the suspect moves them upward or to the left, he's using his cognitive center to develop an answer. If the question is "where were you on such a date?" and he responds with his "memory" side, it's a positive sign. If he answers using the creativity side, he may make it up. The technique works pretty well, but we need to pay attention to the small details.

242

Looking at his file, Angelillo continued, "Makes sense; you were last seen working behind the bar at the Black Cat on September 10th, a Friday. Is that what you're saying?"

"If Friday was the 10th, then yes, that was my last workday," Mark answered.

"What happened next?" I asked the open-ended innocent question in a low, friendly tone of voice. Taylor turned in my direction, and I noticed his eyes looking upward before continuing.

"Well, they offered me to meet the real owner of the bar in Marathon. Nelson was the front man but not the real owner. My DEA infiltration had brought me to the Black Cat, a central location for drug distribution in Miami. I needed to go a step further if I wanted to discover who was behind these drug distributors."

"Hold on a second," Angelillo interjected. "Are you telling us you were gathering information for the DEA about this gang?"

"That was my play, yes! I was deep undercover to gather enough evidence about them. Your raid yesterday came in too early. I wanted to pull the plug myself. I was just waiting for the big boss to arrive. Your operation scared him away for sure now."

Silence fell in the room. So this was his defense. He had not joined the gang but rather went undercover as a DEA informant to catch them. I looked at Angelillo and, with a quick head sign, showed we needed to regroup outside.

"Let's take a break, Mark. Do you want anything? Coffee? Water?" asked Angelillo.

"Water, please."

Both the Lieutenant and I gathered our files, got up, and walked out of the interrogation room. As we exited, we saw Gomez with a bottle of water. He would bring it in and stay with the suspect until

243

we returned. Right behind him, McBain arrived, and the three of us found a quiet space to confer and regroup.

"So that's his defense; he's working for the DEA. Do you guys think it's possible?" asked McBain.

"I'm uncertain we can disprove his statement just yet," said Angelillo.

"He has not contacted his handler at the DEA for a while. Ms. Hester will vouch for this," I added.

A detective walked our way and handed Angelillo a note. He read it, then said, "Hold on for a few minutes."

We chit-chatted while waiting for Angelillo, who took longer than previously announced. Fifteen minutes later, he walked in our direction, smiling, and said, "Let's go back in. Take the lead on the DEA situation, will you, Jason?" Angelillo asked.

"Sure."

We walked back inside the interrogation room and took our respective seats. I started the conversation.

"Mark, you're telling us you're a DEA informant, is that correct?"

"Yes."

"When did you start working with the DEA?"

I kept looking at his eyes, and they shifted right before he answered, "About two years now." We already knew he was an informant once. No reason to lie here.

"OK, as a source, did you have a handler, a person you reported to?"

"Yes."

"What was his name?"

A small pause but then, "Tianna Hester."

"And she was your handler from the beginning?"

"Yes, she was. I met nobody else."

Just like at the FBI, a single person controls the informant relationship. It's simpler that way and limits the number of people who could identify the source.

"So, she's the only person you communicated with," I continued.

"Yes."

"How did you contact Tianna?"

"A few times we met in person, but on most occasions, I called her."

"That's strange, Mark. We looked at your phone records, and you did not make one call to or from Ms. Hester. How do you explain this?"

This time the response was longer coming, and his eye movement was upward.

"The gang got me a new phone once I moved to Marathon, and I was afraid they would monitor my calls or listen in. I have not contacted Ms. Hester for a while. But she's the one I would contact to intervene here."

"Makes sense, Mark, but plenty of ways to communicate in our world today are available, you know? Public phones, other people's phones, e-mail, and confidential phone messaging apps, just to name a few. You didn't discover one other way to get in touch?"

"I was afraid they would discover me."

Angelillo looked at me and retook the lead.

"Were you confined to the house?" asked Angelillo.

"No, but if I had to go out, somebody was always with me, it's the rule of the house, and everybody follows it."

"And who would accompany you?"

"Sometimes Nelson, but mostly one or both of his bodyguards."

"All the time?"

"Yes."

"How did you meet Yang Nelson?" inquired Angelillo.

"We had a mutual friend who introduced us on the beach. We both surf, and that's how we met. While talking one day, he mentions he owns a bar, and I say funny, I'm a bartender myself. We both laughed, but a few weeks later, he asked me to replace a sick employee, which was the first time I worked there. I knew the place was on the DEA surveillance list, so I kept my eyes and ears open."

"Then?"

"One day, Nelson asked me if I wanted to meet his partner in the bar. He talked about him before, but I never met him. I figured it would be a good idea to know him."

"And what was your response?" asked Angelillo.

"I accepted right away. After my shift at the Black Cat, we would drive to Marathon. Nelson's partner is a yacht captain and happened to be in the Keys over the weekend."

"You drove down alone?"

"No, no, I jumped in with two associates of Nelson, Asians, Sato, and Watanabe. We call them Bill and Bob, it's easier."

I opened the file in front of me and pulled the photo of Nelson with the two Asians on the beach. I placed it in front of Taylor and asked, "These two individuals?" He looked at the image and said, "Difficult, I don't see their faces. But that's the way they dress for the beach." I retrieved the picture and returned it to my file.

"What happened next?" I asked.

"We drove to Marathon and arrived in the middle of the night, it's a few hours' drives, and my shift ended at midnight. I reserved at a cheap motel, and we crashed there for a while. The captain was unavailable at first, so we fooled around, had drinks, and waited until Sunday to rendezvous with him."

"Where did you meet him?" I continued.

"A local bar, I don't remember which one."

"And who was present?" I questioned.

"Other than me, Bill, Bob, and the captain, Brad Scott," Taylor answered.

"Can you describe him?"

"I would say around six feet tall, short black hair, blue eyes, protruding jaw, tanned, and he wears a small tattoo on his right temple, looks like an animal, but I'm uncertain. Everyone seemed to take their orders from him, even Nelson."

Taylor correctly described Bruce Steiner. The one thing our raid on the Marathon residences missed was the main man himself. Pity.

Angelillo smiled and didn't say a word. I understood he wanted me to handle this aspect of the talk.

"What discussions took place then?" I continued.

247

"Scott did most of the talking. Billy-Bob just sat there. We discussed the distribution strategy. The hand-to-hand typical drug delivery was problematic if you wanted to increase the volume. I don't know how the subject came about, but soon, the conversation turned to electronic commerce applications once I informed him I once specialized on the subject. That's when he got excited. Nelson's girlfriend already operated a small commerce site for her vitamins. He suggested we do the same thing for the products he sold. I explained how one business could hide the other and how we could take in payments electronically and then ship products anywhere."

"Was he interested?" I asked.

"If he was? He thought the concept would be unique and foolproof. He was smiling a lot."

"And then?"

"He took me to the compound on 92nd Street, showed me around, and gave me my new responsibilities. Starting now, I was to set up the distribution system and work only for them. He stated I was to concentrate solely on this project and do nothing else. Billy-Bob would see to it I concentrated my efforts right here in Marathon. He had forbidden communications with the outside world until further notice. He would pay my consulting fees plus a little more for the inconvenience."

"And how much was that?" asked Angelillo.

"I would receive $1,000 cash every week in an envelope for my services. I figured this approach provided me with a good cover. At the appropriate time, I would inform the DEA to arrest the gang and close the manufacturing plant."

"But you never called the DEA."

"As I explained before, I wanted the top man to be present," shouted Taylor.

Angelillo pulled the file someone handed him in the corridor in the middle of the small table. He extracted an 8x10 glossy picture and put it in front of Taylor, who bent over, looked at it, and leaned back. Pointing at a man in the middle, Angelillo asked, "Do you recognize this individual?"

"Hard to say from that distance," answered Taylor.

Angelillo put another picture in front of him, this time blown up. Mark Taylor's face appeared.

"And now?"

"Looks like me."

"For the records, the First State Bank of the Florida Keys, here in Marathon, provided these two pictures taken October 15th, at 11 AM. Now, Mark, do you see Nelson or his bodyguards in the picture?"

"They were waiting in the car, outside. They've done this before," he suggested.

"It could well be. But would that not provide you a fine occasion to call your DEA handler?"

"I met a representative of the bank, and after I filled out the paperwork, it was time to leave."

"Well, that's not the reason I showed you these pictures. At least not to presume you had plenty of opportunities to reach out to your handler. No, they take these images when a new customer opens an account." As he said this, he slipped a third picture, of Mark Taylor's face, in front of him. "The person on this photo opened a bank account under the name Mark Patry."

Taylor was silent, so was Angelillo, letting the news sink in. He picked up a moment later by presenting Mark a clear evidence bag with a Florida driver's license inside. "Besides all the drug manufacturing equipment found on-site, we located this fake driver's license with your picture, under the name Mark Patry. Any idea why?"

"Part of my DEA cover," replied Taylor.

Angelillo doubted and just said, "Sure." He flipped pages from his file and then stopped and looked at Taylor. "Mark, do you know how they divided the revenues from vitamin and drug sales? You managed the commerce platform where customers paid immediately, and the money came in every day."

"I'm not sure. I made certain everything operated correctly."

"We asked for the FBI digital forensic team yesterday, and they're working next door going through the computer systems seized on site. They resolve financial crimes around the country and are focusing on the platform you helped put together. They quickly found the trick used to separate the vitamin purchasers from the drug users. But we asked them to 'follow the money,' and that's where it got interesting."

Taylor shifted in his chair, looking uncomfortable. He glanced at Angelillo.

"The forensic team gave me their initial appraisal this morning. The revenues from the sale of vitamins and drugs all ended up in the business's operating account at Bank of America's downtown Miami branch. So far, it's not complicated, but I'll spare you the details because you probably know them better than me. The result is the net revenues, the profits if you wish, are divided between three groups:

Sailing the Atlantic, Black Cat Management, and Vitamin World of Asia."

"Who is behind these corporations, Mark?" questioned Angelillo.

"Sailing the Atlantic is Scott's corporation. Black Cat is Yang Nelson, and Vitamin World is Sun My's company. They shared the profits among these three, the proportions I ignore."

"And that's it?"

"Yes, these were the people running the operation, normal they share the profits. So now, you have enough information to convict them of drug manufacturing, sales, and distribution. The DEA should be happy with these results, it took some time, but now it's done." Taylor sat back, crossed his arms in front of him, happy with his performance. He looked proud of his accomplishments.

"Except one little thing Mark," Angelillo snarled. We both turned toward him, waiting for the big reveal. He extracted another sheet of paper from his file and referred to it while presenting the information.

"The forensic team looked for the daily PayPal report, which shows all money transfers using that tool, in and out. It seems a lot of the customers like to pay for their purchases with PayPal. To their surprise, they found no report. Digging deeper, they located a daemon, whatever this is."

I stepped in with the little knowledge I had, "It's a background program that runs all the time, like in the shadows." Angelillo looked at me; his expression told me he did not fully understand the answer. But he continued anyway.

"This 'daemon,' I'm told, kept erasing all the regular PayPal reports so no one would see them. Why would that be, Mark?"

"No idea," as his eyes shifted upward once more.

RC Cameron

"So the team launched the PayPal manual report, and guess what? It listed the transactions coming IN and some going OUT. The system transfers money from the business operations to a bank account at the First State Bank of the Florida Keys. And who owns this account?" Angelillo was sharp, and his voice even sounded theatrical.

"It belongs to a Mark Patry, whose picture you have seen recently. The bank even gave us today's balance. There are over a million dollars in it. How do you explain that one, Mister DEA informant?"

Mark's chin was resting on his chest, defeated. He could not explain why a DEA informant, undercover, defrauded a bunch of crooks. It was not to get them arrested and convicted. At the peril of his life, because if anyone had discovered the scheme, they would execute him, he appropriated money for his benefit. Had we not descended on the compound when we did, all traces of Mark's activities would surely have disappeared.

The twist in the case surprised me. I was first happy to locate Mark but then disappointed by what seems to be the greed he showed in this adventure. I wasn't looking forward to my discussion with Nadine.

Chapter 15

The following day brought out a clear sky and low winds, perfect timing for my return cruise to Pompano Beach. Jennifer had left yesterday in the late afternoon. She missed Damien and the kids. I elected to stick around for the night, no reasons to sail in the darkness unless you're a drug trafficker or a commercial vessel. At around five o'clock, I made my usual martini aboard and sat under the canopy of the top floor. I have received a few text messages from my daughter Cynthia, who insisted I call her about the police intervention. Knowing her, she must follow the Floridian regional news on the Internet and learned the local police with the DEA in Marathon raided an illegal drug manufacturing business. They described the operation in the Sun-Sentinel the day following the raid with some images of the compound and the police force taking in suspects.

Since Denver is two hours behind the east coast, I had time to enjoy my drink, find a restaurant, and call Cynthia afterward. I calculated that she worked all day and would only return home for her dinner time.

The familiar sound of my phone erupted inside the main cabin. I ran downstairs, looked for it for a moment, and got my hand on it before it went to voicemail.

"Hello."

"Hi Jason, Barry Gilmore, how have you been?"

"Oh hi, Barry, nice of you to call. I'm fine, a little tired, but that's because I was not sleeping well in recent days. I believe it's behind me now," I whined.

"Let's hope so. I was checking on your investigation. An article appeared in the papers this morning about a bust in Marathon. Was that you?"

"I must admit so. It went pretty well, and nobody died, just a few injuries, but the best idea came from you, Barry," I said.

"What's that?"

"The digital forensic team. It was your idea," I acknowledged.

"And?"

"We captured most of the gang. Steiner was nowhere to be seen, it's a shame, but the DEA informant we chased was right there, in the middle of the action."

"Mark Taylor?"

"Yes, he pretended to gather evidence or something before calling the DEA, but I was faster than him."

"Faster?"

"I alerted the DEA about the group in an anonymous call to get things rolling. I told the Sheriff it wasn't me, but between you and me, it's a white lie. That the DEA was interested got the Sheriff to follow up on my case."

"Good for you, Jason, but I don't see the link with the forensic team," Barry questioned.

"Thanks to them, the so-called DEA informant or agent got trapped. The team discovered he was siphoning money from the gang and moving it to his secret bank account. Without their talent, we'd never have found this. Thanks again," I replied.

"They're all in prison now?" Barry inquired.

"Well, they're holding Nelson and Taylor without bail; the hearing was this afternoon. The two Asians, Bill and Bob, great Asian names, are still in the hospital recovering from gunshot wounds during the raid. They'll go directly to jail and will not collect $200; they're suspects in the murder of a nice gentleman on my yacht earlier on. The vitamin girl, Sue My, is out on bail, so is the bartender and two other gang members."

"A nice catch overall, Jason!"

"I still would have liked to see Steiner behind bars; that's my disappointment."

"Maybe he'll cross your way one day," said Barry.

I thought about it for a second and recalled his quick departures when the walls of justice were closing in on him, like in Chicago. "I doubt it," I said.

After some idle chitchat, we ended the conversation. I thanked my friend again for his help in the case. I returned to the top level to finish my martini, now warm.

As a typical Italian, Angelillo knew all the right eating spots in the area. When I told him I felt like having a fresh lobster, he directed me to the Keys Fisheries. He mentioned they're located on the north side of the Island, on the water, and have a dock for traveling tourists like me. I prepared to sail around the main island of Marathon, raised the anchor, and motored to the local Marina, just like Angelillo had described. I noticed a small craft behind me as I turned around the corner of the island. The flats in the area are great fishing spots. I supposed he was going out to catch a few, or coming back.

I attached the lines, moored on the dock's exterior, on the ocean side. Dining outdoors on the aft deck while looking at the activity around interested me, so I moved the table outside. Examining the Marina, I could see the restaurant entrance on the left, a visitor's parking lot sat on the right. I got my wallet from the cabin and walked to the restaurant to order my takeout lobster.

The place allowed either a sit-down meal or an order window for takeout. I lined up behind a line already waiting to make their selection. I looked at the menu appearing above the order window, and I liked everything I saw. But I stuck to my guns and asked for a steamed lobster when my turn came to order.

"Jason," someone shouted. They handed me a big white plastic bag protecting a styrofoam box. I retrieved it, and I hurried to the comfort of my home, waiting for me on the water. Once aboard, I opened a bottle of white Chablis and set up my dining table on the deck to enjoy my fresh lobster.

The weather was perfect, with almost no wind. The sun would set in over an hour, plenty of time to enjoy my meal outside. I sat with my back to the ocean, facing the Marina and the restaurant onshore. The takeout window looked busy, and cars moved in and out of the parking area. Horns erupted from that area, and I noticed a small red convertible with the blacktop still in position. He parked at a 90-degree angle to the rest of the guests, taking two parking locations.

The Missing Taylor

With all the traffic, it's not surprising that people tooted their horns. This stupid driver used two parking spots when space was scarce.

A man burst out of his pickup and walked towards the little red car. But then, he stopped, turned around, ran back to his truck, and accelerated toward the exit. Strange.

I looked back at the red convertible, and the visible window was coming down on the driver's side. I wasn't sure what appeared in the window, but it looked like a stick or a broom handle. Then my gray cells exploded in action: a rifle, aimed in my direction. I lunged for the floor, protected by the boat's side hull but just a few feet high. Then a loud bang erupted, and pieces of fiberglass flew in the air. A bullet perforated the ship's hull right in front of my dining table. It also made a hole in my chair. My back hurt like hell, but I managed to crawl toward the safety of the cabin, reaching for the Glock in my bedroom. So much for my hull protection.

Still walking on all fours, I reached the main cabin entrance and peeked at the parking area. Gone was the small red car inside a cloud of dust. Mayhem erupted around the restaurant as people ran in all directions for cover. With no more shots fired, relative calm was returning to the area. Someone must have called 911 because sirens erupted and two police cars burst in the parking lot, all lights flashing. The doors flew open, and the police officers crouched behind them. A witness, hands in the air, walked in their direction and must have told them the shooter had already left the scene. The police officers stood up and reached for their radios to inform the dispatch. Five minutes later, more police cars arrived to secure the premises and take witness statements. I reached for my Oxycontin to relieve my pain then I waited, knowing full well someone would reach out to me.

I walked back inside, poured myself a new glass of wine, my first one lay on the floor of the aft deck, and waited for a visit. About ten minutes later, a voice I recognized yelled out, "Jason!" I stepped out, leaned on the door jamb, and looked at Angelillo, arm drawn but pointing down. "Come on in, Roberto."

# # #

"Right in the middle of the action again, Jason?" Angelillo asked.

"Looks like it," I answered while lifting my shoulders to show I didn't know why.

"What happened here?"

"I followed your recommendation, came to this quiet seafood restaurant on the ocean, and someone shot at me. The only thing I saw was a small red car with a protruding rifle shooting in my direction. It came close. Check out the hull; the bullet passed right through. If I hadn't noticed that car and rifle, the hole would certainly be in my body."

That small red convertible reminded me of something, but I couldn't put my finger on it. Where had I seen it recently? It bothered me my memory was sometimes working at a snail's pace. It must be my natural aging process.

"Don't touch anything; our team will be here shortly. They'll try to locate the bullet to match the rifle should we find it."

"Don't bother Roberto, check the hole in the other side of the deck. The bullet passed right through there and disappeared in the ocean."

"Yea, you're probably right, but they must analyze the scene, anyway. Any idea who could be responsible?" asked Angelillo.

"I would concentrate on the folks just released on bail, then look at the elusive Brad Scott; he's still unaccounted for."

"Yea, it's a good guess. We'll see what the witnesses can tell us. We're gathering their statement now. I believe a man got close to the red car. Maybe he can provide us with a good description of the man inside. Your plans for the rest of the day, Tanner?"

"I'll stay here until your team has combed the scene, find a quiet place to sleep, far from shore, and then head back to Pompano."

Angelillo noted my phone number should he have other questions and returned ashore to join the rest of the police squad taking witness depositions. The Taylor case had developed into a monster. From a simple missing person, it evolved into a significant drug bust while they followed me, kidnapped me, and now shot at me, far from the quiet investigations I wanted to accomplish.

I walked back inside and ate the lobster I had ordered earlier. It was now cold, but hey, I can live with that. I grabbed my notebook and flipped pages of information on my search and entries I sometimes scribbled in the margins. Notes about people I talked to, things they said, stuff I observed. And then, a note jumped at me, and I understood who had just tried to take a shot at me.

I holstered my Glock, exited the main cabin, and locked it before running toward the restaurant. On my way out, I crossed the crime scene team walking toward my yacht. At the restaurant's reception, I asked the person at the desk to call me a cab urgently. I walked outside, waiting for it. I jumped in when it arrived and directed him to Barnacle Barney. Five minutes later, I stepped out of the taxi, threw a twenty-dollar bill to the driver, and asked him to wait for me.

I burst through the front entrance and looked all around the bar. I wasn't expecting to find him here, but I suspected he lived close by. A lady mixing drinks behind the bar got my attention. I walked in her direction. "I need to talk to Tony, it's urgent."

"I don't know where he is, Sir," she replied.

"You have his home address?"

"You must talk to the manager over there," as she pointed to an individual near the front entrance. I hurried toward him, reached for my wallet, and presented my FBI insurance coverage card while saying, "FBI, I need to have Tony's home address immediately."

The tactic worked, to my disbelief, and the manager rushed to his office and returned with a piece of paper with an address on it. "Thanks," I said and left before he asked me to show him the card again.

I rushed outside where I left my taxi driver. He was gone, disappeared with my twenty-dollar bill for a five-minute drive.

I keyed the address into the Google Maps application on my phone to discover Tony, the bartender, lived only a half-mile from where I was standing. Using the app as a guide, I walked toward his home. At one point, I crossed Overseas Highway and continued along the main road. On my left, a residential area appeared with tiny houses, small dwellings, mobile homes, and trailers. It was amazing how these different houses ended up in the same neighborhood. Poverty was my first gut reaction to this housing district. It could have sprung up when the last hurricane passed by and the temporary housing became permanent for people unable to afford to rebuild.

From what I saw on my screen, the residents had access to their district from a single entry point, and then, several secondary lanes joined in. I wandered onto the main street, trying to look like a resident enjoying an after-dinner walk. At the second intersection, I turned left. I was trying to get a feel for the place without walking directly to Tony's house. If he were present and sitting on the porch, he would recognize me. Once I got to the end of his street, I figured his house was the fourth one down the road. Mobile homes surrounded me on each side. I walked back to where I came from to approach his house from the rear. From what I saw, he stayed in a small one-bedroom house with an attached garage.

Using the darkness as my friend, I moved silently toward his garage, hiding behind his back neighbor's shed for a moment. Dogs barked, but that appeared to be standard around here and not the sign of a stranger in the area. I hurried and stopped beside the garage. I held my breath, listening to any sound originating from the house that would show the owner was coming out. Still nothing.

A small window decorated the garage sidewall. As quietly as I could, I moved toward it and peeked inside. It was dark, but the moon coming up allowed me to discover a small red convertible parked inside.

# # #

I retreated to the comfort of his neighbor's shed, not wanting someone to see me on Tony's land for now.

Should I advise the local police?

I could have received an anonymous tip. That's how I got here to verify it. I didn't have a plan either. Should I ring the doorbell and ask Tony to surrender?

As my mind tried to decipher these alternatives, the neighbor's backlight suddenly lit up, and the owner came out shouting, "Who's there? What are you doing on my property? I'll call the police." I froze, looked at the man on his back porch, and stood still, in the hope he didn't see me. Uncertain if the noise or the light woke someone up, suddenly, a new voice erupted, "What's happening here?" This time it seemed to originate from Tony's pad.

I heard footsteps approaching. Someone was coming in my direction, still hidden by the woodshed. Suddenly, the older man appeared with a flashlight in my eyes. I turned around, not wanting a confrontation with the old guy, and walked in the opposite direction toward Tony's garage. I decided on my new plan to escape from this area and call the police.

I quickened my steps and passed the garage. The few street lights and the full moon provided more visibility than behind the house. That's when I noticed Tony, the bartender, come running out in my direction. He spoke first.

"Tanner! I thought you'd understood the message by now."

"Not really. It would take more than a small bullet to convince me," I replied.

"I guess I must find another way to get rid of you." He now strolled in my direction. I tried to recall my one-on-one marine training from back then. It was one thing to remember it, something else to apply it. But I recalled the first advice: examine their eyes. If they look you in the eyes, they'll swing. If they look down, they'll kick first. The other piece of advice I received was not to show fear, don't be the underdog, don't walk back, be the aggressor. And the last rule of hand-to-hand combat is there are no rules; anything goes.

As he approached, I quickly stepped up, surprising him. I then launch a straight right hand directly on his nose, causing his eyes to close and his nostrils to spray a bright red liquid. Even before his eyelids lifted, his right shoulder went back, a clear announcement a punch was coming. As his fist traveled in my direction, I leaned left, avoiding it. My right leg kicked as hard as it could toward his exposed stomach. "Ouch." He bent at the waist, trying to refill air in his lungs. He raised his head and looked straight ahead; I wasn't there anymore. When he rose and turned his face in my direction, a left hook on his jaw dropped him to his knees. His arms stopped the forward motion of his body. He now rested on all fours.

"Stay down, don't move." I wanted to call the police to perform their investigation of Tony, his red car, and maybe a rifle still around. But Tony had other ideas. He got off one knee, planning to get back up and continue the fight. I had no interest in pursuing it. As he was slowly getting up, a hard kick under the jaw knocked him out for good. He now rested calmly on his front side, passed out.

My knuckles hurt like hell, my back too. But I was standing, and he was lying on the ground.

The old neighbor arrived on the scene shouting, "What have you done?"

I pulled my gun from my back holster and pointed it at the ground between the annoying man and me. "Police matters; go away." He understood and turned around.

I needed to call the police, but I debated if I should remain on-site and wait for them. The man lying in front of the garage knew me. A witness was also back there, his neighbor. I should stay. I called the Sheriff's office and reported a man down, close to a red convertible. I heard sirens within a few minutes, and a police cruiser arrived on the scene. I kept my explanations to a minimum: a stranger informed me this person had a small red convertible. I checked the garage through the side window to confirm, and when I walked away, he came out and attacked me. I only defended myself.

"I carry a gun; I could have shot him when he attacked me. I put him down with a few tricks I learned in the Marines." That seemed to satisfy them for now, but they still insisted I go with them to write a statement. I complied with pleasure.

They picked up Tony, who had regained consciousness and sat him in the cruiser. They debated if an ambulance was necessary but decided against it. Already on bail for drug charges, Tony could face new accusations like attempted murder now. His future did not look dazzling.

Chapter 16

Already the ground was warm, and the moist air seemed to rise from the pavement as I walked near Pompano Beach Pier. The DEA and police raid had netted a few rotten apples, but the main man, the cat with nine lives, still ran loose. No matter how I turned the missing Taylor case around, a piece was still absent: Bruce Steiner. Or, as they call him in this part of the United States: Brad Scott.

With May arriving in South Florida, the temperature crept to the low nineties, a signal for the last snowbirds to run back north. Beaches will look empty now until they return in October. Only a few visitors like Florida beaches in the summer. You needed to love the hot temperatures.

Back aboard my year-long residence, I still pictured Steiner's nine lives tattoo in my head. Something annoyed me. He captained a large yacht, but this was not a full-time job. Some days they booked him, others not. He required a roof over his head when not at sea. Where did he stay when not working? I walked to my captain's cabin, lifted my bed, and reached for my backpack where I kept my investigation papers. I grabbed a bottle of water from the cooler, pulled out all the paperwork, and set them on the table in a large pile. When I broke into the yacht rental agency, I photographed several pages and printed them. Would one of these documents show the infamous captain's land location? A discreet person, yes, but a home address was still a necessity. I flipped page after page with a particular interest in those images from my night intrusion.

A sheet dropped on the floor. I picked it up, looked at it in diagonal, and was about to turn it over when something caught my attention. A handwritten note asked to route Captain Scott's next insurance papers to his new address. Deep down, I sensed Laura's help from above, still guiding my steps on this earth, moving a piece of paper in front of my eyes. Brad Scott's home address emerged, on Washington Avenue, in downtown Miami Beach, right under my nose while I stayed at the Marina near South Point Park. With Google Maps, I located his address, only a fifteen-minute trot from the Marina, also within walking distance of the Black Cat bar, how convenient.

Sitting back, I tried to imagine how I could use this new information. For sure, I wanted the authorities to capture Steiner; they listed him on the FBI's most wanted. No doubt my former employer would raid this apartment with Steiner present. They didn't know when he would be there. A miss-timed raid could inform Steiner federal authorities were close and force him to flee in a hurry as he did in Chicago.

To my knowledge, the Miami-Dade police issued no arrest warrants for Steiner either. I could not find a reason to involve them either. After imagining multiple scenarios, I concluded the soundest plan required to stake out his place, and when I could confirm his presence, then call them in.

If I was in Steiner's shoes, what would I do? His group had suffered a significant blow. His chief associates were in jail; a risk existed they talk and identify him. I remembered the man's history from my FBI days, which demonstrated he closed his business, packed his things, and then moved elsewhere. He did this a few times already. But I had to hurry before he moved his circus again. I could catch him right now if it were not too late, but I may have only one chance.

I prepared a bag of goodies, clothes, binoculars, my Glock, and some ammunition. Then I locked the yacht, advised the Marina of my departure, and hopped in my SUV for one more trip to Miami Beach.

By chance, I reserved the same Airbnb unit I once rented in Miami Beach. Only a few blocks from Washington Avenue, I drove to my temporary housing, parked my ride, moved my stuff upstairs, and dressed like a visiting tourist.

Once in front of Steiner's apartment, I inspected the building. Constructed at least thirty years ago, it comprised five stories and over three hundred feet of frontage. At street-level, more than a dozen retail outlets advertised their products or services; a liquor store, a hairdresser, a tattoo parlor, four or five restaurants, a cleaner, a currency provider, one was empty. Above the stores stood four floors of residential units, each having a single-window giving onto Washington Avenue. The building's middle portion houses the apartment's main entrance. Buzzers can advise the owner he has a guest at the front door. The panel contained only a few names, a sign of high resident turnover.

I walked into an Italian restaurant and sat at the bar where I ordered a beer and asked for a menu. During our small talk, the elderly barman told me residents above his head were singles or couples mostly, few children around. The place had plenty of transient folks because short-term rentals were available. If I was interested, I could meet an office person during the day. I finished my beer and strolled to the buildings' main entrance, where I rang Unit 101, with the name "Office" displayed. A loud buzz filled the entranceway, so I pulled the handle and walked in. Straight ahead, a door marked "stairs" and right beside it, a scratched-up elevator. I escalated the staircase, not trusting the antique lift. When I reached the second floor, a sign displayed units 101–110 left, 111–124 right. I headed left and knocked on the business office door. Another buzzer sounded, and I pushed my way in, noticing an overhead camera, viewed by folks inside probably. An obese woman well in her sixties greeted me with a mean-looking face.

"Yes!"

"Good afternoon Mam. I'm searching for an apartment."

"OK, sit down here," as she pointed to one of two old leather chairs in front of her desk. These chairs have felt a lot of cheeks during their lifetime. I sat down, expecting an old spring to rise and attack me. She reached for a small black binder and flipped pages.

"We have either studios or one-bedroom, nothing else. What will it be?"

"A friend of mine once lived here. He had unit 310; was that a studio?" Steiner's home address said 410, and I expected all units ending with the same number to be identical.

"310 is a one-bedroom. Is that what you'd like?"

"Maybe, can I see one?"

From her expression, you knew she hated this question. It meant she would have to get up, obtain keys, walk to an empty unit and show me around. You could sense her feet hurt, her knees resisted, and her hip complained. Without smiling, she continued scanning her binder, found what she needed, got up, and meandered to a small wall-mounted cabinet where she extracted a key from her collection.

"Follow me."

We walked back toward the stairs without hesitation; she pressed the elevator button. After a minute, the automatic door opened with a big bang. She walked in; I followed in apprehension. She pressed number 3. The car crawled almost a full minute to grind its way up two floors; turtles walk faster. We moved in complete silence, having nothing to say to each other. The car finally stopped and bounced up and down like it had traveled fifty floors at high speed. The doors opened, I let her take the lead out the risky lift.

Unhurried, with her feet dragging on the dirty floors in a hush-hush sound, we arrived in front of unit 304. I expected an empty apartment, but she still knocked on the door. Some noise came from inside, and a young black girl in her twenties, dark hair, in shorts and skinny top stood in the opening.

The old lady announced we were visiting and stepped forward. The girl moved aside just in time not to get rolled over.

Turning in my direction, the old lady said, "They're leaving at the end of the month." I bobbed my head up and down, showing I understood the situation.

With mesmerizing comments by my guide, such as, "This is the kitchen" or "This is the bedroom," I absorbed the space's look and feel. Steiner occupied an identical environment. I wanted to know about the living space, in case I had to enter his flat. I thanked the young lady, and we got out of her life, at least for now. She seemed happy.

When we returned to the old lady's desk, she asked, "So, when do you need it for?"

"I'm wondering if a studio would not be enough."

Her face reacted like her mother just died. She was looking at another trip to a studio apartment with her feet, knee, and hip all objecting vehemently.

"Let me think about it, and I'll be back." She replied with a sweet smile. Her agony was over. I got up and walked away, leaving a happy woman in my wake. With the office door closed behind me, I walked to the stairs, looked around, and seeing no one, trotted up to the fourth floor, where Steiner crashed on occasions.

Number 410 sat at the corridor's far end, the last unit. This meant he had a neighbor only on one side. Knowing Steiner was sailing today, I knocked on apartment 409, his nearest neighbor. I was in luck, I heard footsteps coming, and an eye appeared in the door viewer. The security chain rattled a moment, then the door opened. A man in his sixties appeared as a dose of stale air reached my nostrils. The TV blasted game show cries in the background.

"Yes."

He spoke this simple three-letter word even before the door opened fully; I guess he was watching an exciting program. The smell, the noise, and the urgency also encouraged me to hasten my delivery.

"Excuse me, sir, I am trying to reach your next-door neighbor, any idea when he will show up?"

"No."

I reached in my pocket and extracted a full money clip. I flipped a few twenties and a ten-dollar bill to my right hand and showed them to the retreating man.

"The guy in 410 owes me money. Here is fifty dollars for you; let me know when he comes back. As soon as you tell me, I'll run over here and give you another hundred. Would that work for you?"

That seemed to get his attention. "And how would I reach you, mister?"

I extracted my business card with my phone number on it. "Just call me at this number, I'll rush back." That seemed to satisfy him. He reached for the money and the card, closed the door, and reinstalled his security chain.

While still inside the building, I moved down to the main level and examined all the ways in or out. From each end of the property and in the back, I counted four exit-only doors. The front, I knew, had a single entryway providing access to all floors. Down the basement, a metallic door opened with a loud screech to an interior parking lot. Cars sat between big cement columns holding the building together. Having seen what I wanted, I crossed the street and located a Chinese restaurant with a table close to the front window where I could still observe the main entrance. I decided on an early dinner of wonton soup, sweet and sour chicken, and white rice while I kept an eye on my prime suspect's base.

After having gone through two pots of Chinese tea, I paid the server and left him a substantial tip. I walked back to my pad and tried to relax while developing various scenarios, should his neighbor call me. In the end, I fell asleep only to wake up after a terrible dream where several oversized cats attacked me and lacerated my skin with their enormous paws.

Not being in my bed and after a terrible nightmare, sleep did not return. At 6 am, I was ready to leave. I walked along the beach amid several elderly taking in their morning stroll and younger runners using the early hours to exercise before going to work.

Back on Washington Street, I located a place where I could eat breakfast while keeping an eye on Steiner's pad. Around noon, still without a sighting, I walked toward Ocean Drive for lunch and then went back to my apartment for an afternoon snooze, not having slept well.

Around two o'clock, a call from JR surprised me.

"Hey, John, what's up?" I inquired.

"A lot Jason. The Sheriff's office down in Monroe County asked us to arrest Steiner. A judge signed the warrant this morning, so we tried to execute it today. When we contacted his employer, they informed us he was returning from a cruise at the Miami Beach Marina this afternoon. We dispatched officers at that location to grab him upon his arrival."

"So far, so good."

"When the officers boarded the yacht, they could not locate him. Upon further investigation, some passengers reported the captain abandoned the ship using the tender. It was missing, which confirmed the passengers' statements. A drunken rider suggested the captain should be the last one to leave the ship, not the first one!"

"Someone radioed the information to him, probably from the yacht agency. Shit, this guy is so slippery."

"Yeah, it seems. Now we're combing the beaches to locate the tender. So far, nothing, I'm told Steiner could reappear in West Palm Beach for all I know."

"That's a possibility for sure," I replied.

"I just wanted to let you know. This guy tried to kill you once, and you helped annihilate his operation. He might come after you, so be careful."

"I will. Thanks for the heads up JR."

I didn't say I was sitting in Steiner's apartment; I haven't seen him after all. Nothing indicated he would show up at his pad. If the police were looking for him, chances are they have a car sitting in front right now. But the incident on the high seas was recent, and the urgency of executing a warrant from a Sheriff's office is not the top priority for the Miami-Dade detectives.

As my mind debated the issue, my phone rang again, an unknown number on the screen. My watch displayed 4 pm.

"Yes," I answered.

"He's here."

Just waking up, the short message did not register first. I didn't even know the caller.

"You're in 409 on Washington Street?"

"Yes."

"I'm coming right over. I'll buzz you when I arrive. Let me in. I have your money. Give me fifteen minutes, maximum."

"OK," and he hung up.

Things were moving in my direction now.

I changed my tourist attire for a pair of jeans, running shoes, a black T-shirt, and a loose shirt over it. Then, I grabbed my Glock, slipped it into my lower back, and covered it with my shirt. I took additional ammunition and pocketed a compact flashlight. With my phone on my right hip, I was ready.

Excited by the moment, I rushed toward the apartment building.

#

When I reached the Washington Street building complex, I slowed down in case Steiner was watching. A plan was forming in my head. At the building's main entryway, I rang number 409, where no name appeared on the board. A few seconds later, hearing a buzz, I opened the door and charged up the stairs, which I escalated two by two.

On the last floor, I stopped to catch my breath. I opened the door with care and looked toward units 409 and 410 at the end of the long corridor: no movement, no one in sight.

My running shoes were silent as I strolled toward the corridor's end, hugging the right side, trying to be invisible. Without warning, a door opened, and a middle-aged man walked out, startling me. He looked at me as I bent down to tie my already-tied shoe. As he approached me, I stood up. I did not recognize him; neither did he. I continued on my way; he did the same.

I tapped softly in front of unit 409, hoping his neighbor would not hear it. As the door opened a fraction, his face appeared. I put my finger on my lips, asking for silence. He followed my instructions, opened the door wide, and I entered, closing behind me. On my first visit here, I remembered the smell, but once I walked inside, it was noticeable. For some reason, strangers will smell things that residents can't seem to identify, especially in an old folks' home.

"He's there?" I whispered.

"Yes, arrived 15 minutes ago," as he looked at his watch.

I reached in my pocket and extracted a one-hundred-dollar bill which I handed him.

"That was our deal. Thank you." I picked two other similar bills and asked, "Why don't you get a drink, a nice meal, return after midnight, I will watch your place?"

He hesitated, not knowing me, it was understandable. He already had a hundred. But three hundred were much better. He also had to trust me with his belongings. Looking around, he concluded he didn't have much to lose. His decision time was short. He reached for the additional bills and just walked away.

The Missing Taylor

If my suspicions were right, Steiner must have checked for the presence of police officers in front of his building before coming up. He would pack his stuff and disappear from South Florida. He must have significant personal effects to gather; that's why he was back. The risk was great. Things he could not leave behind. I suspected but did not confirm if he owned a car parked in the garage. He would use it to drive toward a state where no one knew of him. His days as a captain of a super-yacht were over, at least here in Miami.

Because he lived at the end of the corridor, he had to walk right in front of my door. I got a chair and placed it close to the entrance. I sat in it, waiting for his next move. My ears were wide open as I continued to debate calling the Miami police. I decided against it for a couple of reasons. One is I needed to confirm Steiner's presence; he could have dispatched someone else to gather his belongings. And second, I believed Steiner had a mole inside the Miami police.

Absorbed in my internal debate, a noise came from Steiner's apartment, my watch not even showing five o'clock. I gazed through the dirty door viewer and saw nothing. Still standing, listening, and looking into the corridor often, I could feel his presence nearby, but I wanted to surprise him. All my senses were alert. A few minutes later, a door opened and then closed. I put my eye on the viewer once more just as the shape of a man passed in front of me. It was too quick to identify my prey.

After a few seconds, I reached for my gun and opened the door as silently as I could. I stepped out into the middle of the corridor and turned toward the man walking away carrying a bag over his left shoulder. By then, he was about thirty feet from me.

"Hold it right there, mister," as I pointed my weapon in his direction.

He stopped in his tracks.

275

"Now turn around, Steiner."

He slowly pivoted to study the person holding a gun on him. His head bobbled left and right; he was trying to identify the threat. The low light in the corridor did not help.

"You're making a big mistake. My name is Scott, Brad Scott. You have the wrong man, and I can prove it," as he reached for his back pocket.

I joined both hands onto the Glock. "Don't move," I said. He stopped abruptly. "No mistake Steiner, I would recognize you anywhere." I stepped forward. He straightened out, one hand on his side, the other one still holding the bag. His face now showed a new level of comprehension, and a smile formed on his lips. "Tanner, the swimming investigator. I knew I'd seen your face before. Are you still upset about your transport back to Miami that night? We only wanted to scare you. We would have released you on arrival, promised."

"And the man on my yacht, you wanted to scare him too?"

"It's difficult to get good help around here. My men should have ditched the plan when they didn't find you on the yacht; they're not all rocket scientists."

At first, a noise erupted, then the door to apartment 408 between Steiner and myself opened without warning, and an elderly lady came out and turned to lock her door, oblivious to the goings-on around her in the corridor. Steiner seized the opportunity, where I couldn't shoot, to turn around and sprint toward the exit. The lady looked in his direction, uncertain what was happening. I dashed after Steiner, still bearing my firearm. The old lady leaned her back against her apartment door, brought both hands to her face, and screamed. I sped past her as she was sliding down her door.

The Missing Taylor

Steiner ran into the first stairway he encountered. Since he still had his bag, I assumed he was armed, and I could not rush around a corner without taking safety precautions. On top of the stairs, I stopped and looked around the corner. I saw nothing, but I picked up hurried footsteps on the metallic stairs. I followed him, halting at each landing to look for my suspect possibly aiming at me. As long as I heard his steps, I felt confident he hadn't stopped to ambush me.

A screeching metallic sound interrupted the running steps. That would be the door leading to the underground garage. I sped up my descent and reached the door less than ten seconds later. With my back glued to the wall, I opened the door wide and looked inside just for a fraction of a second. As I was pulling my head back, I saw a flash beside a large cement column, and a single shot then landed on the closing door, missing me by inches.

I bent down as much as I could, flipped the door open again, and from my position, fired three rounds toward the previous flash without looking. I then surveyed inside the garage and observed Steiner running away from his cover. This time, I slowly aimed, like at the range, and fired a single round at his moving legs. He dropped his long body onto the cement floor, followed by a metallic sound, something skipping. In the hope he dropped his gun, I rushed toward the column and looked around it. I saw a man with a grimace dragging himself with his arms only on the floor, about ten feet away from his purpose. A trail of blood followed him.

"Stop it right there," I shouted as I ran toward him and picked up the revolver just in time. A high-security jail would cater to the cat's last life. I pocketed his gun and then reached for my phone to call the Miami police, unsure if all the noise had not generated an emergency appeal already.

"John, I know it's late, but I have a package for you, a man appearing on the FBI's most-wanted list. Why don't you come over to pick him up?"

After a short hesitation, JR asked for my coordinates which I provided. I would be in the garage waiting, I told him. "Shots fired, and a man is injured, send an ambulance."

Not even five minutes passed when the sound of sirens erupted outside. Four patrolmen, guns in hands, stepped into the humid garage shortly after. When they saw me holding a firearm, they asked me to drop my weapon.

A stretcher soon arrived, and under a police escort, they moved Steiner to the waiting ambulance. They put his belongings in an evidence bag, which will eventually lead to the downfall of his supply chain, as I will learn later. JR arrived just as the stretcher rolled in his direction, and he looked at the man well tied up and escorted. I joined him.

"Nice catch Jason. On my way down, I had someone check the ten-most-wanted list. The man on the stretcher is worth a cool hundred thousand dollars, not bad."

"That will cover my expenses on this investigation, but barely. I have a few folks I need to compensate for their help in this case. But I'll take it with pleasure."

Steiner was still grimacing. He looked at the paramedic. "I need something for the pain, man."

"Don't forget to get the real drugs, buddy. Fakes are all over the market, but the DEA and the police put an end to a dirty gang, at least for a while."

He shot me an insulting look.

I hated myself now. I took down a drug manufacturer, and I was using myself illegally. I decided I had to do something about it.

"When your troubles are behind you in Miami, folks in Chicago are waiting to talk to you. A homemade bomb exploded in one of your garages, remember that? Asshole."

He closed his eyes. It would be hell for him from now on.

In the next hour, I narrated the events leading to the capture of the Cat, from my arrival to the pursuit and the shooting. Two detectives took my statement, but not Freeman; I wondered why.

It was late when I returned to my temporary lodging and fell asleep within a minute from putting my head on the pillow. I will drive back tomorrow.

# # #

After my early morning walk in Pompano, I was having a regular Americano at my coffee shop. The news on the Post and the Times were demoralizing as usual. On occasions, I read the news story from Canada where life appeared more normal.

When my phone rang, it startled me so much I first dropped it. But my iPhone reflex allowed me to catch it before it reached the floor and the standard $149 repair cost. It reminded me of an old professor in high school who raced weekends on ice circuits while I lived in Chicago. On Monday mornings, after his usual weekend race day, he reported his success or demise by enumerating the car parts which needed to be replaced. He remembered the price of everyone: a rear bumper, left or right fender, a side door, and others. Even with a win, he needed some new hardware.

"Hello," I said, not having looked at the screen.

"Jason? It's John."

"Hey John, how are you?"

"Well, it could be better. A sad moment at the station today," he said.

"How come?"

"We arrested Wayne Freeman this morning on charges of conspiracy to commit murder. The district attorney struck a deal with the big Asian to testify against Freeman for reduced charges. It's not my favorite approach, but we had no other way to get a conviction."

"You know John, the police force should remove a bad apple this way rather than keep him. The conspiracy charges will be difficult to prove. He passed along information on where to find me at the Marina. A quick call from a public phone, that's all he needed."

"Yea, I know."

"So you'll have the two Asians plus Freeman for the murder of William Tudor. No sign on who ordered the kill? Can't link Nelson?"

"No, the big Asian is not talking. He received his instructions from Freeman, no one else, he said. As for Freeman, we have not interviewed him yet. We're waiting for his lawyer to arrive."

"How was he introduced to the drug gang initially?"

"We don't have this information yet, but we will. We are looking at his financial transactions over the past years, his access to the national crime database, and several other verifications. We'll find out the truth in due time. In the meantime, his career is over in law enforcement. When he comes out of jail, he'll need a new job."

"Yea, if he comes out. Police officers have a hard time in jail; it's well known."

"I've got to go, Jason. I wanted to give you the news firsthand."

"Thanks, John, it's appreciated."

Early afternoon, back at the Marina, I made an important decision. One I should have made months ago. It finally dawned on me I was addicted to the painkillers, and I needed to bring back my life. The pain clinic had stopped calling me because I never returned their call. That would change from now on. For some reason, I have a better track record of keeping my promises when I tell someone else. I knew who I had to call.

"Hello!"

"Hi, sweetheart, it's your Dad."

I took her through the details of the last few days and the successful capture of a public enemy. I made the story not too dangerous. I didn't want Cynthia to worry about my safety during these sometimes unexplainable developments in my investigations. She was not surprised about the rotten apple Freeman. He deserved everything that was coming to him.

"I've made a decision Cynthia. I will be taking care of my pain killer addiction before it's too late. I'm telling you now, and I'm calling the pain management clinic immediately after speaking to you. I cannot continue this way. I realize it now."

"Great news, Dad!"

"I'm telling you, so you keep on my case. It may be difficult at times for me, but I know I can get through this with your support. What do you say?"

I could hear some sniffing at the other end of the line. I believe they were tears of joy.

"You know you can count on me, Dad, always. Mom would be proud of you too," she said as she wept at the same time.

# # #

A few months after my talk with JR, I received a call from Tianna. Not expecting it, I still welcomed the update about the strange ramification in the investigation.

"Jason, hope you are well. I wanted to inform you about developments after Steiner's capture."

"Are you telling me you're following up on DEA matters with a private citizen?"

"Yes, I am. It will be our secret."

I didn't object, so she continued.

"When the police arrested Steiner, they also seized his phone. On it, they found emails, messages, but also several applications, including one called WICKR. I was clueless about this application, but my colleagues described it. It's a messaging app to send and receive text between parties with a unique feature that once the recipient reads the message, it's destroyed immediately. It's impossible to know what it was; no logs, no history, nothing."

"Sounds perfect for a bunch of criminals or terrorists. Okay, then what?"

"It appears Steiner had been corresponding, using this application, with a French-Canadian man, Eric Mondoux."

"Can't say he's in my contact list."

"Mondoux is a well-known drug trafficker up in Canada, in the province of Quebec."

"I've been up there before; nice place if you like the cold."

"So Steiner communicated with Mondoux while this guy was in jail. The gentleman is conducting business while serving a ten-year sentence for drug trafficking."

"In prison, and he ran his business from there?"

"Yes, in Drummondville, wherever that is."

"Hum, so the authorities stopped this little gimmick?"

"Well, hand it to the Canadians; they are smart people."

"How so?"

"The RCMP seized Mondoux's phone after a search of his cell and placed him in solitary confinement."

"Smart."

"They took over his identity as a major importer of Fentanyl ingredients for North America. If you wanted to make Fentanyl, he was your top man for the job."

"Interesting."

"That's not all. By taking over Mondoux's identity, the Canadians also found four Chinese citizens now blamed for shipping fentanyl components to countries in the area. Steiner organized sailing expeditions to these locations and brought back what he needed to manufacture his own drugs. A simple but deadly result."

"Impressive."

"We have nothing to do with this situation. The Canadians managed everything on their own; hats off to them."

"Quite a story, don't you think?"

"Yes, a happy ending."

"I would have more details if you buy me a drink at the Jet Runway cafe tomorrow, let's say around five?"

"I have a two o'clock appointment at the pain clinic, but I should be able to be there by five. See you then."

Suddenly, I wondered if a husband shares her life or not. I must ask her.

*** THE END ***

Reviews

If you enjoyed this book, let your friends know by providing a feedback where you purchased this novel. That is just about the only way to spread the good news.

If you're not already on my discreet e-mail list, please sign-up from my web page at www.rccameron.com. This way, you'll be informed when the next Jason Tanner story hits the stores.

Cheers.

www.ingramcontent.com/pod-product-compliance
Lightning Source LLC
Chambersburg PA
CBHW031702170626
46808CB00005B/1570